JUNCTIONS

For Doug & Annie,

I share my first-born novel with you hoping you come to love my characters as I do. I absolutely treasure our writer and cousin bonds—
Warmest wishes,
C'Anna 2016

C'Anna Bergman-Hill

ISBN: 0997850000
ISBN 13: 9780997850000

For
David

TABLE OF CONTENTS

NEGATIVE SOUND

What we do not say
creates phantoms
that ghost our peripheral vision
mirages of the unspoken
that shimmer just beyond sight
and symphonies of silence
that echo unheard in our bones

What we do not speak
becomes carnivorous
it consumes our soft parts
leaving hollow rib cages devoid of heart
and graying pelvises
leached of passion

Cynthia Leslie-Bole

PROLOGUE

In Three Scenes

ONE

BIRTH

The lack of conversation in the room was at odds with the circumstances.

Warren sat in the orange plastic hospital chair. His face stoic, gray eyes watching the snow falling outside the window; his thoughts hidden by his blank countenance.

Cecilia half reclined in the hospital bed. Hair disheveled from the night of childbirth, she had eyes only for the infant in her arms. She stroked his cheeks, memorizing their softness, and traced the tiny eyebrows. His small mouth had found her nipple and knew just what to do. It astonished her that it could be so easy, having anticipated only awkwardness. Touching his ridiculous abundance of dark hair, she was overcome with a love for her newborn son. She had not expected this intensity, to be so overwhelmingly besotted. Caught up in this force, Cecelia and the baby were alone in an impenetrable bubble.

The baby slept without worry about what lay ahead.

This suspended scene ended when Pedro and Victoria surged through the doorway, bumping into each other in their haste to enter, shedding coats and scarves. Warren stood up from the chair, politely, automatically. Cecilia glanced up, giving her parents a dreamy smile.

Victoria's eyes went immediately to her daughter's exposed breast. The sight bothered her so she averted her eyes, went to the bedside, took a brush out of her purse and began to smooth the tangles from Cecilia's hair, all the while sending out one comment after another as if to fill the quiet in the room.

"We're late, I'm afraid. Traffic is slow with this snow."

"How are you feeling? That didn't take too long."

She looked, not without kindness at the newborn. "He's a pretty baby."

She brushed more, and then added, "Your hair is a mess, dear."

Pedro finished taking off his coat, tossing it over the foot of the hospital bed. He strode over to the bed, stopping on the way to give his son-in-law a bear hug.

"Congratulations Warren! A son! You're a father." He pounded the younger man on the back, exhilarated, but his eyes were only on his grandson. "1977 is going to be the best year ever! What a blessed day."

His words were genuine but without waiting for a return of his hug or his exuberance, Pedro moved to the bedside. Kissing Cecilia's brow, he bent over to take in the sight of the baby.

"Everything's good, Ceci?"

"Papa, everything is wonderful. Isn't he just perfect?"

Victoria directed her questions to Warren. "Did everything go well? How long will she stay in the hospital?"

"Nurses all said it was an uncomplicated birth for a first, and she can go home this evening."

"No. Oh no. That is too soon. Back in my day, we stayed in the hospital for a week, gave us plenty of time to rest up. Warren, you need to tell the doctor to keep her longer."

"Mother, I'm fine, and I'm ready to go home tonight." Cecilia still had not looked up at her mother.

"May I hold him?" It was her father asking.

Cecilia smiled and Pedro Sanchez lifted the tiny boy as if he had been doing it daily, although it had been over twenty years since he last held an infant. As soon as the child was out of Cecilia's arms, Victoria pulled her daughter's hospital gown together. Cecilia didn't notice, as her eyes had followed her son. Pedro held the baby to his chest and buried his face in the smallness of the little one, inhaling. He began to rock back and forth gently, and soon Cecilia could hear him humming the soft Spanish lullaby she remembered him singing to her as a child.

There was another suspension of time in the room, as even Warren stood and watched.

"Warren, what have you named the baby?" Victoria broke the spell.

"Cecilia's picked out a name."

"Warren's is the last name, so I chose the first name," Cecilia said a little too quickly although her parents didn't notice. She briefly looked at her husband and then away, eyes back to the baby in her father's arms. "His name is Mateo. Mateo Schumacher."

For a brief moment Pedro stopped his rocking. Then resumed. And for those watching, his tears were simply the tears of a grandfather meeting his grandson for the first time.

The orange chair remained empty. The three adults stood around the new mother's bed like actors in a play without a director.

And the baby slept on, safe in his grandfather's song.

Two

DESTRUCTION

They stood each on a side of the kitchen table and screamed back and forth across the solid wooden barricade, shooting for the other's suddenly-exposed vulnerabilities. His venomous words masked an underlying plaintive voice and she never heard the hurt. Her self-righteous defensiveness never gave him a clue of the tender state of her emotions. Alone they stood apart across the great divide of their mugs and toast and New York Times, but together after fourteen years of silence Warren and Cecilia Schumacher blew up their marriage in one horrifying battle.

It was 1991. Mateo's fourteenth year. Cecilia and Warren's secret had lain quietly in a bottom drawer of their marriage, and while it was never revisited, it was not forgotten. This secret seeped out like a deadly gas through the cracks of the days and years, so lacking in odor that

C'ANNA BERGMAN-HILL

they were caught unawares when it suddenly overwhelmed them with violence.

The explosion came about on a gorgeous Saturday, with winter finally saying goodbye and blossoms in full show all throughout town. Only in the deepest woods was there any trace of snow. Very soon the deciduous trees would be putting out lime-green leaves that would grow with prodigious speed to cover the sky view from the windows of the houses in Pine Junction, mixing in with the evergreen pines that filled the woods.

The brothers were not home. Eleven-year-old Rowan was spending the weekend with a friend, and Mateo had left for an overnight trip with his grandfather to attend a flamenco guitar concert in nearby Amherst. The house held an unexpected quiet, and even the dogs seemed to question this unnatural state of affairs. At the breakfast table Cecilia realized with surprise that this was the very first time both boys had ever been away overnight at the same time. A few comments later, when she casually added that Mateo had certainly inherited a passion for music from his Grandfather Pedro, Warren lowered the newspaper and erupted with a force that staggered them both.

"Hell, He sure didn't get it from me! Seems to me he inherited everything from his grandfather."

Cecilia froze at his tone. There was a long, loud silence between them. Startled out of her usual calmness, she stared at her husband and then demanded, her voice cracking, "What's that supposed to mean?"

"Maybe he's really Pedro's son." Warren spat out these words like a man spits out poison too long held in his cheek.

His face was contorted, uncomfortable with his own outpouring. There followed a long pause before Cecilia could manage a thought.

"My God, what are you saying?"

"Do I have to spell it out?"

The air around Cecilia's body felt like it was whirling and the staccato of her heartbeat in her temples filled the room with its volume.

"I am saying that maybe you came back to Pine Junction and screwed around with your father when all the while you were playing at being the demure little library student in New York!"

She gagged. "Unbelievable. How dare you say such vile . . . perverted trash."

"You are the one who is unbelievable, you hypocritical, deceitful bitch."

Warren jumped up and creased the newspaper. The tense movement of his hands belied the surety of his tone. The slight shaking of his upper lip and his long fingers might have been rage, or might have been fear.

Cecilia abruptly stood up too and grabbed the chair for support. Astonished. Outraged. His words punched at her and her own replies were unrecognizable, like the voice of a stranger.

"I can't believe you are talking to me this way. Such filth. Such accusations." She violently shook her head. " . . . so ugly, so hateful, so . . . you're disgusting!"

"Fuck you and your church-going family. Maybe you have all been lying to me all along." Warren's eyes were wild now; he was losing all the control he prided himself on possessing. "All that boy ever thinks about is his grandfather, and you've encouraged it since the day he was born."

She swept her arms up into the air as if guiding a plane to land. Shouting now, causing the dogs to run away, whimpering.

"So he's close to his grandfather! At least my Papa shows him some affection. You ignore him and only give Rowan attention. You can't deny that."

"Rowan feels like my son. Damn you. Mateo, he is like no one's son, or like your precious Papa's son."

Warren was glaring at her, breathing hard. They stared at each other, like strangers. In two minutes everything had changed.

"If he is close to my father it is because Papa has earned that love. Making that evil accusation about my Papa is the cruelest thing I've ever heard. That you could even think such a slimy thought makes me want to puke."

Cecilia looked like she might indeed throw up right there at the kitchen table. The whirling sensation continued and she grabbed wildly for the wall for support. Warren jerked defensively as she made the move and then looked at his clenched fist and smashed it into the nearby cabinet, letting out a growl of pain as he did so, then yelled back at her.

"Oh, you and your Sanchez family pedestal. What a bunch of crap. Talk about wanting to vomit."

They were both terrified but could not stop the torrent. Bitter accusations followed one after another. The fear showed up in their bodies. Warren smashed the wall, breaking through to the old lathe and plaster. Cecilia swept a lamp off the table with a wild motion. The fight took their words and bodies and flung them around the room, but husband and wife did not touch each other.

Holding his injured hand, Warren snarled at Cecilia who was pacing back and forth across the worn wooden floor.

"Well, if it wasn't your dad, why don't you tell me about what was going on with you back then when we were supposedly engaged?"

Cecilia stopped pacing and replied like an ice queen, which goaded him further.

"I told you everything you needed to know at the time."

"You never told me details."

"You didn't ask and you don't need to know any more."

Cecilia sounded in control but she began sobbing, dropping onto her knees.

"I think you owe me more." Warren breathed hard and first muttered and then shouted out, "Fucking bitch. Don't know why I fell for your begging eyes."

"I didn't beg. You have a really screwed up memory of what happened. You're the one who wanted to go on with things. You! You were adamant about that. We had to get married. Everything would work out."

Cecilia's voice was shrill. Warren's face was hate.

"My mother told me not to marry a Mexican. She said you'd lose your looks and then be a bitch."

"What? Now you bring up my race? And your mother?" Cecilia sneered. "What has she ever done for you and what does she have to do with us, or with Matty and Rowan?"

"Leave Rowan out of this."

"You are the biggest bastard I have ever met. I can't believe what you are saying." Breathing was difficult. Pain pressed fiercely on her chest, or maybe the pressure was from the inside out. "Cruel . . . cruel . . . " She lost the ability to formulate a sentence but then her outrage at this injustice gave her voice again. "Speaking of our sons that way. They are just children. How dare you?"

"Children! That is all you care about." Warren felt about five years old but he cried out, "What about me?"

For another hour this unraveling carried on, full of much that was untrue, considerable half truths, an occasional but misrepresented truth, all that had built up. Eventually they ran empty of words. Bodies spent, they collapsed into separate corners, dripping with tears and mucus and sweat, guts pulled out of their bodies and left hanging, raw and putrid. Spent, their ability to think was suspended.

Warren and Cecilia had faced each other at last, but the facade of their marriage sheltered only emptiness. Nothing of substance for rebuilding after this vicious disembowelment. Theirs was the cruelty of resentment left unexamined and unexpressed.

Three

While Warren and Cecilia staggered through the wreckage of their fight, their sons were having a carefree day, each in his own favorite way. Having been mesmerized by the magic of the guitarist, Mateo talked nonstop and ate ice cream with secret sips of his Grand Pedro's coffee. Rowan was equally happy with his best friend's family across town. And the neighbors, whose home bordered the Schumacher's wide garden happened to be out shopping that morning, so when the secret snuck out and grabbed Cecilia and Warren by the throats, slinging them around until they were defeated, it stayed hidden from both the helpful and unhelpful ears of Pine Junction.

Cecilia and Warren never talked to each other again after the fight, unless you count the note that Warren left saying that he was moving to Amherst and that Cecilia should get a lawyer. She never lifted her voice to try to stop his exodus. End of the marriage. It was that abrupt. Of course there were loose ends to tie up for both of them. Besides the divorce and legal issues, there was Warren's business move to a new town. Cecilia kept the house. Mundane and messy details. Cecilia undertook alone the task of telling boys, family, friends, pastor, patrons of the library, and on and on. Life in a small town is very inter-connected. But with no explanation ever given, everyone was astonished and all grappled to form an opinion.

It helped that Warren was not a native and left town after the big blowup. His fourteen years in Pine Junction could be seen as a faint blip on the small town radar. Cecilia moved as if in a daze for some time before seem-ingly regaining her composure, lost in her books and job and garden, drinking endless cups of tea at the kitchen table while looking out the window at the pines outside.

Close inspection showed that the boys were stunned. Rowan separated himself from his family as much as possible, spending more and more time with his friends and their families, immersing himself in the sports, cars, games, and social activities that an eleven-year-old loves. Mateo seemed to be pretty unchanged on the surface, but more and more he hung out with his grandfather. He took a cleaning job at the church and spent hours there with the church organist, Vic Dalloway, playing chess, discuss-ing philosophy and music, and he spent summer days out on his bike. When he was home, he clutched his guitar as though it was his best friend, in his bedroom or out on the hammock with one of the family dogs at his feet.

Four years passed in this manner with absolutely no discussion about what had transpired. That the marriage had ended was the fact. It simply become the new reality. Mateo graduated from high school a semester early, and then instead of accepting one of his college admission offers, he disappointed everyone by fulfilling the dream he had nurtured for several years, moving to New York, guitar over his shoulder, duffle bag in hand. During the next ten years in this biggest of cities, he was as happy as he remembered being since he was a small boy. Mateo created a self-contained life for himself with little thought to family. He exchanged some correspondence with his beloved grandfather, but that contact was minimal compared to the loving and instructional impact Pedro Sanchez had bestowed upon Mateo's upbringing. Pedro missed the boy tremendously but never pressured Mateo in any manner.

Rowan convinced his mom to let him attend, and got his father to pay for, a boarding school during high school from where he managed to come home to Cecilia as seldom as possible, spending breaks with his friends' families or with his father. He went on to college and majored in business, becoming a stockbroker as soon as he could make it happen for himself. He saw his father some, his mother occasionally, and his brother a total of four times in the ten years Mateo lived in New York.

Financially Warren did his duty by the boys and paid child support. But he was erased from the little town of Pine Junction, having left only his name with three people: Cecilia, Mateo, and Rowan Schumacher, who drifted far apart. From all appearances, Warren Schumacher did move on successfully in his life, but regarding his happiness and how well he dealt with the secret that had sundered his marriage to Cecilia, none of the residents of Pine Junction ever knew.

PART ONE

Pine Junction

ONE

No one knew what Cecilia knew about Cecilia.

One night, in the middle of 2004, she woke up in a panic, heart pounding. Another dream. After hours of twisting, squeezing her pillows and staring at the digital clock, what was the point of finally getting to sleep if the nightmares would come? She was sick of this routine. Since the planes slammed into the World Trade Center, Cecilia Sanchez Schumacher could not remember a single good night's sleep. She slumped back on the rumpled sheets and stared toward the darkened ceiling. Not that there had been many good nights prior to September 11, 2001, but now it was relentless, this insomnia. And since the invasion of Iraq in 2003, it had become worse, with the dreams invading what little sleep she did salvage each night. A duo plagued her nights: rampaging thoughts of injustice combined with violent dreams.

Cecilia lived alone these days so her midnight floor pacing and her 2:00 a.m. hot showers were her own little secrets. How she managed to make it through her days being productive and organized, as well as reasonably sociable and civilized, was a wonder to her. And she was all of the above: productive, organized, civilized and on the surface at least, sociable. No library patron would have known of her wrecked heart. No one sitting in the pews on Sunday morning would have seen her calm face in the choir and guessed the tumultuous thoughts wrestling in her mind. When she was working in her garden, or walking down the streets of her home town, she looked picture perfect, in her mid-life now, gracious and dignified.

Her friends and family were well aware of the topic most crucial to her these days, however. She talked of it often with friends and acquaintances, at the grocery store, at church coffee hour or on the phone to old college roommates. But they did not know the intensity of Cecilia's anguish.

Fortunately, this particular bad night was followed by Saturday morning, meaning there was no early rising and work routine required. On Saturday the library opened at noon for only four hours, so her morning was free.

At 9:00 Olivia's cheerful voice drifted up the stairs.

"Ceci. Ceci? Are you home?"

Cecilia groaned, pulled herself out of bed, thrust her arms into her old green robe, and peered down the stairs into the entryway where her sister stood looking up at her.

"Oh good, glad I caught you," chirped Olivia. "I wanted to pick up the cookies you made for the bake sale."

Cecilia looked at her blankly.

"Don't tell me you forgot? The bake sale for my students."

More silence.

"Remember, to raise money for our field trip to Boston next semester?"

"Oh darn, Livia, I am sorry. But you know, I think I have some in the freezer from Christmas. Let me see how they look."

"My God Ceci, I hope the cookies look better than you do. You look awful."

Cecilia shuffled down the stairs and gave her younger sister a glare before moving to the kitchen.

Olivia Sanchez, Olivia Howard, and now Olivia Miller, was a pale version of Cecilia. It was as if someone had photo-shopped Cecilia with her deep brown eyes and hair, her rich tan skin, and produced a second version, identical in details but lacking in vividness. Through the years her family had viewed Olivia as less substantial than either of her older sisters. But these days Olivia was sailing high, in love and full of a glow absent in her earlier life and first marriage. Her attitude towards Cecilia was almost nauseatingly kind. Cecilia felt patronized, but then shook that feeling off as uncharitable. She was honestly happy for her sister. It was a delight to see her content.

"Bad night?"

"Yeah, didn't get much sleep and then had a nightmare." Cecilia sighed and pulled a large container out of the freezer and handed it to Olivia. "Open this and see how this batch has held up. I trust you have other more reliable sources for your bake sale?"

"Yes, although you are usually the one I can count on. I guess you are allowed one screw-up." Olivia peered into the container and pronounced the snicker doodles to be in pristine shape, and if she could just get some plastic she would wrap them in small packages for sale.

"Your cookies are always the first to be bought. You always were the best baker in the family."

"Thanks, Livia. I am honored. Queen of the bake sales, that's me. Here is the plastic wrap and how about some tea? I need to wake up. Have to go to work at noon and it may take me three hours to get my eyes and brain functioning."

Cecilia groaned without realizing she had done so, and after putting the water on to boil, she sank into a chair and watched as her sister began methodically wrapping up packages of cookies. She didn't offer to help.

"So tell me about your dream, sis." Olivia looked up from her wrapping.

Cecilia poured the boiling water over the loose tea leaves before answering.

"Oh the usual." Cecilia tried to lighten up her mood and her voice. "People dying, bombs going off. Families crying over the bloodied bodies of their loved ones. You know, kind of like the evening news . . . ."

"Hm, yes, only without our smirking president talking about how cool it is to shock and awe the world." Olivia mocked..

Olivia was sympathetic. Cecilia knew this, yet she also sensed that Olivia could state her view with sincerity but then move on. In fact it seemed like everyone Cecilia knew in her liberal enclave shared similar opinions about politics, and certainly about this war. But the difference was that somehow others were able to leave their outrage in a box and just go on with their lives. But not her, not Cecilia. She lived and breathed injustice.

Olivia looked at her sister steadily. "I am sorry. This is all pretty awful for you isn't it? The war and the news and all."

Cecilia appreciated her sister's awareness but felt incapable of truly sharing how much she hurt inside, everyday, all the time. Every single civilian death or military death, be it American soldier or Iraqi soldier or Iraqi citizen felt to Cecilia akin to the death of her own child. Every posturing by the American administrative policymakers incensed her enough to throw things at the television. She felt her body filled constantly with red hot anger, until all she could do was go outside and walk and walk and walk.

Maybe she should try more often to explain how she experienced all of this. But she could never get to the level of what she felt.

She took a breath and said to Olivia, "I just don't understand how the American people can believe all this, all this crap," and she drew that word out with such a curl of her lip that had it not been so serious to Cecilia, Olivia might have smiled. "For the life of me, I just cannot see how every American doesn't just rise up and scream back, 'I'm mad as hell and I won't take it anymore!!' "

Olivia shrugged and replied, "I agree with you, Ceci. I do. But it's hard to know what to do that will make any difference. The country is still scared to death about 9/11, and that fear is making everyone paranoid. When people are scared they want someone to tell them what to do, someone who makes them feel good about themselves, like we Americans are so special that God should bless only us, and that we all have to stick together because any dissent marks you as a traitor."

Olivia spoke calmly, but Cecilia looked at her sister thankfully. It was the most outspoken she had ever heard Olivia be.

Olivia continued as she wrapped up the last package of snicker doodles and swallowed her last sip of Earl Gray. "I appreciate that you went to all those peace marches a few years ago, you know, back before we invaded Iraq for their weapons of mass destruction. I felt you were representing the whole family on those marches."

Cecilia absorbed both the support and the irony of Olivia's comments. She rubbed her eyes and looked even more weary.

"Yeah, well, fat lot of difference it did this round. It felt so powerful to be out marching together, kind of like Vietnam war protest days. Only in those days it seemed to make change happen. Not now though. It's a different time. There was ugly stuff then, too, but there was also a sense of solidarity with people working for a cause."

Olivia looked up from her work and nodded. "Don't forget, we had not been attacked on our shores then, and we had a draft too, so everyone was affected. Now the military can buy their army from the poor and those who can't see a better future. The draft gave us a much wider perspective. But Ceci, I am not sure you want a draft back, do you? Not with Rowan and Matty or even my Julia in their twenties.

Believe me, Livia, I have wrestled with that possibility over and over again. I would be furious if whatever current administration happens to be in Washington forced our sons and daughters to fight its misguided war. At least there is some sense of choice now. But oh my, the horror of it all.

"I just feel so helpless to stop anything." She went on, speaking to herself. "Am I crazy? But no, it really is a murderous uncalled-for action, and I'm part of it unless I do something . . . I'm guilty too."

Cecilia tried to pull herself together, not fall apart completely, and finished her rambling self-recrimination weakly.

"Guess it's time for me to write another letter to the editor, maybe the Boston Globe or NY Times, and see if they will print it. Local papers will put it in, but people may be tired of my voice."

Olivia put the cookies into her cloth bag and shook her head at her sister. "You write very well, Ceci, and no one ever gets tired of your letters. They make people think about important issues. So go for it." She paused a second. "Especially if it helps you exorcise some of your anger!"

As she walked by Cecilia on her way to the door, Olivia stopped and put her hand on her sister's shoulder.

"Well, give me a hug. Thanks for the cookies. Maybe you should go camp by the White House in protest. But for me, I guess I'll go ahead and sell snicker doodles and fudge to raise money for my students to go to Boston to study American history and see how democracy works!"

Cecilia gave Olivia a wry smile and a hug and saw her out the door. Olivia, in teacher-mode, always looked very purposeful.

When Olivia drove off, Cecilia returned to her kitchen, to her old sofa under the window and hugged her second cup of tea between her hands, letting the steam engulf her face, eyes closed, wondering and thinking. Had she been more optimistic when she was younger because there was more to be optimistic about? Had things really become more evil and hopeless? Or had her world view changed as she had gotten older? Or maybe it was menopausal hormones messing with her mind. Sometimes she could drive herself crazy.

Just a week earlier Cecilia had tried a conversation about the Iraqi war with the oldest Sanchez sister, Maria. As was often the case the conversation with Maria had not felt satisfying to Cecilia. Dr. Maria Sanchez was a well-respected professor of history. In the eyes of the rest of the Sanchezes, Maria was confident and accomplished, but unapproachable. Maria was a dynamic force but not reliable for compassionate listening.

In contrast, this morning's conversation with Olivia left Cecilia feeling understood. It was a pleasant sensation. Still, Cecilia sensed that Olivia had plenty to distract her from thinking too much about the political dissatisfactions: new husband, grown daughter still not fledged, a huge garden to tend. Plus Cecilia suspected that Olivia's daily interaction with children would keep her focused on the future. Surely a person would need to have an attitude of hopefulness if she interacted with little ones every day.

As for Maria, she was not sensitive to the level of despair that Cecilia lived with. Their politics were not much different and their values were similar at a deep level. But when Cecilia tried to explain her horror at what was going on across the world, she felt Maria glaze over. Maybe Cecilia was imagining that reaction in her big sister. Cecilia knew that she and Maria played out their hopes and beliefs differently. Cecilia considered herself a spiritual being, and her church life was one very important aspect of that spirituality. The music, rituals, and mystery of worship filled and fed her soul. This was not Maria's style at all. Maria was a nature buff and an outdoors woman who kayaked, hiked, and ran marathons. From all appearances, Maria slept well.

Cecilia put down her cup. She almost smiled. In the midst of her anguish, she had to admit perhaps therein lay the biggest difference between the sisters. Maria slept well. Cecilia did not. As she washed out her well-used tea cup, Cecilia wondered if the sleep issue was the symptom or the cause. Ah. That was something else to think about, and Cecilia spent too much time thinking as it was.

Maria had no children. No wonder Maria slept better. Cecilia rested her hands on the counter, brows furrowed. Behind the center stage of sadness Cecilia felt regarding the Iraq debacle lay her heartache at the disconnection between herself and her sons, Rowan and Mateo, her beloved boys. Now in their twenties, there were no harsh words, but they were simply not a part of her life. She missed them like an arm being ripped from her body, but only when she let herself dwell on their loss. As painful as it was, she did not allow their absence to rise to the surface very often. Yet she knew it was there, like a bubble of sadness in the core of her. It was not only that she missed them, but she was convinced that her own actions were responsible for the fissure in their idyllic childhood.

Cecilia went upstairs, shed her big robe and stepped into the shower to try to be soothed and awakened at the same time. She let the water pour onto her face, through her hair, down her breasts and her belly, and turning around, her back and legs, a body now matured but still lush, full of warmth and appeal. The water felt like heaven.

This moment of relaxation was broken too soon by her own self-monitoring, reminding herself to check the web site started by a California minister who kept a daily tally on deaths in Iraq, both civilian and military, local and American. Since the first bombings of Iraq, as a daily ritual, Cecilia added one stone each morning to her garden shrine.

TWO

Mateo Schumacher shoved back a strand of dark hair and gazed around him, his guitar resting comfortably across his back and his duffel bag against his leg. His ride gunned the engine and disappeared around the curve of the country road and the sound slowly faded. The silence that surrounded him pressed into his skin, making him sweat. When the quiet was shattered by the fierce squawk of a blue jay, the young man jerked, looking around to see if anyone had seen how startled he was. No one around.

Among the pines, some deciduous trees were pushing out vibrant baby green leaves. It had been late spring when he left and now it was on the far edge of springtime yet again, 2005. Here, two hundred miles from his city home, the barista stood at the crossroads without appreciation for the cliché that was playing out.

Ten years ago, eighteen-year-old Mateo began a new life and became an urban man. Ten years of waking up to the sound of the garbage trucks, loud voices and smashing bins, yet Mateo had no trouble sleeping. For ten years, the rooftop chords of his guitar were sandwiched between the sirens below and traffic helicopters overhead. Ten years of car horns and buses farting around him as he rode his bike confidently alert down the crowded streets. Ten years of the swoosh of the coffee machines at the Urban Perk Cafe, accompanied by off-color shouts back and forth among his work mates and over the counter to the endless stream of customers. And ten years of the neighborhood buzz only slightly muffled through the walls during late night squeezes at his girlfriend's apartment. For ten years, city living had roared around him. And he was content.

Mateo wasn't sure whether he was taking the high road in coming back home or starting a quick trip to disaster, but he was not a coward, and he was here, and so he took a deep breath, picked up his bag, hoisted the guitar case back up to its familiar position, and brushed the hair out of his eyes again. Between the thick trees the mid- morning sun lit up the road that curved in front of him.

Pine Junction, Massachusetts, was a mile down the road, and his walk gave him a chance to think about what might be ahead of him. Once he had received the message from Pine Junction's First Congregational minister, a call he had not returned, he had thought of little else but old times. His memories were both bad and good. However, thinking about the past brought about a growing sense of shame that he had so completely left it all behind. With the impetus of newly discovered guilt, Mateo abruptly found someone to take his shift at the Perk for a week, made a weak explanation to his girlfriend that left her confused, and posted a note on the cafe bulletin board requesting a lift out of town that next day. Conversation with the young woman who provided his ride helped the trip pass quickly from city streets to the busy interstate highway north to a country highway, all leading to this road. Ahead of him lay the town of Pine Junction.

THREE

Mateo's intended stop as he walked around a bend in the road towards town was the church itself. It was the first building one came upon along the narrow road. Mateo knew this road well, as a youth having ridden his bike almost daily to the junction in the road where the highway swept by. The sign in front of the church listed the same Reverend Rex Randall who had left the phone message on Mateo's cell phone a few days earlier. Reverend Randall was new to the church since Mateo had last attended a church event. How he had tracked down Mateo's phone number, and why he had decided to make the phone call was something Mateo wanted to find out.

At his age, Mateo's lean body was almost always hungry for something, be it food, conversation, sex, or music. Life was a physical sensation for Mateo, and he wanted as much as he could have of everything that felt good, looked good, tasted good, sounded good, and just generally interested him. But he was pretty laid back about it all, because he had found that getting what he craved was fairly effortless.

In Brooklyn where he eventually settled, there was always someone ready to make connections. A coffee shop as busy as the Urban Perk provided a never ending opportunity to converse. Mateo was quick at his work, could talk and make the most complicated drinks at the same time. He thrived on conversation. If no one familiar was around, Mateo did not feel uncomfortable striking up a conversation with a complete stranger, be it on the subway or street corner. Conversation was easy in Mateo's world.

So was sex. Many friends found themselves admiring with envy but somehow no resentment how easily relationships worked out for Mateo. He was appealing for his physical presence as well as his unthreatening charisma. While his relationship with his current girlfriend was a committed one, prior to meeting Catherine at a cello recital, he had moved from one woman to another without ever apparently injuring any of the women's fondness for him.

But it was making and hearing music that fed Mateo's soul. The driving force that pulled Mateo to New York was his desire to live with music, right smack in the middle of music, whenever he wanted it. His pay as a barista gave him just enough money to hang out at cafes, clubs, and concerts. Mateo himself was not ambitious and only mildly disciplined, but he had innate talent and he exuded passion for a wide spectrum of music and musicians.

Music was in Mateo's head one hundred percent of the time. At this very moment as he approached the traditional front entrance of the First Congregational Church, he was having a flashback to one of the hymns he grew up hearing when the former pastor, Reverend Carl Prescott, selected the songs. Mateo still shared Reverend Prescott's love of a good rousing hymn. Right now "Blessed Assurance" filled Mateo's head in full glorious memory.

As musical memories swirled through his mind, he had a different growing concern. Where could he find a good cup of coffee in Pine Junction? Mateo's love of coffee went well back and had been reinforced daily by his work in one of the best coffee shops in the New York area. With each step he took now, Mateo was feeling the need to satisfy his craving. He contemplated the virtues of the brew; coffee was ritual and relationship and comfort and more. In a sudden bout of irrationality, Mateo felt panicked. Coffee right now was alarmingly absent.

Perhaps a good cup of coffee would help Mateo put together the mystery of the phone call soliciting his return to Pine Junction. Rex Randall's words had been brief, but a sense of urgency had survived the crackling cell phone reception for which Pine Junction and vicinity was notorious.

"Mateo, this is Pastor Randall from First Congo Pine Junction. Your mom is not . . . uh, is not doing well. You could make a big difference here."

The phone line went dead before briefly coming back to life . . . . "I ran into Dane Faber last winter at the pharmacy . . . "

After this unfinished sentence the phone signal faltered and whatever else Reverend Randall added was lost completely. This last cryptic phrase, however, brought some name recall tugging at the back recesses of Mateo's memory, vague and without context.

Now Mateo stood in front of the traditional white steeple of his home church, hoping that somewhere in Pine Junction someone had opened a good coffee shop over the last ten years.

FOUR

"**B**lessed Assurance" was not just in Mateo's mind, it was coming from behind the front doors of the sanctuary. Organ music at full blast, meaning the church was empty and Vic Dalloway was indulging himself as only an organist in an empty church can do when given a fine instrument to play. Mateo grinned and stood there enjoying it from outside the door.

Then suddenly just as the song reached, "This is my story, this is my . . . " the music stopped abruptly and various loud thumping sounds were heard. Mateo leapt up the stairs, pulled open the double doors, and found Vic on his knees in the narthex closet, muttering to himself.

"Vic. You okay?"

"Damn mice!" was the reply from Vic who didn't even turn around to see who was standing behind him.

Mateo was smiling again. Some things had not changed a bit in the ten years he was gone. Vic and the mice had a long battle going.

"What'd they get this time?" Mateo asked him.

"Pilgrim Hymnal" came the muffled answer from deep inside the closet. "Ah hah." Vic's hand found the mouse trap and he unwound his slender body, agile for a man approaching sixty. The common opinion was that the full-body workout demanded by playing the huge concert organ was all the exercise Vic Dalloway needed.

He stood with graceful ease and faced Mateo. He stared for a second before the familiar guitar over Mateo's shoulder and the big wide grin gave the younger man's identity away. "Well, son of a gun! Mateo Schumacher!! If this doesn't beat all, eh?" Before either Mateo or Vic knew what happened, Vic grabbed Mateo into a big warm embrace. Then just as quickly he released him, embarrassed for his untypically demonstrative showing.

"Hey, Vic. How's it going? Aside from the mice I mean."

"Winter was never-ending, it's already a bad year for rodents, budget for choir music has been decimated . . . but otherwise I won't complain." Vic looked Mateo up and down. But it was an affectionate appraisal, and he added, "Cup of tea?"

Inwardly Mateo groaned. Tea. But he knew he would no more get coffee from Vic than he would from his mother.

Mateo followed Vic's long strides down the side aisle of the sanctuary past the stained glass windows that lined each side of the church. He gave them as quick a check as he could on the run and was glad to see no damage. As a high school student one of Mateo's jobs had been to clean these windows. He knew every story, and every glass piece on all twelve windows of the old church

They went into a door near the choir loft, to the choir room, Vic's own personal sanctuary. It was unclear whether Vic ever went home to the stark apartment he rented in town. He was rarely seen there, even by his landlord. This corner of the choir room was Vic's kingdom. Here was the same ancient plaid recliner that Mateo remembered. On one side of the chair was a stack of musical scores, organ and choir music. On the other was the familiar pile of Agatha Christie mysteries to which Vic was addicted. On the back wall, there was a sink and his electric tea pot as well as a toaster oven and microwave. A small refrigerator completed Vic's homey corner.

Also on the side table by the old recliner was a pack of cigarettes. Long years after most of the parishioners had given up the habit, Vic continued to enjoy his cigarettes. To Vic's credit, he was a very considerate smoker. He wandered a considerable distance into the woods that surrounded the church, enjoying his tobacco in solitude before returning to his church garden and organ.

Once when Mateo and his friends had been in elementary school, they followed Vic into the woods at a safe distance hoping that he would throw out his cigarette butt with enough left for the friends to have a smoke. But Vic carefully put out his cigarette, and brought the butt back to the church where it was thrown out discreetly. The boys never saw the subtle smile on Vic's face.

Now Mateo pulled up a chair from the choir circle and watched while Vic made the tea. Vic's back was straight.

When he turned around, Mateo noticed a few more lines on his face, but otherwise Vic seemed unchanged.

Mateo took the tea cup with an inner sigh. Tea. Where was his coffee? Vic looked at him directly now.

"How's mom?" Mateo finally said.

"You really don't keep up, do you, eh?"

Mateo suddenly had the urge to take a deep drink of tea and buried his face in the cup, while Vic kept his gaze on him relentlessly.

The loquacious Mateo found himself speechless. Silence seemed the only recourse at this moment. Or perhaps flight. But to where? He had come this far, and really, what could he expect? From this perspective, ten years did seem like a long time to be gone and incommunicative.

Finally Vic took mercy on the young man and shrugged. "Hey, I know how it is. I was young once too, if you believe that. You might recall I was born in Canada, in Manitoba. Left home when I was twenty-five. Never contacted my folks for five years. At least your mom knows where you live."

Mateo put his tea cup down with surprise, and found his voice. "Really? You mean you just left the country and disappeared?"

"Yes. Don't look so shocked, Mateo. I don't think you have too much to be sanctimonious about yourself!"

A grimace passed over Mateo's face. But his curiosity got the better of him and he pushed on with his questions. "Why? Where did you go? Did you eventually get in touch?"

Vic looked like he was a little sorry to have opened this Pandora's box, but he was a fair man and so he continued to sit in his chair and drink his tea with more satisfaction than Mateo.

"Dad put me through music school in Winnipeg, which is all I ever wanted to do, but he complained with every check he sent to me what a worthless study music was. How it would never get me a job. How I would never make any money. What a disappointment I was to him. My mom never said anything. Never stood up for me, and never did anything but sigh and look defeated. Not sure why they even put up the money for my studies. They didn't come to my recitals even, much less my graduation."

At this point Vic stood up and puttered with making some more tea. Mateo sat still in the silence. Finally with his back still to Mateo, Vic spoke again.

"At least the beatings stopped when I went away to school. Dad knew I wouldn't have taken it any more so he kept his belt on his pants once I turned eighteen. I went back home after graduation and worked two years in the family department store to pay them back for every penny of my education."

Mateo shifted his gaze and didn't know what to say. Vic finished up his story simply. "I left. I sent word through a go-between that I was alive but didn't want to communicate. Gave them no contact information." He paused for a very long minute before completing the longest personal story he had told in years. "They died. Five years seven months after I left, both gone. Cancer got both of them within four months. Hard to fathom. My uncle tracked me down and I went back for the memorials. I had no brothers or sisters to help me clean out the house. Found a scrapbook in my mom's drawer. Chock full of programs from my recitals and newspaper clippings from my concerts. I have no idea where she acquired them . . . . Not much more to say. Not much I could think of to do, so I came back to the States and my music."

Mateo sat with this unveiling, his own mind full of a jumble of thoughts. Finally he blurted, "You know, my mom never beat me. We didn't even fight. My dad, either."

Vic's response was short. "There're a lot of ways to disconnect. People let each other down."

This unexpected encounter was going into uncharted territory for both the young man and his elder.

Vic cleared his throat and asked, "Seen your brother lately?"

"Nah. Last time I saw Rowan was maybe two years ago. He came to the City and took me out for lunch, expensive place, food was over-rated, but the cocktails were good, and the coffee too. He picked me up in a black BMW. Dressed like GQ . . . . We didn't have a lot to talk about. Mostly he told me about his stocks. Guess he's a broker now . . . . He didn't talk about Mom or Pine Junction at all. Didn't ask about my life either . . . . Guess I wasn't interested enough to ask too much about his . . . . He sure did spend the money though."

"Hope it was his money he was spending." Vic stopped at Mateo's quick look. "Ah well, of course it was.

Don't know what I am talking about. Gossip you know. Too many old gossips around here." Then he quickly changed the subject. "You met the new pastor yet?"

"Reverend Randall? No, what's he like?"

"Good man. You don't fall asleep during his sermons. He manages to keep the old folks happy and the young families like him too. He understands music, even caught him playing the organ once soon after he arrived."

Mateo looked startled at this news. Vic was notoriously protective of the magnificent Casavant Freres pipe organ. "Really?"

"Never did it again. We came to an understanding. But I have to admit, he did know what he was doing . . . for an amateur." This sidewise praise was quite remarkable coming from Vic. "Problem with your brother, he never did respect music. He had no soul for it. Sad." Vic shook his head.

Mateo found himself overwhelmed by all the new stories. Feeling a need to escape led him to stand up, dump out his cold tea into the sink, and ask if Reverend Randall was in. Vic affirmed that he was, and then began to look around for the mouse trap and his peanut butter jar to load it up. As the two headed for the door they bumped each other. Mateo deferred to the older man to let him pass out the door ahead of him. As Vic moved down the aisle back to his organ and mice, he called behind him to Mateo, "Take care of Ceci," which gave Mateo one more tidbit to ponder. Ceci was his mother's pet name, the name only used by her intimates or dearest friends. Vic Dalloway had not been on that list ten years ago, or at least not to Mateo's knowledge.

To cover his confusion he called out to Vic's angular back, "Mice get anything besides the Pilgrim's Hymnal?"

"Bach's Brandenburg. Damn those rodents!! Not a page left un-shredded!"

"You know that by heart, Vic. Not to worry," he laughed.

FIVE

When Rex Randall arrived in Pine Junction four years earlier in the spring of 2001, he was in an enviable place in his ministry and career, namely, at the peak. At fifty-five, he was seasoned, a real veteran not just "of the cross" but of a great array of human crises, global and personal, both of which took considerable patience and wisdom to mediate. His strength as a pastor was his unfailing love for people, having long ago learned to forgive others and himself. No one left a conversation with Rex Randall without a sense that whether they had agreed or not, there remained between the two individuals a deep respect. Rex's skill was not one that can be taught, and Rex had achieved this only in fits and starts over time. His years as a local church pastor had given him an unmatched opportunity to observe a vast variety of human relationships.

When he arrived in Pine Junction Rex was old enough to know strength and humility both, and young enough to have the energy to carry out the necessary duties and still have a fire in his belly for his congregation.

Pine Junction was not the most demanding parish work he had done in his three decades of ministry. But when he had discerned that it was time to leave his large suburban church, it was a decision made all the clearer by the death of his wife Beth. He, in his grief, longed to be where trees outnumbered people.

Several years had gone by since the Pine Junction church had lost their long-time institution of a minister, the Reverend Doctor Carl Prescott. The coming together of Rex Randall and Pine Junction First Congregational Church was a peaceful marriage. When Rex immediately relocated his office to a smaller but sunny room with big windows overlooking the woods behind the church, he was able to redirect the shock of the long-time members who were thrown off by this unheard of notion of change. Rex simply turned the much larger former pastor's office into a Deacons and Elders meeting room, with a sizable library of memorabilia from the Carl Prescott era. All were happy.

Rex won over Vic Dalloway within a week of his arrival by deliberately crossing the line. He played the church's phenomenal pipe organ despite having been fully forewarned of Vic's proprietary feelings. When Vic showed up with indignation in his face, Rex was able to not just calm the livid musician, but also to discuss the beautiful instrument and music in general with deep knowledge as few had ever been able to do before. Rex agreed that he would be far too busy to spend any time at the organ. So they both walked away satisfied, feeling they had their places on the team. Rex still suffered daily from the loss of his Beth, but he found that the work in Pine Junction fulfilled him and the setting suited his soul.

On the day that Mateo arrived in Pine Junction, Rex was not in his office. He was spending the morning in happy solitude mending the fence that went along the side of the church property. Carl Prescott would never have done such a thing. The old timer led the life of a clerical student and worship leader. But Rex was made of different stuff, and during the week days he could as often be found with a screw driver or hammer in his hand as a book. With the current caretaker out on a disability leave, it seemed natural to Rex to pick up some of the slack around the building. This maintenance work felt to him like a working meditation.

When Mateo entered the church office after saying goodbye to Vic, a young man stuck his head out of the supply room and inquired if he could help.

"Reverend Randall in?"

"Out fixing the fence." Pointing out the door, the office manager rolled his eyes affectionately, not being himself inclined to get grubby. "Go on out. You can leave your bags here if you like. I'll watch them."

Mateo divested himself of his belongings, and feeling lighter but almost light-headed, he started out the door. Behind him the office manager called out, "Tell Pastor Randall it's time for his coffee break. I just made a new pot. Pastor's dead serious about his coffee. That will get him in."

The words were music to Mateo's ears, and he turned and grinned conspiratorially with the young man now busy at his computer.

Behind the church there was a courtyard, almost Spanish style, somewhat architecturally out of place with the New England-style building. On one side of the courtyard was a building with a few classrooms, and along the back side of the church property was a Fellowship Hall, where much of the life of the congregation happened. The buildings made a U shape to contain the courtyard. On the fourth side of the courtyard a fence separated the church property from the trees of the open woods, the woods of Mateo's childhood play, the woods that brought Rex such solace and gave Vic a private place to enjoy his cigarette.

Here at this fence Mateo located Reverend Rex Randall, the man who had sparked this whole odyssey. Finally Mateo hoped to find out what was going on.

Rex Randall was a tall man, slim except for a slight middle aged paunch. As a young minister, he had been well known in the social justice circles not just for his passionate sermons, but also for his mane of vibrant red-gold hair, worn long to his shoulders. Over the years, his theology had evolved along with his hair; the focus and the fervency was not gone, but like his hair, just tempered. Now his hair was much shorter, just slightly curling around his ears, and his still reddish beard was speckled with gray. Kind eyes shone with intelligence behind his glasses, which were at this moment sliding down his nose as he sweated in the effort of his work. In work clothes, Rex was a comfortable-looking man. In suit and tie or clerical robes, he was distinguished.

Lost in his work, humming a song that Mateo almost recognized, Rex did not notice Mateo's approach. When Mateo cleared his throat Rex looked up calmly, seemingly not surprised to be disturbed. His glance was questioning in Mateo's direction.

"Reverend Randall, I'm Mateo Schumacher. You called me."

"Ah. Mateo. How good to meet you." Rex reached out and enthusiastically shook Mateo's hand. "I wondered if you would come. Never heard back from you. I was on a hike the day I called from my cell phone. Our coverage here in Pine Junction is pretty abysmal, so I wasn't entirely sure I had gotten through to you, or whether you would consider coming. It's wonderful to see you."

His response was so enthusiastic that Mateo was put at ease. Not knowing what to say first, he relayed the message from the office about the coffee being ready. This elicited the hoped-for response from Rex, as he smiled broadly, gave one last whack with the hammer, and turned towards the church motioning Mateo to go ahead of him.

"May I offer you a cup of coffee? Derrick makes the best coffee in town."

"You don't know how good that would be," Mateo replied without any attempt to conceal his eagerness. "I just spent some time with Vic, and all I got was tea."

Rex laughed. "With all due respect to Vic's immense musical talent, he and I do feel differently about our beverage of choice. Let's give you a welcome more suited to your needs."

A few minutes later as they sat down in the pastor's small study, hammer placed in the middle of the expansive wooden desk between piles of books, Mateo sighed a happy breath, because truly the multi-talented Derrick did make a cup of coffee good enough to satisfy a city boy like Mateo. Whatever else was to come next in terms of demands to relive his past, Mateo felt a sense of relaxation steal over him for the first time in a week.

SIX

Rex sank into his wooden desk chair, tilting it back to an alarming angle while not spilling a single drop of coffee on his work shirt, clearly a skill honed with much practice. This was his thinking posture. He swiveled his chair so that he could both address Mateo across the desk from him and have a clear view out the window into the woods outside. He sat balanced in a comfortable silence while both men fully appreciated their coffee. As a rule, Mateo was not one to engage in silence, but then nothing was normal about this day. For this moment he felt in no hurry to learn more about his mission here in Pine Junction, at least not until this first cup of coffee was treasured. Time seemed to have slowed down ever since he stepped out of the car back at the highway junction.

Setting his empty cup down on the desk, Mateo finally spoke. "My mom, what's wrong with her? is she really sick?"

"Not physically sick, Mateo." Rex looked at the young man for a moment and then asked him, "When is the last time you talked with your mom?"

There was a long pause while Mateo seriously tried to remember when this might have been. "Well, she sent me my birthday card in January, but we didn't talk. I mean she left a voice mail, and I sent an email, but no phone call." He scrunched up his forehead trying to be more specific. "I guess it was our Christmas phone call. We always talk on Christmas Day."

Rex gazed thoughtfully at the younger man, and it crossed his mind how sad it would be for him if his children didn't come see him at the holidays, particularly once the intensity of the Advent and Christmas liturgical season was over. With Beth gone, his children had been extra sensitive not to leave him alone in the post-Christmas period. Apparently Cecilia didn't spend much time at all with her sons, at least that was his impression so far.

Both men sat in thought.

Mateo continued where his mental meanderings led him. "I don't remember anything unusual in anything she said. I think she mostly asked about me, my music and my girlfriend Catherine. I'm sure I asked about my grandpa and grandma because I always do, and she said they were doing pretty good in the retirement home." He was perplexed. "What do you mean, she isn't physically sick?"

"Mateo, I can't confide what Cecilia has discussed with me in private conversation of course, although she doesn't share too much with me, but it has not been an easy time for her recently. Your mom is almost apoplectic with anger at our present administration in Washington, and she has felt very personally how devastating this Iraq War is for our country and for the Iraqis. I know this has all been a huge struggle for her, and she is wrestling with how to manage her reactions and passion about that conflict and politics in general. But that alone is not why I called you."

Clearly Cecilia's political opinions or dilemmas were not something of which Mateo had any knowledge. "Well, I do know she came into the City to take part in some peace marches, but then so did a lot of people, for all the good it did. And I remember one time she made a comment about not wanting a draft so that Rowan and I wouldn't have to join the military. She even asked me once a couple of years ago whether I had any notion of enlisting or joining the Guard, and I assured her that it never crossed my mind."

"Well, like I said, Mateo, I don't think that is the center point of the problem right now. Your mom will wrestle with those issues because that is the kind of person she is. She really cares about these things at a deep moral and emotional level. But I believe there is something else going on for her, closer to the heart of your family. That's why I called you."

Rex dropped his chair back to the upright position and leaned forward across the desk to face Mateo more directly and continued. "This last month your brother came to Pine Junction. He was here at the church to attend the wedding of a school friend, and I took the opportunity to take him aside and try to share, with all discretion of course for your mother's privacy, that . . . um, that I was concerned for her. I'm afraid I was too vague for him to take me seriously, or something. Rowan pretty much blew me off, kind of an 'I don't want to talk about it' response is what I got, frankly." (What Rex was too diplomatic to relate to Mateo was the disinterested look Rowan had given him, and the curt dismissal with an abrupt departure to get another drink.)

At this point Rex rose and left the room with both coffee cups to get a refill. When he returned, Mateo was standing by the window looking out. Rex handed him the coffee and Mateo took it gratefully and sat down again.

"Well," Mateo started, "Rowan never was much of one to take on a conversation, especially not a personal one, or a topic that is, you know, kind of overly emotional, at least in his mind. I haven't been around home either, so it's not like I am in touch with anything that's going on obviously . . . but with Rowan, well with Rowan, there never was a time we could talk about deep stuff, you know, what I consider important topics. He is pretty much straight up. What he lets you see is all business and that is all that seems to matter to him. Dunno if it is avoidance or just who Rowan is." Mateo breathed in suddenly, stopped talking, and spent a few minutes sipping the coffee lost in memories of the years he spent growing up with Rowan, and how things had changed at one point in their relationship, or maybe just how they had grown apart when they were no longer small children.

Eventually he looked up at Rex who had not interrupted. Mateo took the next step. "Okay, so you approached my brother, got no help, and then you called me, someone you've never met. How'd you get my phone number anyway?

And here we are. You've said my mom is not physically sick, so I guess that leaves one thing, that somehow my mom is having a mental breakdown, however you say it. But she seemed normal on the phone just three or four months ago." He looked hard at Rex. "So what's up? I think it's time to spill it."

Rex nodded, walked to the office door and closed it securely. He grabbed another office chair and pulled it next to Mateo's, but then he paused.

What business was this of his?

SEVEN

"There isn't much I can tell you, Mateo." Rex finally began to speak, choosing his words carefully. "In fact, I believe it's your task, or better yet, your opportunity, to learn what would be helpful to bring to light here."

Mateo stared at Rex, with no comprehension whatsoever.

Rex tried again. "This is a small town Mateo, and while I am new here, relatively, Pine Junction is like communities everywhere. There are secrets no one knows about, and so-called secrets everyone knows but no one talks about. And there are topics of conversation and gossip that sometimes have no resemblance to what the truth of the matter might be. Sometimes what really happened is so distorted by time and retellings and various interpretations and half truths and perspectives . . . . " Rex knew he was not being clear or helpful at all. Why was it so hard to begin?

Mateo just shook his head. The comfortable feeling he had experienced when first entering Reverend Randall's office was rapidly turning into bewilderment. "What am I doing here, man?" He muttered, and then spoke louder, "Why the hell did you call me?"

Rex stared out the window for a very long time before answering Mateo's justifiable question. Just when Mateo was about to grab his guitar and leave the room, the minister spoke with a firmness his voice had not possessed before.

"Mateo, you have only known me for about thirty minutes, but I am hoping you can trust me and stay with me on this."

Mateo didn't answer but sat back in his chair to listen.

"Sometimes in your life you just have to lead with your gut feelings, and that is what I did when I called you. And you're right, I was putting myself out there given that I don't know you at all. But now, when amazingly enough you showed up here this morning, well, I just know we're on the right track. I also believe that you're probably the only one who can help or at least uncover some truths to help your family"

Rex continued, "It's my impression that your immediate family is somewhat disconnected, and so I cannot be one hundred percent sure what you can do." At this he turned from the window finally, and gave Mateo a kind but penetrating appraisal. "I have a lot of confidence in the quality of folks you are, you Schumachers and Sanchezes, so I am hoping you are willing to jump in and give it a try."

Mateo sat for a moment. His understanding was nil, but he did understand now that what he needed to know was not going to come from Rex. The mystery of the situation appealed to his curiosity.

"I have no idea what this is all about, but I got myself here, so I might as well figure out what comes next. Ya know, I've been thinking it's been a long time since I have seen Mom or Grand Pedro, so maybe I'll stick around a few days."

But before Rex could respond, Mateo burst out with frustration, "But for God's sake, give me a clue . . . ."

Rex hesitated a second and then spoke with emphasis. "Mateo, your mom is experiencing some debilitating sadness, above and beyond the grief of the war, as bad as that is. We've talked for hours about the war, and I share her anger. But I believe there is something more that has caught up with her recently. I'm just crazy enough to think that if you showed up it could bring her a healthy distraction and a great deal of joy to be reconnected to someone very important to her."

"What's that supposed to mean?" Mateo bristled at this remark. "Since when are you so involved in my family?"

"My apologies if that sounded accusatory. Let me reshape what I was trying to say. If your mom were sick in the hospital with some terrible illness, I would certainly track you down to give you the news and solicit your help. And of course even in that case you could ignore my call, and continue on with your life. Sure. But what I am seeing is a sickness of heart that is just as serious, in my opinion."

Rex put his hands on his knees and leaned toward Mateo. "I think if you take the time to get reconnected with your whole family, pay attention, really listen, and maybe not ask aloud but ponder the questions that will come to you, Mateo, you may be able to take part in some healing. Of course if things get dicey, I would suggest that you get some professional help. I have to say that as a minister. I have to be careful because although I have seen what seems like everything in my long years as a pastor, I am not a therapist. I must tell you that."

"Why is this any of your business?"

"Certainly I am treading on thin ice in terms of my ministerial role, Mateo. And that's the truth. I will put that right out to you. But as I said, this is a time when I felt I could no longer only be a prayer partner. After I talked with your grandparents and your Aunt Olivia, I felt the strong directive to call you."

"Did they ask you to contact me?" Mateo was sidetracked in his indignation. "Why didn't they call me themselves?"

"I suggested myself that they should call you, as family member to family member, but they said they were not comfortable contacting you about your mom. They asked me to be their messenger, and yes it could be interpreted as interfering. I don't have much more to tell you, and yes it's vague, but I'll promise to be here for you as a sounding board if you need me."

Mateo furrowed his brow as he scrunched into the chair. He thought briefly of how uncluttered his daily life had been in the past ten years. That life seemed like long ago, even though he had only this morning jumped out of his own wrinkled sheets, taken a shower in his mildewed bathroom, and joked with the neighbor downstairs as he left the house with duffle bag packed. Now everything seemed to be full of the complications of attachment. Family attachment, he realized, is what he had been avoiding for ten blissful years. What possible reason did he have for returning to what he normally blocked out, to the turmoil and anxiety of family life and the unspoken secrets that always seemed to be hiding under the surface of them all . . . Mom, Dad, Aunt Olivia, Aunt Maria, Grandma Tori, and even his beloved Grand Pedro?

Rex looked at the young man with sympathy. The minister could almost read Mateo's mind. He fervently hoped that Mateo would choose to rekindle the ties that were so ripe for further disintegration. Quite frankly, the jury was out. Rex was somewhat of an optimist but even he could see the potential for a painful lack of resolution within this family.

The introspective thoughts of both Rex and Mateo were broken by Derrick's knock on the door. "Excuse the interruption, Pastor," he apologized, "but I am going to lock the office door for lunch and wondered if you want me to bring you . . . uh, both of you, some lunch?" He glanced at Mateo sitting somberly in his chair looking as though he was waiting for a root canal.

Rex had a better idea, hoping it might lighten the atmosphere. "Let's all go out for some lunch. Chinese or pizza? Sort of our only choices." He laughed ruefully thinking of

Mateo's endless culinary opportunities in New York. "My treat," he added to sweeten the pot.

Mateo nodded, and after Derrick went back to his office, Rex made one final appeal to Mateo. "Listen, let's have some lunch, maybe invite Vic to come along, and not talk about any of this for an hour. That will give you a chance to decide whether you want to hang around Pine Junction and get your life complicated, or go back home and forget I ever called you."

"Sure," Mateo stood up, then paused, and softly added one more statement that sounded a great deal like a question. "But you never explained why you mentioned the name Dane Faber in your message."

Perhaps Rex didn't hear Mateo as he was shutting the window and grabbing his jacket. The pause was enough of a hiccup to give Derrick a chance to come back in with an extra umbrella, which he handed to Mateo. "Rain started," he announced and the three men walked out the door together, the question still hanging in the air.

EIGHT

The village of Pine Junction had one main street that divided around the town square, the Village Green. Side streets branched off in all directions. Unlike other small New England towns that found their quiet streets becoming busy highways, Main Street in Pine Junction remained a quiet road that intersected with the busier county highway a mile away, at the point the locals called "The Junction." The town itself was therefore not overwhelmed by through traffic. Even in 2005 Pine Junction remained a quiet refuge, far removed in ambience but a relatively short distance in miles from the major university center of Amherst. Every morning, half the residents would drive off to the Amherst area for work, and the rest would walk down the streets to their jobs in the village or catch the yellow bus for the short ride to school.

Yang Chow Very Good Chinese Food on the Village Green was bustling at noon for takeout orders as well as with the local sit-down diners who squeezed into the tiny outdated space. One of two restaurants in Pine Junction, the restaurant had been open since well before Mateo's childhood.

The same owners, now getting older but assisted by their son and a newly arrived niece, kept the little place going, the establishment looking as it always had and the food tasting much the same since Mr. and Mrs. Chui first arrived from Taiwan via New York City to open their restaurant. It wasn't originally named The Yang Chow Very Good Chinese Food restaurant, but soon after it opened when patrons were interviewed the first night by the local newspaper, a youngster of the town had proclaimed it to be "Very Good." And after the Chui family saw the write-up in the paper, they decided it was a good omen and quickly changed the sign in front of the restaurant to read "Yang Chow Very Good Chinese Food," and it remained thus ever after.

When the four men walked in from the church that day, Mrs. Chiu spotted them from the kitchen, shouted for her niece to watch the food on the stove, and bustled out to greet her favorite man outside of her family, Mr. Dalloway. All but one of the four Chui children spent their childhood working in the restaurant immediately after school, the exception being the eldest son who spent his after school hours practicing the piano at the First Congregational Church under the tutelage of Vic Dalloway. Mrs. Chiu gushed and thanked Vic today as she did every time she saw Vic for helping her son reach his goal to be a concert pianist. For the rest of her life she would remain grateful to Mr. Dalloway, as she insisted that Martin should address his first music teacher.

After thoroughly embarrassing the reserved Vic, Mrs. Chiu then greeted Reverend Randall and Derrick Jackson and was turning away when she recognized Mateo. This called for more expressions of joy and welcome, and it was only her lack of confidence in her niece that made her flee back to the kitchen.

Mateo grinned despite himself and said, "Well, it is great to feel welcome."

After ordering their food, the four men sat in casual conversation.

Derrick was aware that something was going on between Pastor Rex and this young man, Mateo, who was back in town. Derrick knew Mateo from high school days, but he was a couple of years younger and didn't know him well. So he pondered what this something might be, while chatting about his goal of starting a new restaurant in Pine Junction as soon as he acquired enough capital.

Meanwhile Vic was discussing Martin Chiu's latest concert tour but soon was grousing about his battle with the mice in the organ music. "Right in the chancel. Of all the nerve! I think Emma Grant left some cookies behind the curtain in the choir loft and that brought out the mice." But underneath he wondered what had brought about his intimate disclosures earlier that morning when Mateo had arrived, catching him completely by surprise.

Rex responded to the conversation topics around him, and threw in comments regarding the fence repair project which would keep the deer out of the church garden. But his internal voice was running through the morning's dialogue with Mateo. He was not at all as confident as he tried to appear that he was on the right track, but he also felt strongly that something had to happen for Cecilia and her family, and that something was better than nothing. He just hoped he had not pulled Mateo into a situation that was bigger than he could manage. But he had already started the train rolling, so Rex had no choice but to stay on board.

Mateo listened to the others and answered questions about his life in the city, his job, and club life, but deep down he was running through what he knew and did not know about his family situation. While he still had some desire to flee the scene, much to his own surprise he had an ever increasing sense that he could never be content if he didn't attempt to unravel whatever it was that tormented his mother. And he was beginning to be drawn back into the charm and warmth of his home town, even while he was still fighting a suffocating sensation.

As they wrapped up their leftovers and got ready to go back to work, Mr. Chiu came over to give his greetings, and he questioned Mateo as to why he was in town. Mateo looked at Rex, then spoke to the whole group. "I am here for a visit with my family, probably be here for the week. Hope to get back over to have some more of your pork and eggplant. You know how much I love it." Mr. Chiu smiled broadly and gave Mateo a slight bow of thanks. Rex found himself letting his breath go out quietly, not realizing he had been holding it tight in his chest.

The rain had stopped after lunch when the four men parted ways, Vic to the church garden, and Derrick to the office. For a moment, Rex and Mateo stood silently beside each other in front of the neon Very Good Chinese Food restaurant sign. As Mateo held out his hand for a handshake, ready to take off for his old home, Rex cleared his throat and said, "One more thing, Mateo. I was in the drug store in January waiting for a prescription to be ready and met a stranger at the cash register. Since there are few strangers in Pine Junction, I introduced myself as pastor of the church, and in turn he said his name was Dane Faber. I had no idea who he was or why he was in a drug store in Pine Junction. All I know is that he then asked about your family, seemed to know they were part of First Congregational, and he specifically asked about you. It caught me by surprise and I gave some sort of reply. I was tempted to ask how he knew all of you. I just had a strange sense that it was more than a casual inquiry. But at that point he left quickly."

Rex paused briefly. "That is all I know. All. Honestly. I'm figuring you must know more than I do, that he might mean something to you. After that day I was down with the flu, and then went out of town to a conference and had almost forgotten about the encounter. In fact I have not mentioned this to your mother or grandparents." He shrugged. "And I am not sure why I haven't said anything to them. Some gut feeling to keep it to myself. But I haven't forgotten the man's inquiry. It seemed odd to me at the time, and perhaps that intuition is behind my phone call to you, Mateo. I just don't know."

With that, Rex shook the hand that Mateo had not moved. Rex turned to go before Mateo could think of an appropriate comment or question, Rex calling over his shoulder, "Remember, if you need a sounding board, I am here."

NINE

O n a corner of Main Street sat a traditional brick
building, the 1920's era Thompson County Public
Library, Pine Junction Branch. Several times it
had come close to being replaced, but the old building was
spared every time by those fighting for its historic value, or
simply by lack of funds. So Cecilia Schumacher spent her
career in the same brick building she and her sisters had
frequented as a child. She felt secure in this building surrounded by cliffs of books going up the shelves on every
wall. In the back office, light streamed in the tall windows
and the woods stretched out behind. Even during the darkest days of her life, the library had been an island of serenity.

Upon going up the steps of the library and through the
coat room, the patrons walked into an entryway where the
librarian's desk sat with good proximity to greet the new
arrivals. To the right was the children's room with books
and little tables and chairs, plus a rug area with bean bag
chairs where Cecilia held story time. To the left of the librarian's desk was the main room of the library for adults
and older students. Wooden floors, tall stacks of books,

and an occasional narrow window gave the room a warm old-fashioned appeal despite a row of computers lining one wall. Behind the front desk was a door to the back room office for the staff, which consisted only of Cecilia and Tiny Jones.

Tiny lived down the street with his wife Leticia who reigned as queen of her beauty chair at the local hair salon. She had cut or styled almost every head in town. At home she was royalty in her kitchen as well, cooking satisfying Italian food for anyone who wandered in at dinner time. She was a generous woman, as was her towering husband Tiny. Tiny's warm heart was perhaps his biggest asset, and his long tenure as library custodian and general fix-it man was due as much to Cecilia's compassion as to Tiny's overall skill at any particular task.

When Mateo and Rowan were small children, the babysitter would bring them to the library to have lunch with their mom. The boys would help the sitter make sandwiches, then walk the few blocks down to the library, hopping up the steps and, struggling, open the large heavy double doors. Cecilia would greet the boys with a hug and kiss, and then escort the last patron out the door for lunch closing. The next hour would be spent in the back office with Cecelia and Tiny listening to her boys describe their morning activities. She would tell them stories about people and books. These were very simple but precious hours in Cecilia's memory, and when Mateo and then Rowan went off to first grade and stayed in school all day, she missed these lunches. She had to relearn how to spend her time and developed the habit of taking a walk during summer weather and eating her lunch with a book. When the library entered the digital age, Cecilia found herself eating her lunch by her computer, reading email and news blogs.

On this particular day, when Mateo made his third stop in town, it was at the library. He took a moment to appreciate the S curve of the metal stair railing that had intrigued him since he was a little boy. He remembered running his hand over this railing in fascination until Rowan called him names and told him to hurry up. Mateo may have been the older brother, and thus held some supremacy, but Rowan was the practical fellow of the two. When the younger boy was tired of waiting around for Mateo's peculiar distractions, he would not hesitate to boss Mateo around.

But now Rowan was far away and Mateo stood in the quiet street with no apparent observers, so caressing the smooth metal bar gave him a moment to think about what might come next. It was unprecedented for Mateo to come back to his home town and pop in on his mother at work, so he considered how his mom would react, caught completely by surprise by her son's appearance, particularly if she was in a fragile state of mental health. He gave himself a pep talk. He simply needed to go the rest of the way up the stairs, open the door and go in.

So he did. And the first person he saw as he entered the foyer was Tiny, pushing a broom methodically across the worn wooden floors. A broad smile spread across Tiny's affable face, and he dropped his broom and gave Mateo a bone crushing squeeze. Mateo finally extricated himself and gave Tiny the high five hand clap that they had practiced endlessly when Mateo was a small boy. Mateo peered around Tiny looking for his mom, but he only saw a couple of library patrons look up from their books in curiosity at the commotion. Tiny followed Mateo's gaze and shook his head.

"Your mom's not here today, Mateo. Substitute Mr. Rawlings came out for the week. Your mom's home, kinda sick lately."

Tiny looked uncomfortable, so Mateo smiled and replied, "Great to see you, Tiny. You're looking fine, real fine. How's Leticia?"

"Doing good. Had'ta have bunion surgery last fall, on her feet too much. But she just made a batch of cheese raviolis, so come over."

"Thanks, Tiny. Tell Leticia hello, and I'll come if I can." Mateo gave one more look around the familiar book-lined rooms to either side of the main desk, gave Tiny another hand slap, and went back down the stairs of his mom's library sanctuary. Today, apparently, the library's peaceful qualities were not working for her.

And at the back of his mind was a memory, his mom telling him, just last year, with some pride, that she had received an award from the state library association for achieving the best attendance of any librarian in the state.

TEN

Mateo lugged his duffle bag and guitar back down the library steps, partially glad for the short reprieve from the face-to-face encounter with his mother. He was not really worried about how things would proceed once the first meeting was behind them. His communication skills had never deserted him before, and he felt that things would just unwind. But there was no question that he was unnerved about the first few moments. He hadn't walked more than ten feet away from the library when his cell phone rang.

It was Catherine. Mateo adored his girlfriend. But in the hours he had now been in Pine Junction, he had not thought of her once. His life with Catherine was completely associated with Brooklyn, and the surroundings where he found himself the last six hours seemed alien to the uncomplicated hours he spent with Catherine. Looking into her eyes he could talk for hours. He loved watching her elegant arms move back and forth across the cello strings. But most especially he relished the hours spent on her mattress, her long shimmering brown hair framing her breasts as it hung covering both her body and his with its softness.

Hearing Catherine's voice as he stood outside the Pine Junction Library disoriented Mateo. So his "Catherine! Hey. Hi." when he heard her voice did not sound as warm as she might have been expecting given the affectionate man who had left her bed two nights earlier.

"Mateo. How are you? Where are you? I've been thinking about you."

"Uh . . . ." Mateo was not quite sure what to say. "Listen Catherine, I have some things I need to do right now. This isn't a good time to talk. Can I call you back later? I can send you a text."

Now it was Catherine's turn to fall silent. But only for a moment. "Mateo what the hell is going on? You don't tell me where you are going. You leave me this fucking ridiculous note that doesn't make any sense. Where are you anyway?" Her voice was getting shriller as she became more distressed.

"I'm in Pine Junction. Gotta see my family. Nothing's wrong. Well, I don't know, maybe something is wrong, but babe, it doesn't have anything to do with you, with us."

Catherine, somewhat mollified, calmed a bit. "But Mateo, why can't you tell me what is going on? Maybe I can help." He could tell she was getting worked up again. "Damn it, Mateo, I thought we had a relationship, and now you just go disappear like this. What am I supposed to think?"

He heard the catch in her voice and unlike her usual confident self, she choked out, "Is there someone else?"

There was a long silence as Mateo sank down into the bench next to the library steps. "Listen, for now I just cannot think of anything besides what's going to happen next. I can't explain it all. Too complicated. I'm sorry I can't talk more now."

He stared at the store front across the street. Finally he added, almost as an afterthought, "Oh no, there isn't someone else. Don't be crazy."

Mateo knew his words were not comforting to Catherine but he was desperate to separate his worlds, leaving Catherine in his other world where he would soon return to slide right back into the perfect life that included her. But first he had to put his full concentration on what he needed to uncover here in Pine Junction. It never occurred to him that Catherine would be understanding and perhaps even be of some help.

"I'll call you later Cate," is all he could manage. He clicked the off button on his phone, forgetting to listen for her "Goodbye."

Mateo sat still for a few moments on the bench, staring at his phone, knowing he had handled things very poorly. His only hope was that he could explain to Catherine when this was all over. He was on a one-track mission, and it was taking all his focus to put his phone away, stand up and walk the few more blocks to his family home, dragging his guitar and duffle bag along with him. He was beginning to feel like a refugee.

ELEVEN

Mateo moved purposefully up the walk to the house that had been his home for eighteen years, through the yard that held so many memories of play time. But he didn't stop to dwell on these formative experiences. After all the interactions of the day, he was approaching mental fatigue. He needed to keep moving in order to not abort his mission and retreat.

Mateo skipped up the stone steps, two at a time as had always been his habit, and not wanting to walk in on his mother, he knocked on the door. There was no response, so after an appropriate wait, he rang the doorbell, which also brought about only silence. He finally tried the door knob, found it turned, and entered.

Mateo called out, "Mom. Mom, it's Mateo."

While he waited for her answer, he relieved his shoulder of the duffel bag and guitar and stretched his muscles. After hearing nothing but the refrigerator click on in the background, he walked from room to room without finding Cecilia anywhere. Upstairs was next, looking into each bedroom, and it was only when he stepped into his mom's bedroom, saw her unmade bed, that he glanced out the nearby window and caught some movement at the back of the yard. It was his mother viciously attacking the ground with a garden tool of some sort. Her frenetic flailing was quite relentless. A large pile of branches surrounded her.

After watching for a minute trying to figure out what she was doing, Mateo ran downstairs and out the back porch and across the lawn. "Mom! Whatcha doing?"

Cecilia was in a lather. Sweat was pouring down her back and neck, and her face glistened. "This buddleia has to go! Butterflies never come, not enough flowers." Her words were interspersed between grunts as she continued to hammer the hole around the thick roots. "Can't see my rose bush, and it doesn't have a chance to get healthy with this big old behemoth in the way. But these roots feel like they are embedded in rock. I just can't seem to make any progress." She paused a moment and finally seemed to take in who was standing beside her. She finished her thought, "I have to get these roots dug out . . . " while taking in the new development that was beginning to penetrate her frenzy over the buddleia bush roots.

"Mateo! My God. It's been such a long time!" She stared at him as if he were a vision. "What are you doing here?" Then as if realizing how rude that sounded, she quickly added, "I am so glad to see you. This is incredible. Oh my God, it's really you!!" Cecilia was too stunned to hug her son. They stood there just a few feet apart.

Meanwhile Mateo was looking at his mother as if he was seeing Cecilia for the very first time. Her face was shiny with sweat, pink blotches on her cheeks. Her dark brown hair had streaks of gray running through it, but was still thick and wavy, attractive even now with pieces of leaves and branches caught in it. Her unusually expressive eyes seemed to be swimming with tears and looked tired. Clutching the pick, her hands were dirty. She had forgotten to put on gardening gloves when one hour ago she had realized the buddleia bush was an invasive eyesore, an impediment that must come out instantly. An elegantly framed woman despite the extra pounds that mid life had brought her, today she was dressed in an old shapeless pair of jeans and a dirty green sweatshirt with a couple of rips in the fabric. Mateo thought she looked older than he remembered, but when had he ever taken the time to truly look at his mother?

Rather than standing there in discomfort, Mateo simply took the pick axe from his mother's hand. "Hey Mom, you look like you could use some help. Why don't you take a break for a bit. My turn."

Cecilia released the tool, and stepped back, caught quite off guard. She moved a few feet away while Mateo took over the attack on the roots. They were solidly tangled into the soil, but his new energy soon had them loose enough to pull out of the ground. He helped his mom pull all the roots, branches and new leaves into a pile at the back of the yard, trim them down to a disposable size, and fill in the hole in the ground, while she tenderly appraised her rose bush, its bare branches now better able to produce the lovely yellow-orange blooms come summer time.

Under the guise of this work, mother and son both adjusted to the new situation.

Cecilia brought out some iced tea and the two, so long separated from each other, collapsed into the wooden Adirondack chairs at the back of the house. The air was steamy after the midday rainfall and held an almost tangible small town quiet. Mateo spoke first. "Mom, I stopped by the library and Tiny said you were home sick, or at least I think he said you were sick, and all week too. But you sure aren't laid up in bed. What was going on with that bush?"

"I just realized why I was so bothered by that corner of the garden. It was that bush. I planted it five years ago and it was supposed to bring hundreds of butterflies but it didn't put out any flowers to speak of and then my beautiful rose bush never got enough sun . . . but I didn't realize until today that it was that stupid bush that was causing the problem and I had to get it out of there and I couldn't wait until Tiny could come for his spring yard clean up because it just had to come out right now." Her voice was becoming frayed, breathlessly on the verge of tears, which Mateo noted with alarm. "So I tried to cut it down, but those damn roots were just stuck, so I had to work at it so hard . . . I thought I would never get it out, but I had to do it!" These last words were spoken with a vehemence that shocked even her, so she stopped talking, and a tear escaped down her cheek.

"Hey Mom, are we talking about a bush here? I mean, it's just a bush, right?"

"Oh Matty, you are right of course. It is just a bush, but it made me so angry." Cecilia stopped again, unable to talk for a moment. Pulling herself together she finally looked at her tall son who so resembled his father that it took her breath away. "I am kind of losing it here lately . . . "

She continued. "I really am sorry. Pretty crazy welcome home, huh? And what a surprise. I can't believe you're here. Don't know what brought about your appearance, but I can't tell you how grateful I am for your help with the buddleia. That damn bush was going to kill me. It was me or it!" She started to smile and Mateo joined her, and soon they were both laughing at the absurdity of it all, a laughter that touched only the surface of things, but it did release some emotions in desperate need of escape.

"Well Mom, you must be hungry after all that exercise. Got any food in the house? I know how to cook now. I'll make you some dinner."

Cecilia smiled wryly. "Well this is a turnabout. The son comes home and cooks for his mom. Okay, today you can show off your cooking, but the next meal is on me." Then she stopped as if regretting her words. "I don't mean to put pressure on you to stay, I mean . . ." She floundered a bit, then finished her thought, "I don't know what brought about your visit, but you're a sight for sore eyes, as my mother always says, and however long you can stay will be a joy."

"Relax Mom. I'd like to hang around the old town for a few days. I had a vacation from work and just took a wild notion to come check in on you and Grand Pedro and Grandma."

After washing his hands and inspecting his mom's refrigerator (not very well supplied, he noted, and not very clean, more along the lines of a college student's fridge than his mom's usual standards of neatness), he tried to casually ask her again. "So are you playing hooky from the library Mom? Tiny getting on your nerves? Too many books needing shelving?"

Cecilia just shrugged her shoulders. This was a habit she had deplored when her sons were teenagers, and she had upbraided them many times about how rude this gesture was. Now it seemed to cloak her in a sense of defeat so Mateo didn't remind her. Clearly something was disturbing his mother to the point that it was affecting her work life, and this was serious indeed. He sighed and realized that explanations were not all going to come tumbling out all neat and orderly merely because he asked a question. He was less than one afternoon in the house with his mother, and nothing whatsoever was clear except she was not her usual tranquil self.

Cecilia went off to take a shower. As Mateo scrambled some eggs (hoping they were not too dated) and made a salad of sorts, the door bell rang. It was Rex standing there with a bag in his hand. "Hi Mateo, I thought you might want this." In the bag was a coffee maker and a bag of coffee, fully caffeinated.

"The coffee is courtesy of Derrick as is the coffee maker. He has three. We thought you might find it nice to have since we are aware that your mom is strictly a tea drinker. The first bag is on us, we sell it at the church, fair trade fundraiser, but your next bag you can pick up yourself at the office from Derrick, $10 per bag. It's ground at fine setting for this coffee maker."

Mateo chortled. "I like that Derrick more and more!"

He looked back into the kitchen. "Mom's in the shower. We were wrestling with a bush in the garden this afternoon." Mateo looked at Rex with an expression that was both an appeal for help and a defensive I-can't-explain-it look. "I'd invite you for dinner, but there really isn't much in the house. I'll get out to the store tomorrow."

Figuring that Mateo looked competent if somewhat bewildered by whatever was happening, Rex gave him a slap on the back and headed out the door. "Gotta run off anyway, have a finance committee meeting and that group is never late! Be in touch!"

Mateo went back to his eggs, stirring them contemplatively, hearing the sound of his mother's shower turn off in the bathroom at the top of the stairs. But he felt reinforced by the contents of Derrick's bag. And for some reason, despite the total oddness of the day, and the uncertainty ahead, he was not unsettled. Strange.

TWELVE

After their simple meal Cecilia did the dishes while Mateo made himself a satisfying cup of coffee, glad he had learned to drink it black since there was no milk in the house. He heated the water for his mom's tea and found she had switched from Earl Grey in the past years, and now Darjeeling was her favorite. The two sat down at the kitchen table and Mateo considered broaching once again his mom's withdrawal from work, her frenzied attack on the buddleia bush, the depleted state of her refrigerator, and the unkempt appearance of her kitchen. He was tired of being given the run-around, however, so he opted out of the interrogator role and suggested they play a game of Cribbage or Scrabble instead. While he had not given it a thought in years, this was one of the activities he had shared with his mother on countless holiday trips and winter evenings.

Cecilia agreed and found the Scrabble box after some rummaging through the depths of the hall closet. Mateo located the dictionary on its familiar shelf. It was a great relief to while away the evening hours in a spirited game. Mother and son were competitive yet fun-hearted about games, which is probably why they had always enjoyed playing together. And it was the perfect antidote for Mateo as he relaxed into being back home after the strange series of conversations he had been having since morning. Cecilia too found her spirits lifting as she temporarily forgot her churning angst, allowing herself to fall under the spell of a miraculous reenactment of lighthearted time spent with her son.

Two hours later both were laughing as Mateo challenged his mother on a particularly obscure word when Mateo's cell phone rang simultaneously with Cecilia's house phone. This stopped them both in mid move, as Mateo reached instinctively for his phone, and Cecilia looked almost fearfully at her own phone across the room before standing up to walk over to it.

Mateo had turned off his phone after Catherine's early afternoon call, fearing a second or third call, and kept it off while helping his mom with the garden, fixing dinner and eating. It was rare for Mateo to have his phone turned off, and he had just absent-mindedly turned it back on in the last ten minutes. And now it was ringing, connecting him again with his real life.

He saw that he had six messages, two were calls from Catherine. And it was Catherine again calling him. Mateo gave his mom an apologetic look as he got up to move to the other room, but Cecilia didn't notice as she was standing by her own phone apparently deciding whether to answer or not. Mateo let his own phone call go to voice mail while he watched his mom with dreaded fascination.

"Mom, aren't you going to answer it?"

"Well, maybe not, probably just a telemarketer," she replied with a twitchy look.

"Oh, have you been harassed by sales pitches? You should get yourself on those no-call lists. Just let it go to voicemail now and we can hear who it is."

In a panic she lurched at the phone and with a rush spoke into the receiver saying, "You have the wrong number, goodbye." She hung up the phone, but didn't turn around to look at Mateo immediately.

Mateo stared at her but Cecilia returned to the table and sat down indicating to Mateo that they could finish the game. Mateo forgot about all of his own phone messages as he sat down, completely baffled.

When the game finished, she asked him whether he had written any new songs. Mateo pulled out his guitar, tuned it, and shared a couple. Cecilia closed her eyes as she curled up in her favorite overstuffed chair to listen. When his songs were over, he continued to play the guitar gently in chords and soft ruminations. She eventually stirred herself and stood up stretching, saying she would go up and make up his bed. Mateo himself spent fifteen minutes in the shower, letting the hot water run over his face and body, as if to wash away all that the day had brought, the new information and confusions both.

After he left the steamy bathroom, he saw the door to Cecilia's bedroom was closed with a light underneath. Mateo was just as glad not to engage anymore, and he firmly closed his old bedroom door, grateful for the clean sheets his mom had put on his bed. It was only as his head hit the pillow that he remembered Catherine's phone call, but he decided he could not engage in an emotional discussion right now, especially since he knew he bore the blame for the misunderstanding. He didn't have the energy for the necessary conversation, and he was too confused himself about what was going on, why he was in Pine Junction, and what he might be able to do about any problems once he figured out what those problems actually were. So he turned his phone off once again.

Despite it all, Mateo dropped off to sleep immediately into a deep oblivion that Cecilia could only envy.

THIRTEEN

S ettling in to his reading chair later that same night, Rex began to consider the history behind Mateo's family, some of which Rex knew as factual, some gossip, and some nuances which he had discerned by observation.

Victoria Lessing, Cecilia's mother, was raised in a fifth-generation Pine Junction family who immigrated from England and Germany so many years before that few besides the keeper of the family tree gave their European background much consideration. The Lessing family was solid New England, absolutely tied to the land of Western Massachusetts. Victoria grew up a big fish in a small pond. She carried that birthright without any idea it was not the same for everyone else.

The youngest of two children, she lived her life in the large home her parents had inherited from the Lessing grandparents. The house had been in the family for almost two centuries, a family that was dwindling in number as one generation followed another. Victoria spent many hours in her large bedroom reading and writing poems, sure she would be the next famous American poet although later she considered that poppycock, to use a phrase of her day. She had a horse to ride and tennis to play at a nearby club. She took it all for granted. While sociably capable, overall her preference was to be alone.

The Lessing parents were conservative in many regards, but well educated, well off, and also long time members of the local Congregational church. They were typical for their time and place. Victoria dutifully went to college and began to earn a teaching credential. She was an avid reader and continued to write for her private satisfaction but rarely shared any of it. Her parents were certain that Victoria would follow the Lessing tradition of marrying into a good New England family and raise some babies. They conceded that if Victoria really wanted to teach for a short time, that would be acceptable while she waited to make the right marriage.

Nothing in Victoria's upbringing or behavior up to this time would have indicated that she would not follow her parent's wishes, at least on the surface. But home from college near the end of her studies, she attended a community event in Pine Junction and looked into the eyes of Pedro Sanchez for the first time, and from that moment on she never considered any other life than with him.

Victoria was briefly seen as a rebel and gossip abounded. The blond-haired daughter of Pine Junction stability was being courted by an outsider, a man from a foreign part of the world, a man who looked different from most of the town at that time, and was, the rumor circulated, actually born in Mexico.

Victoria did not set out to defy her parents' expectations, or to shock the town. She simply fell in love with Pedro Sanchez and never looked back. She was strong enough to do this. Pedro clearly did love Victoria, but Pedro was resilient and intuitive enough to know just how to blend into the community, when to charm, when to be serious, how to learn Pine Junction history and traditions. He understood that by marrying this lovely woman, he would be marrying the town itself. And he decided he liked that idea.

As Rex reached to switch on his reading lamp, he had to admit he had only surmised those last thoughts, but talkative Pine Junction old-timers had told him more details about the Sanchez family at the time of their marriage in the 1940s and the following years.

The young couple did not flaunt nor deny Pedro's different background. They did not even advertise his veteran status, although people learned of it, and being a World War II veteran helped some with his assimilation. Pedro became the token Latino in the small New England town, but it did not take long for the Sanchez couple to become mainstays of Pine Junction. Without fanfare they made Pine Junction history as the first multi-cultural family in town. Such was the grace of a personality like Pedro Sanchez and the firm attitude of Victoria Lessing. A natural born student as well as a teacher, Pedro did most of the adaptation.

Victoria's parents did not live long, and so the little Sanchez girls born three in a row between 1950 and 1952 did not know their grandparents except as shadowy figures in their memories, and soon Victoria came to feel that she had no family other than the one that she and Pedro created. Her Lessing relatives were few and far between. She seemed to be the lone remaining figure of a legendary Pine Junction family. And Pedro's family was never mentioned.

Victoria became a life-time teacher even when her girls were young, which was unusual in the 1950s. At the high school where Victoria devoted her days, she was perceived to be a strict but fair teacher who encouraged her students to read and think and be creative, but always with a respectful distance between teacher and student. To her neighbors, she was seen as a master gardener who rarely sat down to enjoy the lush garden she maintained. She was always there to help with a casserole when someone had surgery, but with her teaching hours and raising her daughters, she was rarely around for chatting over the fence or coffee klatches the other town women enjoyed during the 1950s and 60s.

She and Pedro were known for hosting elaborate dinners, and community events were frequently organized in their living room. She was active in the church in many ways, as much as a woman was allowed to be in those days. Victoria was seen as hard working and efficient, and an authority on many topics. She was also a dutiful mother to her three daughters, but it was noticed that the girls went to their father for comfort and conversation. Pedro was "Papa" to the girls. She insisted on being called "Mother."

Rex stirred in his old chair and poured himself another glass of brandy. He was surprised at how much he knew about Victoria Sanchez, given that his conversations with her over the past four years were generally conducted with little self-revelation on her part. Rex had experience reading between the lines with the parishioners in his congregations, however, and he now realized he had been thinking about this extended family more than usual lately. As for Pedro, he and Rex had shared many delightful hours of conversation. Pedro had an ability to listen as well as talk, but when you thought about it afterwards, there was much he did not share. Still Rex knew pieces of Mateo's grandfather's life.

Pedro Sanchez got his foot in the door of teaching languages in Pine Junction by being the only one interviewed who could actually speak Spanish and knew Latin when he applied for his first position at the Consolidated High School. But over the decades he established himself as a gifted teacher and he was able to expand his courses to include music as well as some history and government courses. Because of his skill at making his classes relevant and fascinating, several generations of young people graduated with a fine classical education and well-practiced critical thinking skills.

When Rex Randall moved to Pine Junction and met the Sanchez family among his parishioners, he found them agreeable and well educated, with a dignity in all that they did. They were community and church leaders. They were a dominant family who had made great contributions. For instance, the Lessing Memorial Organ, a magnificent Casavant church pipe organ so cherished by Vic Dalloway, was only to be found in this tiny town due to the patronage and memorials sponsored by Victoria's parents in memory of Victoria's only sibling, her brother who died in the War. Musicians came from all around the area to hear the organ's robust sound. It was in getting Victoria to tell him the story of the organ that Rex had learned more about her childhood.

From the old timers and gossips, Rex realized that everyone in town envied the Sanchez marriage and were perhaps jealous of the strong unit this couple presented. True, the Sanchez daughters' relationship mishaps brought the family down from the pedestal. Maria stormed from man to man, with disastrous results. Only a few years ago had she settled into a solid relationship with a woman, and people acknowledged her obvious happiness. Olivia had the misfortune of seeing her marriage go south when her philandering husband flaunted his new affair in front of the whole town. Humiliated, she sought refuge along with her teenage daughter Julia in Cecilia's home for a few years before quietly eloping with a compassionate electrician. Olivia and Brad moved out of town so she didn't have to live in full view of her third grade students and their families and all of Pine Junction. Cecilia's marriage had suddenly vaporized in the course of a day, or so Rex was told, after almost fifteen years of seemingly flawless existence in the house with the picket fence near the town green. What was equally astonishing to Rex was that to this day, no one in town had any clues what happened. Cecilia, as friendly and active as she was in church and community, remained cloaked in a mysterious aura.

Rex jerked as his old fashioned mantle clock chimed midnight. The whole evening gone and he had not looked over the finance committee minutes. Reflecting on this family had consumed his whole evening. Really, Rex thought, he was neglecting his church responsibilities, and yet it was so much more interesting to consider the story of this enigmatic family.

Even in his short tenure in Pine Junction, Rex knew it was hard for anyone to imagine the town without the influence and powerful presence of first the Lessing, and then the Sanchez family. But eventually old age and illness had proven to be a great equalizer. And it had sparked a humility in Pedro and Victoria that had escaped them earlier in their lives. Not that anyone would have thought that they had been anything but gracious, but they lived as if they were invulnerable in their intelligence and health. Bad things happened to other people. It had been a rude adjustment then when ill health struck Pedro in the form of Parkinson's disease.

His Parkinson's symptoms developed slowly over time, at first not causing too much concern, and the couple made some minor alterations in their lifestyle to accommodate the changes. Later a few more challenges cropped up, but the husband and wife worked as a unit, and life continued with civic and teaching duties, trips and dinner invitations. Even their daughters could not pinpoint what was subtly changing about their dad, or what the source of their mother's tension might be. Both Victoria and Pedro retired from teaching in 1999 while in their mid seventies amidst many tributes. Up to this point, only their doctor knew of Pedro's diagnosis. But upon retiring they shared the medical news with all three daughters, who reacted in degrees ranging from denial (Maria) to hysteria (Olivia) to stoic practicality (Cecilia).

When Pedro and Victoria gave up the facade of maintaining their ever-capable face to the community and let their situation be known in church and elsewhere, the community rallied, but the two had for so long been such a self-sufficient unit that they didn't have many close friendships.

After their retirement, the couple sold their long-time home and moved in with Cecilia for a few years. This time in close quarters helped to strip away some of the cloak of invincibility that Cecilia had always perceived around her parents. Once Cecilia had let it slip to Rex that she had lived her life feeling a degree of inadequacy because she had not met the standards with which she perceived she was raised. She joked that the little girl inside her would have put it this way, "My parents were perfect. I could never live up to my parent's impenetrable marriage and good citizenship, their job performance, and lack of discord."

The few years that Victoria and Pedro lived with Cecilia started to crumble that perception, but before any clear opening could happen, Pedro's physical disability became more pronounced and his medical needs greater, and Cecilia became overwhelmed balancing her work life with what had suddenly become daily elder care. While Victoria was apparently healthy, she was not as strong as she needed to be to fully care for her husband, and she seemed to be needing to rest more. Her criticisms became more frequent, and Cecilia found herself taking her mother's comments personally, causing irritation, which she tried to swallow. Cecilia simply could not adjust fast enough to having her once powerful parents suddenly needing care, and right in her own house. It was unsettling to all the daughters, but neither Maria nor Olivia helped much, both beginning new relationships at the time of their parents' decline.

From his vantage point, Rex observed this strain on the family, and finally he suggested that Pedro and Victoria check out the retirement home in the next village of Lakewood, an establishment where they could make the transition from independent apartments to assisted living and to nursing home care, and, Victoria grimly remarked, finally to the grave. Pedro and Victoria were appalled at the symbolism of this move, but could not avoid reality any longer, and when Cecilia did not make more than the smallest objection to them moving on, they knew it was inevitable. They moved to Pine Crest Senior Village.

The longer Rex lived in Pine Junction, and the more he observed and became acquainted with his congregants, the more he sensed a sadness running through this fine family. Yet if he hadn't been so aware of the decline in Cecilia's stability recently, he would have just let this mysterious family live their lives. Families are all different, he knew, and have different expectations from life. It was certainly not his role as a pastor to analyze and fix his flock. And especially not when they had never asked for his help.

On his last visit with Pedro and Victoria at Pine Crest Village, however, this proud couple had come as close as ever before to asking for Rex's help for Cecilia because they had been distressed by her recent behavior, missing work, not answering their phone calls, the slovenly state of her home, her distracted manner. They wanted his help in getting Mateo on the scene. Rex was reluctant, but while out walking and thinking one day, he pulled out his cell phone to call Mateo despite his trepidation. He was going on faith and a personal and professional liberation he felt he had earned at this point in his life. Yet when Mateo did not respond to his message, he did not feel confident enough to call back again. But now the young man was here in Pine Junction, and Rex was holding his breath, trying not to interfere, but hoping for something positive. Something to help this talented, enigmatic family.

Rex finally made his way upstairs. While brushing his teeth he decided he felt optimistic.

His brief encounter with Mateo had given Rex a degree of hope. Something about this young man was more alive, more connected, than he had seen in any of the rest of the family. Perhaps the years away from his family had given Mateo a clearer vision. Perhaps it was just the personality Mateo was born with. True, Mateo seemed to have operated over the last ten years with Teflon ability to skate along through life, that was clear even in a brief encounter. Yet, Mateo had shown up. He had not fled. He was here now. And Rex was convinced that this was good.

It was 2:00 a.m. before Rex fell asleep.

FOURTEEN

Mateo woke from a dream-filled sleep, led into wakefulness by his nose, a sweet aroma that brought him to consciousness. He blinked a few times getting oriented. His first reaction was that everything was absolutely normal, with his familiar Red Sox pennants and musical posters on the walls. His second reaction was that everything was terribly out of kilter.

He wandered downstairs following the clatter of pans to the kitchen where he found Cecilia whirling from stove to counter with flour in her hair and a dab of chocolate on her cheek, humming and oblivious that her oldest son was standing in the doorway staring at her with sleepy eyes and messy hair. On every counter top cookies were cooling on racks and paper bags.

"Mom! What the hell?"

"Don't swear, Matty," she replied automatically, as she straightened up from the oven pulling another pan of brownies out.

"Hungry? Have a brownie."

"Come on, what's with this baking frenzy? And where'd you get the eggs and all? Last night the fridge was empty."

Cecilia didn't pause, busy mixing up another batch, this bowl looking like chocolate chip. "Bake sale today, fundraiser for new choir music. I almost forgot. Had to get up at 5:00 to get to the farmers market before all the eggs were sold. They open early on Saturdays and always sell out."

Mateo looked at the kitchen clock. "Mom it's 9:00; you've done all this since 5:00, plus gone to the market?"

He looked around again. "You must have ten dozen cookies here." He counted a minute and added, "Fifteen!"

"I want to make sure we have enough," she replied.

"So were you supposed to bring all the cookies single-handedly? There aren't enough people in Pine Junction to buy this many cookies."

Cecilia stopped finally and looked at him and then looked around the kitchen. Her face was deflated and Mateo briefly felt sorry for his words. But really, this was ridiculous. It was irrational.

He walked over to his mom and gave her a hug. "Hey mom, how big is your freezer? We can package the extra up and you can send a batch to me every month. Believe me, my friends will devour them!"

He made his voice light-hearted, and as always with Mateo, Cecilia soon cheered up and a smile flickered across her lips.

"I guess I may have over-done it a bit. Not sure what came over me. I think I just panicked when I realized I'd forgotten all about the sale."

Mateo picked up a snickerdoodle and ate it in two bites and then reached for another.

"You never used to let us have cookies for breakfast."

"You're responsible for your own health now," she retorted, biting into a brownie herself.

"I want to go see Grand Pedro this morning," Mateo said. "Do you want to go?"

"I'm committed to the bake sale all day," his mom replied and took her car keys off the hook and handed them to Mateo.

"You remember how to drive?"

"Like riding a bike."

Truth was Mateo hadn't driven for three years since renting a car with a girl to drive over to a Long Island beach, but the town of Lakewood was only nine miles from Pine Junction, and he wasn't worried that he wouldn't be able to drive his mom's old Volvo down the county roads.

After showering, making some coffee, and taking three more cookies for the road, he got directions from Cecilia to Pine Crest Village. The drive was short and pleasant, a reminder of his long bike rides as a kid along the gravel and paved roads that ran through the woods.

Mateo was greeted at the front desk by a welcoming receptionist who had him sign in and pointed the way to the Sanchez apartment. After knocking twice and getting no response, he was standing, unsure of what to do, when another smiling staff person came by and asked if she could help.

"I'm here to see my grandparents but no one is answering."

Before he could protest this affront to his grandparents' privacy, the aide popped her key card into the lock and pushed open the door, calling out loudly "Mr. and Mrs. Sanchez? Look who's here to see you."

Mateo glanced over the aide's shoulders to see his grandfather sitting in an easy chair, looking at a book. Pedro looked up with delayed reactions, absorbing the scene in painfully slow degrees. When Mateo stepped around the aide and towards his grandpa, calling his name, a smile spread across Pedro's face.

"Mateo. Matty my boy! You're here."

He tried to stand up but fell back into the forgiving chair. Tried again, this time more successfully and Mateo was able to catch Pedro in a hug before he fell back again. Mateo carefully eased Pedro back into his chair and retrieved the book that had fallen from his lap, setting it on the lamp table.

The aide meanwhile had gone to look for Victoria who had not emerged from the bedroom despite the commotion Mateo's arrival had caused.

"Ah Mateo. Look at you. Look at you."

"Hey Grand Pedro. How ya doing?" Mateo almost choked on his banal words. Clearly things were very different from his last visit to Pine Junction when Pedro and Victoria were still living independently.

But Pedro was smiling a contented smile as he kept his eyes on his grandson, soaking in the sight as if Mateo might disappear any moment.

"Ah Mateo, I've got Parkinson's disease and there are days when I feel like my name isn't Pedro Sanchez anymore.

I feel like my new name is Parkinson." He laughed ruefully and added, "I am glad this disease is named after a reasonable name like Parkinson and not after someone named Snodgrass or Fuddrucker."

Mateo threw his head back and laughed, adding, ". . . or Fartly, or Pisser?"

Pedro's deep laugh echoed through the normally sedate room, "It feels like a pisser, so maybe Pisser would have been more accurate than Parkinson's."

The aide, Tina, poked her head out of the bedroom in amazement to see the older gentleman (for this is how Pedro always struck her, dignified and refined) and the good-looking young man, perched opposite him on the ottoman, both laughing like buddies at a bar.

Behind Tina, Victoria Sanchez walked carefully out of the bedroom and, at the sight of her husband and her long-absent grandson so comfortable together, an expression of mild resentment flickered across her face. But a split second after these emotions pricked at her, the sight and sound of Pedro laughing pushed any negative thought out of her mind.

She quickly covered the fatigue and pain she had been hiding for so many months now as she moved across the small living room to greet her grandson. When Mateo looked up he saw Victoria's usual regal bearing, and only secondarily noticed the stress lines around her eyes and mouth, and how much older and thinner she looked.

Tina smiled happily at this unexpected family reunion and announced she would return with some coffee and treats to celebrate.

His grandparents quizzed Mateo about his new life; and, with such an appreciative audience hanging on his every word, Mateo talked on and on, describing his daily life, his friends, and encounters at work. When he mentioned Catherine, he felt a twinge of guilt for how he had neglected her. But when he began to talk about concerts and theater his grandfather's eyes lit up with special attention and Pedro queried him with question after question, only interrupted when Tina returned, letting herself in with no more than a cursory knock unnoticed by his grandparents. She set down a carafe of coffee. "Decaf," she whispered apologetically to Mateo, admiring his thick eye lashes. "The only kind of coffee we have around here."

Mateo smiled back much to her delight and took the cinnamon roll on the tray and, thinking of the sugar high he was on that morning, sunk his teeth into it.

After she left, Pedro began reminiscing about the times he and Mateo had shared when Mateo was growing up. While Victoria contributed a few memories, it was mostly Pedro and Mateo with one "remember the time . . . " on top of another. When they finally drifted to a pause, Pedro sighed in a long breath and said to the boy, "You know Mateo, in many ways, you were, you are, my best friend." After another pregnant pause he added, "After my dear Tori, of course."

Mateo nodded. He had not thought of it in so many words, but of course it was true. His relationship growing up with both his brother and his father had not been adversarial, but he lacked common ground with both. Mateo had never been short of friends from toddlerhood to the present day. He created no boundaries that limited potential friendships or interactions, treating all the same, male, female, rich, and poor, with no regard for differing age, culture or ethnicity; all received the same open acceptance and eagerness to engage. And yet, who had been his first and best friend? Certainly it was his grandfather who had helped him fall in love with music and with whom he could talk for hours. And now Mateo sat here in this senior apartment with his best friend, wondering how he could have neglected this kinship, how he could have been so clueless about the ravages of disease and aging in this beloved man.

Into this deepening awareness Victoria spoke with a purposeful voice. "When did you arrive, Mateo? Have you seen your mother? She's not doing well. Not at all."

Mateo reflected that this was the same expression Rex Randall had used on the phone with him. Had that been less than a week before? Didn't seem possible.

"Grandma, I got here yesterday and saw Mom after lunch. Had lunch with Reverend Randall, Vic Dalloway and the new church administrator Derrick."

"And how is your mom now?" Pedro's voice was calm but sad.

"Man, she is doing some strange stuff! Attacking bushes, baking hundreds of cookies early in the morning, not answering her phone." Mateo shook his head. "And she took a whole week off work! Mom the working maniac! Mrs. Reliable. What's going on?"

Mateo added, "I feel like my whole world is going crazy, once again."

From somewhere deep inside an old pain rose up and caught in Mateo's throat. He had pretty much figured that enough time had gone by and that he was sophisticated enough to not feel his old pain. Certainly every one he knew had experienced pain of some sort. But this was his own pain, and vestiges of it still reached out from the past at unexpected moments.

Pedro shifted in his big old easy chair and winced. Even in this old standby comfort spot, his body could rarely find ease from its malaise. He also felt mental discomfort as he thought of his three beautiful daughters, all three whose relationships had been stressed and dysfunctional. He took a quick glance at his Tori, grateful for the solid life they had made together, which only amplified his puzzlement about his daughters. They were all good women: talented, bright, and successful, yet unable, until recently at least, to form partnerships of love and continuity. Now it seemed that Maria had found zest and compatibility with her Rosemary. And Olivia and Brad seemed to share a love of a most settling type. But then there was Cecilia, such a rock, the stable one of his three girls, perhaps the one most resembling her parents until that day fourteen years ago when everything fell apart. No explanation was ever provided, not even to family members, just that terrible announcement that Warren and Cecilia were no more, and life started anew for the four members of that family with changes that rippled out to touch the rest of the extended family.

True, afterwards Cecilia had settled into a stable and predictable life for many years while her sisters' lives fell apart. But now Maria and Olivia had regrouped only to have Ceci recently behaving so irrationally as to cause general alarm, even in a family that didn't interfere or probe.

Pedro asked Mateo, "Did you by chance hear from Reverend Randall?"

Mateo nodded. Then he asked his grandparents.

"Grand Pedro, Grandma Tori, do you know someone named Dane Faber?"

The blank looks on their faces told him as much as their "No, who is that?" Mateo was more confused than ever but let the subject drop and went back to his mother.

"When did this all happen, with Mom? When did she start acting so weird?"

Pedro and Victoria looked at each other and considered for a minute.

"Three months ago, perhaps."

"Must have been four months ago."

"Maybe longer. Hard to say exactly. She's been preoccupied for years now with the Iraq War, sometimes obsessively so." Victoria sounded disapproving but Pedro shook his head.

"No, that has been a big issue for her, sure, but it has been for many of us."

Victoria's voice didn't relent, "Ceci's been way too invested in this conflict, unable to hold a conversation without bringing it up. She's anguished over death and military force, and it's making her ill. She should be able to let it go, or at least think of other topics. Or if nothing else she should know that others don't always want to hear about Iraq. I mean it's not like one of her sons was involved."

Mateo wasn't sure how to take all of this strong feeling from his grandmother, and once again noticed how worn and drawn she looked and how she massaged her arms and legs like they hurt. He was just going to ask her if she was feeling alright, but Pedro continued to speak slowly and quietly about Cecilia.

"No, I think it is fine to be passionate about a cause and God knows we'd never be anywhere without people who refused let go of their principals. Still, I don't think that's what's happening with your mom. Maybe she is getting early dementia." He stopped while they all three considered this horrible idea, then he continued.

"Something's come up for your mom and it's bothering her enough to disturb her normal rational functioning, like not going to work."

Mateo remembered, "You know, that's what Reverend Randall said, too. He doesn't think this is just Mom's anger about the war."

Pedro nodded. "I like this Rex Randall. A good sort."

"I tried talking to Mom directly last night and this morning and didn't get anywhere."

"But Mateo, you are the only one who can help." Victoria sounded more curt than she meant. Her energy was spent and so was her ability to be diplomatic. "Rowan's worthless and neither Maria nor Olivia can help. Neither can we."

Mateo felt a burden put on him and for a moment looked obstinate. Pedro intervened.

"Listen, Rowan's a good enough fellow, just not the type to figure this out. Too self-absorbed yet. But Mateo, it is not your job to fix your mom. Never. You've shown up. That's what counts. If you're able to get to the bottom of things and help your mom, wonderful! If not, at least you showed up."

He paused and added even more softly, surprising himself that the words came out aloud, "You showed up. That's better than I did."

Both Mateo and Victoria stared at him.

Pedro furrowed his brow and thought, "What's the matter with me?" Lately he had been revisiting the past all the time. This new pattern was exacerbated by the fact that he didn't have the concentration to lose himself in his books anymore, his means of escape since childhood. He didn't elaborate aloud to enlighten either Mateo or Victoria, but he couldn't stop his inner thoughts. "I made a good life. I have so much. But sometimes I know I missed out on doing the right thing. I didn't go back."

The old man turned towards the young man he loved so keenly. "Don't worry about having to do more, Matty. You showed up."

FIFTEEN

A s Mateo left his grandparent's apartment, promising to return the next day, Tina arrived to take the Sanchezes to lunch. Tina looked admiringly at Mateo's retreating figure before turning her attention to the Sanchezes. Victoria took out her hairbrush and smoothed down Pedro's thick white hair, once so jet black. She lovingly tamed an errant strand and then used the brush on her own light gray hair, cut in a practical style.

Tina helped Pedro into his wheelchair. He could still walk but the wheel chair helped him get down the long hallway to the dining room, and he conceded it was better to arrive with dignity in a wheel chair than to risk stumbling.

Tina pushed Pedro out the door, but Victoria stopped and told Pedro, "You go ahead. I am a little tired and don't have an appetite. I'll heat up some soup here in our kitchen if I get hungry."

Pedro nodded, thinking that Victoria needed more time to think about Mateo's visit. "Okay darling.

Remember, it's Saturday and I have a chess game in the lounge after lunch. I'll be back up by 2:00."

Tori put her fingers to her lips, kissed them and pressed those fingers to Pedro's mouth. They smiled at each other and Tina thought how sweet it was that these two were still in love after all the years.

Pedro went off to lunch and Victoria stepped back into the apartment, leaning her back against the door for a few minutes. Maybe a shower would clear her head and renew the energy she needed now to deal with the constant pain throughout her body.

After his lunch, Pedro played several stimulating games of chess with Malcolm Frank, an old teacher friend now living in the Village. While Pedro found critical thinking more difficult these days, there were days when his brain felt as sharp as ever. Perhaps it was the visit from Mateo that had lifted his spirits and his mental capacities. Even his hands didn't tremor as much as usual; not one chess piece was knocked over by the extra movements of his clumsy fingers. Malcolm didn't have a chance today in game after game and finally good-naturedly threw up his hands in defeat.

Tina returned Pedro to his room and helped him into his easy chair. They could hear the shower running and Tina asked if she should check on Victoria to see if she wanted something to eat.

"Oh no, let her enjoy her shower. We have some food in our refrigerator," Pedro assured Tina, so with a friendly wave she left him to take a nap in his chair. He soon fell into a deep sleep. When he woke he looked at the clock. He had slept for 45 minutes. He sat for a moment pulling himself back from the dream state. He had been back home at his mother's table, eating a tamale, which was odd because, although it was one of his favorite foods, it was something she had never made for him as a child. In his dream, voices were arguing around him in Spanish. Try as he might, he couldn't understand what was being said.

After a moment the dream left him and he returned to the present. Pine Crest Village. A sudden nauseating dread washed over him, but he couldn't comprehend what it meant at first. Then he knew.

The shower was still running.

He made a choked noise, and then pulled himself to standing and staggered as quickly as he could to the bedroom. Out of the corner of his eye he saw Victoria's clean clothes laid out on the bed as was her practice. He lurched to the bathroom door and pulled it open.

"Victoria? Tori! My Tori!"

The room was dripping wet, but no longer steamy. He pulled the shower curtain aside with a sweep of his unsteady hand and found her, crumpled on the shower floor, with the cold shower water pouring down on her relentlessly, as it had for hours, going from warm to tepid, to cool to cold, over the time she had lain there.

Strange sounds poured from Pedro's throat. With all the coordination he could muster, he fell to his knees and, putting his arms around her, tried to pull Victoria out of the shower, but he did not have the strength to do so.

Screaming, he staggered to push himself to his feet again, turned off the water, and pulled the Life Alert cord, before kneeling once again to gather his precious Victoria in his arms and hold her unconscious body next to his heart.

And so Tina found him minutes later when she arrived to check on why the Sanchez alarm had sounded. There was dear Mr. Sanchez on his knees half in the shower, clothes now soaked, holding his naked and unresponsive wife in his arms, crying a sound that Tina would never forget the rest of her life: a wild bellow of grief.

The paramedics put the unconscious Victoria on a gurney and placed Pedro on another and took them both to the hospital, accompanied by the Director of Pine Crest Village.

Phone calls were made to their daughters, but all calls were met with Voice Mail.

"Damn!" exclaimed Tina, and then she thought of the church.

Mateo and Cecilia were sitting with Vic behind a table full of goodies. After leaving his grandparents Mateo had brought his mother a sandwich and joined her. Of those who knew Mateo from the City, few would have pictured Mateo Schumacher sitting in a church Fellowship Hall selling cupcakes and cookies to those who stopped by. But there he was, drinking some of Derrick's good coffee, exchanging stories with Vic, and keeping a sideways watch on his mom.

Rex opened the door and motioned to them. Drawing them close to him he explained succinctly. "We just got a call from Pine Crest Village. They've been trying to reach you."

"Oh my God. It's Papa?"

"No Cecelia, it's your mom."

Cecelia stared at him. "Mother?"

"Yes." Rex put his hand on her shoulder. "I don't know much except that she's at University Hospital, unconscious. Your dad is there too and he's very shaken. Why don't you let me drive you over."

Like a robot, Cecelia followed Rex out the door. Mateo grabbed her purse and followed, giving a shocked look at Vic who stood there silent and concerned.

Once in the car Mateo asked whether Olivia or Maria had been called. No one knew, so Mateo took his mom's phone from her trembling hands and made those calls. He was able to get through to Maria who said she would meet them at the hospital. At Olivia's house a young woman answered, Mateo's cousin Julia. Her bored voice changed when she heard Mateo's voice and yet again when she heard the news.

"Mom's been in the garden all day. I'll tell her."

When they arrived at the hospital they found both Pedro and Victoria in the ER being seen by a doctor. Pedro looked utterly defeated, a worn old man. He was sitting in a chair right by Victoria holding her hand. IV's stuck out of her other arm, but she was not responsive. The only sign of life was her faint and irregular breathing.

Cecilia rushed to her father's side, but the doctor asked Rex and Mateo to wait out of the room. The two men sat suspended in the waiting area. Mateo was extremely grateful for Rex's presence and thanked him for the ride and for staying with them.

"Of course," is all Rex said. As a pastor, he had found himself in a hospital many times since Beth's long illness but it still brought back mixed memories, both sweet and sickening.

Cecilia eventually emerged from the room and walked directly over to them and addressed Rex as much as Mateo. Her voice was monotone, but it ended with a sob.

"Mother's unconscious. They don't expect her to make it. Can you believe this? Mother has bone cancer, and she has been hiding it from all of us. She knew. But she didn't even tell Papa."

"She's dying of bone cancer, just like that?" Rex was surprised and his words came out rather bluntly. "That doesn't make sense to me."

"What?" Cecilia lifted her face to Rex and shook her head. "No, that is not what I mean. She has bone cancer, but she had a heart attack in the shower and collapsed. Probably the cancer had just stressed her too much, on top of worrying about Papa. Who knows? Whatever, she's slipping away."

Cecilia sank down into the plastic couch in the waiting room and lowered her head into her hands, her shocked face disappearing behind a wave of hair.

SIXTEEN

C ecilia had no more uttered her stark news to Rex and Mateo when both Maria and Olivia arrived at the hospital. Cecelia looked up at her sisters and they saw the stunned look on her face. She repeated the news to them in her flat, disbelieving voice. Olivia immediately succumbed to convulsing sobs, and Maria bombarded Cecelia with questions which went unanswered. Cecilia had nothing more to offer. The three sisters were at a loss, caught completely off guard. Their mother was invincible.

As Rex saw all three of them go inward with shock, he tried to bring them back to the current reality by reminding them that Pedro could use some support. Before the three women could focus on Rex's words, Mateo decided for them.

"I'll stay with him." The young man jumped out of his chair, took ten strides down the hall to find his grandfather slumped in a chair next to his motionless wife, gripping her hand, his head down. And so it was that Mateo sat next to his grandfather in the next hours with his arm around him, holding him, only getting up to escort Pedro to the bathroom and to bring him drinks of water, which were accepted, and food, which Pedro had no interest in eating. The daughters moved in and out of the room like lost little sheep, unable to stay anywhere for long.

Mateo was with his grandparents when Victoria stopped breathing. She was breathing irregularly, then more and more slowly, and then not at all. As she had lived, with reserve and dignity, so she died. Being found naked in the shower was the only part of her dying that would have horrified her.

With his grandmother's death, Mateo Schumacher entered a new phase of his adulthood. It was a transformative twenty-four hours. Reunion and unexpected death. But more than that, it sealed the bond between Pedro and Mateo which had endured many years of separation.

Pedro's grief was beyond his family's imaginations. On one hand it was simple - after almost sixty years of marriage he had lost his beloved companion. And on the other hand, his loss was compounded by complexities. He came back to one staggering question: if Victoria knew she was so sick, that her body was riddled with cancer, why had she not shared this with him and sought treatment? He asked himself this over and over again, and often a sense of deception clouded over the pure agony of losing his Tori, the only woman he had loved, the woman who had sealed his acceptance in his new home of Pine Junction and assured his claim on a new beginning. His Tori who had faithfully helped him achieve the stability he had longed for during his tumultuous childhood and his service in the army during WW II, an experience he chose to not discuss, ever. His Tori who never pushed him to face what he could not or would not talk about. And when he had nightmares, she would sooth him with her strong body so the horrible flashbacks would recede, and once more he was the astute, refined Mr. Sanchez, master teacher, church leader, city councilman, father of three daughters, a man who by all appearance was at peace with himself.

Even from Mateo the past stayed hidden. Pedro Sanchez was a genuine grandfather to Mateo. It was the purest endeavor of his life, with no hidden agenda, no ulterior motive, only unconditional love. The time and attention he gave Mateo was his greatest gift. But he never shared the stories of his life with the boy. He never talked of the pain and horror, the ambiguity and beauty, of his childhood in Arizona. Never. And his references to his time as a soldier in the European front were few and far between, and he never let Mateo dwell on questions regarding these parts of his life. His life began when he moved to Pine Junction. This is what he wanted to believe, and others, even his family, were content to accept this. It was very comfortable to accept this version of Pedro's life. But even though he put forth this unquestionable life story, only his mind bought it. His body and soul knew there was more and without some degree of acknowledgment of the first twenty-four years of life, body and soul had backed up a huge amount of unfinished business.

And now Victoria was no longer by his side to stave off the intensity of the memories.

SEVENTEEN

"Hey Catherine, yeah, well this is Mateo. I know you are pretty pissed off at me. I know I have screwed up ... No excuses, but things have been pretty crazy here. So if you even consider talking to me again, well, I mean I would understand if you won't and all ... but I was thinking that if you would be willing to give me another chance, we could talk sometime. I don't know when I will be back in Brooklyn." ... pause ... choked voice ... then controlled ... "Cate, my grandma just died ... I'm feeling kind of surreal. No one knew she was sick. This is just killing my Grand Pedro ... God, it hurts me to see him so out of his mind depressed ... hopeless like." Deep breathing and a gulp ... "Well, you know, everyone here is in a state of shock. Like my mom, I can't figure out what is going on with her, and now this ... Anyway, I am sure you are pretty ticked at me, but I gotta stay around here awhile ... I'll call Mike at work and let him know ... Hope he gives me some more time off." ... Another pause .... "Well, that's it .... Up to you. Just wanted to let you know that I've been thinking of you . . . despite what it looks like. . . . Oh yeah, this is one of those long rambling phone messages that I know you hate. . . . but things are kind of screwed up" . . . . long silence . . . "but . . . I love you."

EIGHTEEN

Soon after Victoria's passing, while doing some cleaning for her father, Cecilia lifted some new looking nightgowns in her mother's drawer and uncovered several beautiful old journals. Her librarian fingers touched the leather covers, tracing the engravings and bindings.

Feeling shivers running through her spine, yet unable to resist, she curled up on her parent's bed and opened one journal and then another, looking at the dates. The first one she glanced at made her smile and shake her head. Cecilia sometimes had trouble remembering her own childhood, but to imagine her own mother at age . . . well, what age? She looked again at the childish handwriting. Victoria Lessing, age seven.

Hummingbird
Tiny little humming bird
I wish I could tell you with a word
How pretty you flash
In and out of the flowers you dash

Shiny red, green, gray and black
Into the sky and then right back.
I wish I could be
As pretty as thee,
and fly high into the tree
Free to be me.

"So sweet." Cecilia murmured under her breath, and she turned the page, this journal full of page after page of Victoria's childish reflections, mostly on nature, sometimes on her horse, with illustrations in bold colors. Nothing but a little girl's imaging of her life, simple and straight forward. Cecilia was touched nonetheless to have this connection to her mother's childhood.

She closed that journal and looked at the doorway, certain that she would not want her father to catch her at what was feeling like a violation of her mother's privacy. She thought again, her dead mother's privacy. No matter, it still felt like intruding, yet she chose another journal to open.

And so she spent the next hour, reading poem after poem. And it was all poetry in various styles, no narrative. There was free verse, haiku, some in old fashioned traditional poetic formula. There were great gaps in the dating of the books. Had her mom destroyed some of the books, or had she simply not written every year of her life?

As Victoria got older the tone of the poems changed from happy-go-lucky child, to disengaged teenager, to love-struck young woman. All natural transitions, Cecilia observed, yet, it was almost impossible for her to see her stern and practical mother feeling any of these emotions at any time in her life. But it was clearly her mother's distinctive handwriting, childish at first and then evolving into Victoria's classic old-school elegant penmanship. There was no denying who had written these pieces.

Cecilia finished reading of her mother's teenage years, poems of loneliness at home and school, and those that told of liberating rides on her horse, the horse being the "only one who understands me . . . ." Putting down this journal, Cecilia noticed a loose page stuck in the back. She pulled it out and saw that it had been torn out of a different journal, different paper and lines. But it was written in Victoria's handwriting. It looked like it had been crumpled and then smoothed out, as if the author had first thrown it out and then decided to save it.

Wounded
By Victoria Lessing age 16

Little girl halts, then hides behind the third stair
rail.
Out of bed to fetch her lost toy, she stops, pale.
Inside her small chest, her heart thuds as if it
might fail.
Her breathing is soft, now almost is still.
She would run away but she has not the will.

She hears ugly voices below in the summer's dim
light,
As suppressed resentments boil into a hateful fight.
The child hears words full of bitter anger
and spite,
Argued fiercely, not under their breaths,
now too clear.
Leaving their unseen little daughter trembling with fear.

This is the night that will change it all.
Onto nightgown and bare feet, shame
starts to fall.
When she looks into the mirror at the end
of the hall
Tomorrow and always she will see a differ-
ent face.
The old child will be gone, vanished without a trace.

"You monster! I never wanted another
child," Mother hissed.
Wildly Mother threw her glass, but the
martini missed
Its mark, but more shouts hit his face like a
wicked kiss.
"It is all your fault," she screamed, and
Father was blamed.
Standing up to full height, he cursed and
roughly exclaimed.

"You're drunk!" Father growled, then with a quick
switch
He strode out of the garden with a sneer so rich,
"She's just like you, an uptight little witch,
Yes, there's no love lost," was his last damn-
ing shout,
Leaving Mother alone to her gin and her pout.

The day went as usual, the family on their
separate paths,
Perhaps she had dreamed all that had cut
such a wide swath?
But when she looked into the mirror she
felt that night's wrath.
For years the child waited but nothing
more was said.
Still she knew she was wounded, although
she was not dead.

A new sense of awareness came over her
then and there,
Bitter lessons she learned, although they
didn't seem fair.
People cannot be believed, they don't really care.
I am not worthy of value, Pain should
never be laid bare.
Trust was wounded forever that day on the
stair.

Cecilia found her own eyes filling with tears for the child in the poem. Then she thought, my mother. This child is my mother. Cecilia felt a cold ache inside her.

Once again she glanced out the bedroom door and listened for the door. Nothing. Her Papa must be staying longer down in the cafeteria today. Maybe that was good. Perhaps he was resuming some interest in others. Or perhaps the staff was short-handed and had just let him sit in the dining hall too long. Pedro could walk back to his room, but in his grief, he seemed unwilling to exert the energy required. He was passive in his heartbreak.

In another journal Cecilia was relieved to read affectionate poems about her mother's love for Pedro during their first courtship months. Another short whimsical poem was written for Olivia as a five-year-old. All about the garden. Well that makes sense, both Victoria and Olivia being avid gardeners. Cecilia stopped herself. Past tense for Victoria. This would take some getting used to. Of course she would share this poem with Olivia. Of course she should share all these poems with both her sisters. Of course. But what would Papa think? She couldn't admit to finding Victoria's secret journals, could she? Did her Papa even know about these?

She picked up yet another book, feeling guiltier all the time. It opened to a page in the middle. The title caught Cecilia's eye. "Alone," it said. "Well I can relate to that," Cecilia had to admit. But she had never thought of her mother in those terms. Victoria had simply never let anyone see her as vulnerable.

Alone
(written by Victoria Sanchez, dated 1970)
All day I churn with people.
Yet at night I lie alone even as I share my bed
with my one love.
Alone.
How can one care for someone so deeply
and still feel all alone.

He is my life, and I have been his.
I have always thought it to be true.
But while we walk together
year after year after year,
While we share the children I have birthed,
and lay together in intimacy to bring them
life,
While we held each other in calm or in
passion,
There is still something that makes me feel
alone.
Secrets he holds all these years.

At first the mystery of an elusive and differ-
ent past
was exotic, appealing.
But we can't get past this closed gate.
Who are you?
What troubles your sleep?
Why do you distance yourself and go away

some place I cannot enter with you?
Why do I feel so alone when I love you so deeply?

This aloneness creeps into my heart
and from there into my face and mouth and head.
I feel the sternness come over me.
I cannot stop it.
I feel myself criticize and blame and judge.
It is others who suffer, not him
Others, not him, who make me feel as a child,
unwanted again.
I lash at them, and hurt them.
I know I do.
I can see it in their eyes.

I am at these moments wretched.
Because I am alone.
No, it is because I am lonely.
And I have been lonely all my life.

"Oh, Mother! Oh, I am so sorry," Cecilia whispered. She felt confused, distressed, emotions she had never associated with her parents before. She could not even begin to know what to do with the information she had just absorbed. It was like having her sense of herself as the child of Victoria and Pedro Sanchez made into a different movie than the one she had played a role in all her life. And all of that in one hour and with just these few words from her mother's pen. From her hand and her heart, it seemed.

When she heard the door open, Cecilia jumped as if caught stealing. Under the cover of the friendly voice of Tina chatting with her father, Cecilia quickly gathered up the journals that lay around her in the bed and pushed them back into the drawer, dumping the night gowns back in a disheveled pile to cover up the books. Then she stopped and opened the drawer again and folded the nightwear more neatly. Her mother's influence had not left the room.

Sticking her head out of the bedroom she cheerfully greeted her father and Tina. But her head was whirling. What to do with this new view of her mother? How to find out if her father knew about these books and had read his wife's poetry? Should she share this all with her sisters? Should she just take the books and burn them in her fire place without reading another page? What was the right thing to do?

All that night, the words her mother had written jangled in Cecilia's mind, and she felt wiser . . . and more disturbed. By the end of the next day, her prevailing mood was that she had been left in the dark, and she was perturbed that her mother had not shared more of her life with her daughters, more of who she really was. Over the next days and weeks though, Cecilia's thoughts morphed and changed like a lava lamp, moving from just plain sadness to delight in the richness that had lain under the surface of Victoria's stern demeanor. And then Cecilia felt again the sense of betrayal. It was some time before she decided what step to take; meanwhile, every time she visited her Papa, her eyes and thoughts would travel to the dresser drawer.

NINETEEN

The days that followed Victoria's death unfolded in a slow blur for the family, each in his or her own way.

Maria wasted no time and made an appointment with her therapist to talk about the death of her mother. And she spent hours sitting on the old sofa or out in their kayaks, processing with her sympathetic partner Rosemary. Maria thought that through the years she had left no stone unturned in her analysis of herself and family. She was always trying her best to make sense of her life, and during the last few years she felt like she had made progress. The unexpected death of her Rock of Gibraltar mother, whose presence she and the others had pushed against and also taken for granted, rocked Maria's boat. After a long talk one night, she and Rosemary found themselves laughing about the word "rock" and how it could have such opposite meanings.

Maria reached out and grabbed Rosemary's hand and held it tightly in hers, bringing their entwined fingers up to her lips. She kissed that precious hand. "As long as we can keep laughing together, I think I'm going to get through this, Rosie."

Rosemary agreed. "I have no doubt of it. And I know it's not easy. I remember how hard it was to lose my dad, how you supported me. His was a simple uncomplicated death, and your mom's caught everyone by surprise. But you're going to get through this, Maria. You will."

Olivia, on the other hand, was extra emotional about any and all of life's occurrences outside her classroom, and it could be argued that she was closest to Victoria, so when her mother so suddenly departed, Olivia went to bed for a day, and then two more days, and another, and yet another. Her husband Brad attentively brought her cups of hot chocolate and attempted to coax her up with toast and lemon curd, but Olivia remained in bed.

And then Julia appeared at her bedside one day, sat down, and said "Mom, we have to talk."

Olivia rolled over and turned a bleary eye on her daughter. There was something in Julia's tone of voice and bearing that was new, more authoritative. Olivia didn't move but she kept her eyes on her only child. Julia had long appeared stagnant, but she now spoke with certainty.

"Mom, I've been thinking." She waited for a response.

Olivia roused herself to answer. "Jul, I really cannot think too much about anything right now. Is it important?"

Such a brush-off normally would have crushed whatever emergent spirit was bubbling up in Julia. But somehow the new Julia persisted.

"Yes, Mom, it's important. Do you think you could sit up and listen?"

Olivia was silent a moment but Julia didn't move, and the phone didn't ring, Brad didn't walk in the door, the dog didn't start barking, the door bell didn't ring. All was silent. Just Olivia, dank hair, swollen eyes, sweaty nightgown and all, finally raising her head from the wrinkled pillow to face her daughter, who sat on the bed, dressed in an old tee shirt and jeans, one tattoo showing on her forearm, and another on her midriff half covered by her short shirt. Her face was clear and clean and youthful, not at first glance gorgeous, but, on second look, simply lovely.

It was this that caught Olivia's attention. Her daughter had been an adorable child, cute enough to attract attention. But in adolescence she seemed to disappear into herself, become invisible, and each year through high school and on to college just accentuated this impression. Moving back home had seemingly sealed this invisibility, or so Olivia feared. Any physical attractiveness was hidden behind blandness. Nothing else had changed. Julia had not gained weight, or developed a skin problem, nor had she failed to bathe or brush her hair, but her simple beauty had been lost behind apathy. She was frozen in place.

Now at this moment, sitting calmly on her mother's bed, Julia Howard was a picture of serenity, and a glow emanated from her.

Olivia didn't sit up but her eyes opened wider and she nodded her head. "What is it, Jul?"

"Mom, Gramma was sick and no one noticed. No one looked at Gramma, not really. Maybe not even Grandpa. No one, Mom, not even me. It was like she was invisible. She was really sick and no one knew. No one saw her. I think that's terribly sad. I think it was wrong. Everyone took her for granted. I think she must have felt unseen, even though everyone thought she was a strong person. Even though everyone counted on her, she really was invisible."

Olivia's eyes closed. After a long pause, she murmured. "You may be right, Jul."

Then she opened her eyes and looked at her daughter and repeated, "You may be right. But what can we do about it?"

"Oh, Mommy!" Julia's voice was shaking, not with uncertainty but with the opposite, with conviction." I don't know what you're going to do about it, but I know that Gramma would never be lying in bed for days doing nothing. Gramma would be doing something. And I think that when someone dies we should honor them in a way that is like their life. Gramma did things. She was always doing stuff. So I think we should honor Gramma by doing something. And I can't tell you what to do for Gramma. But I know what I'm going to do."

Olivia sat up slowly staring at her daughter as if hypnotized. "Go on."

"Well, Gramma used to tell me something. Remember when I used to go spend time after school with her, after you and Dad got divorced? Well, she and I would talk, and we would work in the garden. And she told me something I was good at. She said she thought I would make a good botanist, because I could remember the names of plants and was good at drawing them. You remember how I used to draw trees and flowers all the time?"

Julia went on before Olivia could embarrass herself by admitting that she had not noticed this skill in her own child. "Well, I think that it's true. And I'm tired of just existing day after day, kinda lost, you know. I've decided to go back to school to study botany, or maybe biology because I like organisms, too, and I think cells are interesting and all . . . ." Although Julia finished in a flurry, there was still a certainty about what she was saying that flabbergasted her mother.

"Julia, your Grandmother only . . . " Olivia choked on the word, ". . . has only been gone a few days, and you have already figured all this out?"

"Yeah, well, you know, Mom, sometimes you just know, like all of a sudden, but when you know it, you realize you really knew it a long, long time, like it has been coming over you quietly, like sneaking up on you for years, but all of sudden you turn around and Boom! - there it is, completely clear, like, totally focused." Julia laughed a little self-consciously, but she seemed elated.

"So anyway, that's what I wanted to tell you. And I'm working on that plan already. I just wanted to let you know." She got up from the bed, and looked steadily into her mom's eyes. "I don't know what you're going to do, Mom, but I suggest you do something that will make a good memory of Gramma, something that makes her life important."

Julia walked to the door calling over her shoulder, "I'm going to see if I can find Matty. . . . I want to see him while he's in town." And she was gone.

Olivia sat for at least ten minutes without moving, even her hands were in repose. Then she swung her feet off the bed and as she stood up, Brad walked into the room returning from work. "Hey hon," he said. "I just saw Julia headed down the road. Where's she off to?"

"I think she's off to her future."

Olivia continued. "Brad, will you help me take a first step into mine?"

"What do you mean?" He looked at her with some concern. He loved his wife but knew she was fairly prone to high emotions. "How're you feeling today?"

"I'm going to take a shower."

"Okay, that'll feel good. But what do you need from me?"

"Can you help me?"

Brad grabbed her hand and gave a whoop, then looked chagrinned.

Olivia's face crumpled, and she sobbed out, "Brad! All I can think about is my mother lying in that shower with the water flooding over her, first hot, then warm and then so cold, and she lying there, unable to move. Oh, such cold, cold water. I haven't been able to face getting into the shower. Please help me. Come in with me. Please."

"Sorry Livia, I forgot myself, but it isn't everyday that a man gets an invitation to shower with such a good-looking babe."

Olivia tried not to, but she was soon smiling at him, and then they made a mad dash for the bathroom, clothes falling to the floor, until both were under the flowing water, bodies pressed together, lips pressed, and the tears flowed along with the water down their legs and swirled down the drain and were gone. Gone.

TWENTY

For the first day or so, Cecilia found herself obsessing over her mother's secrets, reminded of her own. She went about her life as if sleepwalking, with less frenetic fury than the recent weeks. She asked for an extension on her leave from work, which was granted.

One day Mateo came in on Cecilia in the kitchen having heard snorts and gasps that he couldn't pinpoint as laughter, rage, or sobbing. His mom was doubled over in her chair, grasping her stomach, cackling in a most uncontrolled manner. And it was, he finally discerned, laughter.

"Okay, Mom, explain the joke," he asked nervously.

"Oh, Mateo," she managed to sputter, "for days now I've been fretting about my mother's secret. I know this's awful and not funny at all, but I just realized what I was saying . . . Victoria's Secret!! Oh my God, Victoria's Secret! It's so ridiculous. My mom would be appalled, and yet she set this up . . . in a very roundabout way. Victoria's Secret . . . but it hasn't been very sexy at all."

Cecilia wiped her eyes and looked at her son apologetically. "Why is it, Matty, that sometimes we laugh at the wrong times? And once I started, I simply couldn't stop. Oh, I have to tell you that it felt good to laugh."

"I'm sure it was good for you to laugh, Mom."

He paused, then added, "I wonder if we'll ever figure out why Grandma Tori didn't tell anyone about her cancer? By the way, did you hear back from Rowan?"

"Yes. He says he'll come for the memorial service." Cecilia tried not to show the sadness she felt at Rowan's casual attitude about his grandmother's passing.

Mateo continued to watch his mother carefully while spending as much time with his grandfather as possible. He felt overflowing with family responsibilities, so one day while walking by the church, Mateo sought out its sanctuary, drawn in by the sound of Vic practicing. He slipped in and sat near the back, hoping not to disturb the organist as he played. For more than an hour Mateo sat meditatively in the pew, becoming wrapped up in Vic's music as it swelled large and churned out the rich sound.

He started out thinking about all that had happened since he arrived in Pine Junction. Mateo felt the pain and loss his grandfather was living these days, as well as the shock of his mother and aunts. He wondered about his grandmother's behavior in keeping her illness a secret from everyone. Dr. Troyer said it was clear she had been getting sicker for months, but she had weathered on, hiding the worst of the pain behind a stern countenance and her fatigue behind the work she was doing to care for her husband. Mateo thought of how little he had known his grandmother. His thoughts ran on. He had not forgotten the original reason he had come to Pine Junction: his mom's erratic behavior and figuring out who Dane Faber was, but on neither matter had he come any closer to gaining clarity.

Mateo let the problems he was facing flow away with the music and the peace of the sanctuary. His eyes lingered on each stained glass window, and he could feel his teenaged arms working at cleaning the panes, section by section. Beyond the stories they told, the colors and designs in each window were beautifully designed. Soon he was relaxed.

This is how he sat when Vic stopped playing and, without turning around, called to Mateo. "Tea?"

Mateo didn't know if Vic deliberately offered the tea just to be ornery, or whether he really didn't know of Mateo's preference for coffee. Well, let's just play his game, Mateo thought. He had always enjoyed Vic's sardonic humor. "Sure."

"How did you know I was here?" he added.

"Have a sense when I'm not alone in here," Vic answered. "Most of the time it is just me and the ghosts, but when someone walks in the door the ghosts don't like it so they disappear. I can sense it."

Mateo recalled now the stories of the ghosts who not so much haunted the old building as simply resided therein, only in evidence when the sanctuary was empty. Vic was clearly on good terms with the ancient ones, and during his long tenure, Reverend Prescott had come to a comfortable relationship with the ghosts also, occasionally talking to them about the past. It was the single slightly off-beat behavior of the otherwise very traditional Reverend Doctor Carl Prescott. The church as a whole took these other-worldly beings semi-seriously but did not dwell upon them. They were a given, part of the folklore and history of the church and had never caused any harm. Mateo wondered how Rex Randall had adjusted to a place where paranormal activity was considered normal.

Mateo met Vic again in the choir room to hold an undrunk cup of tea, symbol to Vic of care and communication. When each was sitting in a chair, cup in hand, Vic asked his first question, voicing not concern for Mateo or even Pedro, but for Cecilia. "How's your mom doing, Mateo?"

"No worse than before Grandma died, Vic. In fact, in some ways she's more functional."

"What do you mean?"

So Mateo described what he had observed about his mother before the terrible day of his grandmother's death. "And since then, she has seemed kind of stunned, but not so crazy. Not doing such bizarre things like attacking bushes and baking thousands of cookies at 5:00 a.m. or refusing to answer her phone." He added, "Of course she was laughing hysterically just this morning. She was laughing that grandma had a secret and that it was Victoria's Secret."

Vic's face was blank, so Mateo clarified, "You know, the sexy women's clothing store is named Victoria's Secret . . . . I guess it just hit Mom as hilarious and she started laughing and once she started she couldn't stop. She almost made herself gag she was laughing so hard."

Vic nodded. "Yes, this grief business, especially when it's a shock, can produce some strange reactions. Nothing is normal for your mom now."

Mateo agreed, but said, "I'm not sure things were normal before Grandma died either. But then I start to wonder if anything was ever normal anyway, or what normal even means."

Vic didn't have an answer for that, but added that he was going to go visit Cecilia that afternoon and bring her some new music. Mateo mentioned that he was going to go take a walk in the woods before going back to see his grandfather that afternoon.

They parted, but before they did, Vic put his arm around Mateo's shoulders, although he didn't say a word.

"Thanks for the music, Vic. It restored my sanity, as always."

As he walked down the church steps Mateo caught sight of his cousin driving by, and waved her down. "Hey Julia. I was just off for a walk. Want to join me?"

Julia's smile was open and joyful. "Matty, I was looking for you. I wanted to tell you about my new plans."

The two cousins spent several hours walking the fields and woods of their childhood, while Julia bubbled over with her plans for school and a science career. Mateo listened happily because it was a great change of topic in the recent emotionally charged weeks, and he had never seen his cousin so animated. Her energy helped revive his spirits as much as Vic's music. And for the first time he learned a bit more about his grandmother. Turns out that perhaps no one knew Victoria as well as her granddaughter Julia. Those two had forged a quiet bond that few had noticed. Unfortunately, neither Victoria nor Julia had figured out how to let this bond bloom to bear more fruit for either of them. But Julia, with sudden clarity, was not going to let her grandmother's memory and influence be wasted.

Mateo reflected that it had been a therapeutic and instructive afternoon, and he drove over to see his grandfather with new hope in his heart.

TWENTY-ONE

Rex and Derrick picked up several take-out pizzas and a couple of six packs of beer and joined by Vic, knocked on Cecilia's front door. Not every minister would have approached a family to plan a memorial service with beer and pizza, but it was Rex's style to be casual so that the family would be comfortable.

Everyone in the family except Rowan had arrived by the time the church men knocked: Cecilia, Mateo, Olivia, Brad, Julia, Maria and Rosemary, and of course Pedro himself, looking like a mere shadow of himself.

As they were about to begin, Vic realized he had not brought his music planning book, so left to retrieve it back at the church. Advantage of small town living, thought Mateo. Everyone realized that they were hungry. No one had eaten much since Victoria's death. They dug into the pizza with unsophisticated zeal, and only Pedro needing coaxing to eat a few bites.

There was a knock on the door and a ring of the doorbell almost at the same time. Wiping pizza off her lips and swallowing the last of her beer, Cecilia opened the door to greet a total stranger, a young woman who stood in the doorway looking determined but nervous.

"Yes?"

"I'm looking for Mateo Schumacher."

"Can I tell him who's here?" Cecilia asked while opening the door wider.

"My name is Catherine Luna, and I'm sorry to intrude. I didn't realize you were having a . . . party." Catherine hesitated at the word, realizing too late that her choice might not be appreciated.

"Come in Catherine. I'm Cecilia, Mateo's mom. He's in the dining room."

As Cecilia stood aside, Catherine looked through the entry way and into the dining room and there she saw the man she wanted to see, the motivation for her long drive into unknown territory. Her rushed request to her father to borrow his car came as soon as she heard Mateo's voice message on her phone, days after it had been left. Despite, or perhaps because of, her heartache about Mateo, Catherine had almost convinced herself that she had given up on him. Consequently, when she dove into her musical practice sessions that week, she did not check messages for days, trying to lose her pain in the discipline of her music.

Mateo spotted her standing by his mom and a smile spread out over his face. "Cate!" He stood up recklessly, smashed his beer down, dodged around the chairs and people at the long dining room table, and rushed to greet her. Before she could say a word he had grabbed her up in huge hug, swirling her around in a circle, her feet not touching the ground, her dark hair swinging out behind her head, and he only put her down when she cried out in agitation. "Mateo, let me down! I have to get to a bathroom and you're not helping any by squeezing me! It's been a long drive!"

Cecilia, hovering nearby, took Catherine's hand and led her straight to the bathroom off the entry way. Mateo stood there waiting for her with the same grin on his face, feeling goofy but as happy as he had felt in a long time. She had come to him. Later he would wonder and ask about the details of how she had rearranged her life, and somehow found him, what that had taken, but for the moment he just glowed inside that she was here, right here in Pine Junction.

When Catherine opened the bathroom door, he quickly stepped inside pulling her back in, closing the door behind them. "Ah Baby, I can't believe this. You're here. How did you find me? How did you get here? Oh God, I'm so glad to see you. You can't believe how good you look. Umm, how good you smell. How good you taste."

She was relieved to have such an unconditionally warm reception, but having been brought up with good manners, she wiggled out of his arms and reminded him that his family was out in the dining room waiting for him.

Mateo was so happy that nothing could throw him. He took her by the arm and they entered the dining room together, side by side, arm in arm. Vic had returned, and apparently it was he who had been in the right place at the right time to guide a puzzled Catherine to the home of the Schumacher's when she stopped at the church upon arriving in Pine Junction. She hadn't a clue about where to begin looking for her boyfriend since Mateo had unplugged himself from his phone recently.

Introductions were made all around. Catherine was handed a beer and a plate with pizza, and she settled back into a chair while Rex once again reconvened the gathering, now relaxed even more than the mere beer and pizza could have induced. Even Pedro came out of his somber state to feel a few degrees of delight in the happiness of his grandson. A smile awoke in him when Mateo made a special point of introducing Catherine to him, and she warmly took his hand and responded with a natural grace.

"Okay folks," Rex cleared his throat. "May I suggest that we start with a word of prayer. We have a memorial service to plan and we want to make Victoria proud of us."

And so the evening began. Mateo had to agree with his grandfather's assessment of Rex Randall as a "good sort." The pastor was able to lead the family with tender humor as they planned the service for their wife and mother and grandmother. All during the evening, Mateo's eyes were on Catherine and hers on him. He no longer wondered how he found himself in this place with people so familiar and yet so long shut out of his life. He was here now, and it was the right place to be. The sight of Catherine, so intent to be with him, tied the past and present together. He knew in the back of his mind that there was more he needed to discover, but, for this moment, he was as happy as one could be under the circumstances.

While the planning conversation went on between the church men and the family, the young man's arm rested on the back of his Grand Pedro's chair. Mateo stroked Pedro's back without awareness of the gesture. Catherine saw it, and if there was a defining moment in her love for Mateo, it was this one.

Catherine finally pulled herself out of bed the next morning, with no help from Mateo, who could have held her there forever. His euphoric state of mind was checked by Catherine's more disciplined one, and he rested his head on the pillows with pleasure as he watched her get dressed with the morning light coming in behind her. The big windows were open to the spring air and framed the trees outside. The gauzy curtains moving gently softened the dark green of the pines, and the deciduous trees in their spring explosion. Thousands of childhood days Mateo had awakened to this view, but today he felt this familiar scene would be forever enhanced by the sight of Catherine standing in front of the window pulling on her jeans, and then bending over to put on her bra, her hair slipping across her shoulders. Mateo gazed hungrily at her breasts as they slowly fell into the bra's hold.

He leaped out of bed and fondled her. She laughed but kissed his forehead in an affectionate "I love you but not now" message. Mateo held her face in his hands and kissed her full on the lips. He was overwhelmed with desire, but slowly let go, in all fairness to her and her schedule. He slipped into his own jeans, and headed out the bedroom door calling over his shoulder,

"Pancakes on your plate in twenty minutes. Be there."

TWENTY-TWO

Victoria's service was scheduled for the following weekend. After talking with his boss, Mateo had a bereavement leave tacked on to the vacation week he had taken from The Urban Perk, so he stayed in Pine Junction. Catherine spent that one night and then returned to New York to get back to her rehearsals and return her father's car. She drove off with a promise to return for the memorial service.

Alone now in his apartment, Pedro was feeling the absence of Victoria so keenly it hurt like a knife, and the next moment he felt her presence with such reality that it first comforted him and then swiftly devastated him when the true situation washed over him.

Tina and the other aides were attentive. They were all fond of their Mr. Sanchez, horrified at the terrible way Pedro had found his wife. His agonized keening was a sound Tina couldn't erase from her dreams.

It was Mateo who really kept Pedro sane in those first weeks, faithful in his attendance to his grandfather. Mateo knew just when to sit in silence, when to tell stories and

gentle jokes that stirred the humor for which Pedro was famous. It was Mateo who knew how to help his grandfather
speak aloud the stories he needed to tell about his wife,
to release the missing just a tiny bit, centimeter by centimeter. When Rex made a pastoral visit, he was amazed at
the intuitive presence Mateo possessed, and at the love between grandfather and grandson. "Wish I could bottle that
'something,'" is what Rex thought. On that first day when
he was repairing the fence behind the church, if someone
had told Rex that the young fellow who approached him
was this same Mateo, or that any of these events would
have unfolded in this surprising way, Rex would have had
a difficult time believing it.

One afternoon, Mateo sat with his grandfather in
the apartment, and it appeared that they were both
reading. They both had books in front of them, and
Mateo was at least reading some of what was on his page
although his mind was ranging far and wide. Pedro was
staring at his book, one of his old favorites, but he was
reading the same sentence over and over again. And yet
it was gently comforting to be sitting next to Mateo with
a book in his hand. It was a familiar activity, one he had
done countless times in his life with Victoria by his side,
and so it helped him get through one more hour of his
newly devastated life.

Mateo suddenly remembered. "Ah, I forgot something
in the car. Betty Troyer brought over some flowers for you,
Grand Pedro. They are from her garden, of course, and
she said they were Grandma's favorite early spring blooms.

She had to run to a meeting at church and asked if I could bring them to you. I'd better get them into some water. Be right back."

Pedro managed a wan smile while Mateo grabbed his car keys and headed to the door. Walking around the corner of the building, he took a moment to leave a message for Catherine. He couldn't bear not to talk to her many times a day now.

Returning from the parking lot, flowers in hand, he saw two men standing by the receptionist. Wendy waved Mateo over to the counter and the two men turned to watch him approach.

One man was perhaps sixty years old and the other was younger than Mateo. The older man wore a tweed blazer, plaid shirt, and neat khaki pants. His trimmed hair was black and gray equally mixed, his eyes deep brown, teeth straight and white. Behind him the younger man slouched. Although more casually dressed he looked quite similar to his companion. He was slim, with long hair shoved behind his ears. The younger man looked much less comfortable standing in this particular spot than the older man, who seemed self-possessed.

"Yes?" Mateo asked.

Wendy seemed a little flustered. "These people want to see your grandpa. But since I saw you just walk out the door, I wasn't sure I should let them go on to his room."

At that moment Mr. Gribble, a resident of notoriously bad hearing and bad manners, came up to the counter loudly asking if his daily newspaper had arrived, single-mindedly demanding Wendy's attention. Mateo motioned the two men across the entry room to an empty corner.

"We are here to see Mr. Pedro Sanchez."

It was the older man who spoke, quietly. His bearing was dignified and nonaggressive, yet why did Mateo fell a sudden wave of threat? Without thinking about it, he moved his body to the left, guarding the hallway as if the two men were pushing their way down the passage and into Pedro's apartment.

"Mr. Sanchez's not available to see anyone right now," is what Mateo said, but his manner clearly said, "Get the fuck out of here and leave my grandpa alone."

This nuance was not lost on the younger visitor who bristled, but the older man calmed him with a motion of his hand, not even turning his head. He held Mateo's eyes in his own steady gaze.

"We are aware that Mr. Sanchez has suffered a bereavement recently, and it is partly for that reason we have come, to offer our condolences."

Mateo was not the sort of young man to engage in defensive altercations, or bear hostility towards others. He was not a competitive male, measuring his worth against other young men, or daring others in order to maintain his machismo. With his easy going manner he was always the first to defuse confrontations when others clashed. So he was unprepared for the hostility rising up in him as he stood there facing the two strangers.

The older man added, "We were saddened to hear of the sudden death of Mrs. Sanchez."

"If you know of my grandmother's death," Mateo said, "then you'll understand why my grandfather is not seeing anyone right now, especially," and here he looked the young man square in the eye, "especially a stranger."

At that, Mateo turned to walk away, but the younger man could not keep his tongue in check any longer and snarled out the words, with no accent but the language of resentment, "Not a stranger, man; this is his fucking son."

Mateo stopped in his tracks for a long moment, while he absorbed what he heard. Business was going on as usual in the large entry hall of Pine Crest Village. Mr. Gribble shuffled away with his paper, the housekeeper pushed her cart down the hallway, Wendy picked up the phone and greeted a caller. Finally Mateo turned around.

The young man's eyes were beautiful, and they were raging. They were searing into Mateo aggressively although he made no physical move. The older man sighed and put his hand on the arm of his companion.

"Please excuse my son. Armando is quick to anger. You must be," and at this he checked a paper he held in his hand, " . . . Mateo, or Rowan, if you are Mr. Sanchez's grandson, and I can certainly understand your protective stance. However, I have been tracing my father for many years, and I have proof that Pedro Sanchez is my father, so in this information, my hot-headed son is quite correct." He turned to his son, "I am sorry now that I brought you along, Armando, if you cannot have more respect for those who are grieving."

His look at his son quieted the young man for the moment.

Meanwhile, Mateo stood unmoving. His mind was blank, in a white-out, non-existent, simply nothing, shock.

The thought of Pedro waiting in his living room ultimately roused Mateo enough to try to think what to do. His hands squeezed Betty Troyer's flowers too tightly until the stems bent, unnoticed, in his hand.

"And your name is?" Mateo's voice was cold and foreign.

"I am sorry for my lack of protocol," the gentleman responded, for he was deporting himself with sensibility despite the bizarre situation. "My name is Javier Jimenez . . . . " He paused. "To be correct, it seems that my name is Javier Jimenez Sanchez." He held out his hand to Mateo to shake, but Mateo would not respond in kind.

"Well, Mr. Jimenez, or whoever you are, there is no way I'll let my Grandpa hear this nonsense when he can barely make it through the day with his sadness. No way."

"We have come too far and waited too long to go away. I am sorry if the timing is inopportune, but I am not going to bide my time any longer. I have been searching for my father for years." There was a pause in Javier Jimenez's precise pronouncement. "And in many ways I have been searching for my father all my life. There is no more time to wait."

Mateo's breathing was difficult right now. He wanted these men to go away, disappear and never come back. He wanted to pretend that he had never heard what had just been said, wanted to erase the words. But since he had heard the words, his best hope was that this was some sick scheme to get money from his Grand Pedro. Yet, there they all three stood, and apparently these men and their words were not a bad dream, leaving him no choice but to deal with it.

Mateo had one thought: Rex Randall. "If you need any help, I'm here for you." Wasn't that what Rex had told him that first day? Mateo needed more than a cup of coffee now.

Trying to call on some calculating intelligence was a stretch given his pounding heart and building rage. Mateo took a breath. "There's no way I'll subject my grandfather to such . . . " he was going to say, "such shocking news," but that would imply that he gave it credence, and he wasn't going to concede that to these two. So Mateo just concluded, "But I'll meet with you somewhere else and bring someone who'll check out your claim. That's it."

He waited while the older man considered his proposal, and the younger man muttered under his breath. Mateo tried not to hear what Armando was saying.

Javier finally replied, "You probably cannot imagine what it feels like to come so close, and not push past you to see my father, but I also respect your caution. So I will agree to meet with you and your 'third party' on the condition that you promise me that you will not move your grandfather away from me once you realize I am correct."

Mateo considered that a moment, and only wanting them gone from this place he finally agreed, taking the proffered hand for the briefest of handshakes.

"Meet me at the First Congregational Church in Pine Junction at 4:00," is all he said as he turned back towards the Sanchez apartment, resisting the urge to slam the door when he got there, but shutting it firmly and locking it.

He turned to his grandfather and put a casual look on his face. "Sorry to take so long. Wendy at the front desk had a long story to tell me."

Pedro accepted this readily, and nodded in agreement. Mateo looked at the damaged flowers and motioned that he would go to the bathroom and get a vase for them.

Once in the bathroom, he closed the door and threw the flowers into the sink. Mateo sat down on the toilet seat breathing hard, trying to pull his thoughts together coherently. He could not spend one minute dwelling on the ramifications of the visitor's message because right now, he had to figure out how to deal with the matter with the least damage to his Grand Pedro.

First, he didn't trust the men, so he called the front desk where he received apologies from Wendy when she realized that Mateo had not been welcoming to these visitors and had sent them away. Mateo asked her to be extra vigilant about visitors for his grandpa. Then he called Tina and implied that some shysters had been intimidating his grandpa, and the family was very concerned. "But," he cautioned her, "please don't breathe a word about this to anyone, and don't call the sheriff, not yet." And he asked her to keep a careful watch on his grandpa because he had to leave for awhile. Tina readily agreed, responding seriously to Mateo's tone of voice.

Next Mateo called the church, crossing his fingers that Rex would be there so he could fill him in on what had transpired. Mateo realized that it must be a legal matter, but he trusted that Rex could help him chart that path. He was too emotionally charged to do anything further himself, and he had the sense to recognize his vulnerability. His only focus was to get the right help so he could back off and absorb this presumptive claim from these total strangers.

When Derrick answered the phone he detected the charge in Mateo's voice. He told Mateo that Rex was on his way to the dentist, but he would contact him on his cell phone if it was critical. Mateo didn't hesitate. He pleaded, "Please, do it, please!"

Without further questioning, Derrick agreed.

"Tell him." Mateo choked. "I need to meet him at the church before 4:00. It's important. Derrick. I need help."

"I'll call you right back," Derrick promised and clicked off.

Mateo kissed his grandpa, dozing in his chair, leaving him with a cheery, "Bye for now," and he left the apartment, carefully locking the door. Mateo checked in with Tina one more time before making his way on a run to his mom's car, looking over his shoulders every ten feet, in his paranoid state half expecting to see Armando with a blade in hand.

TWENTY-THREE

Armando's earliest memories were of his mother's smell. In his olfactory memory it was a comforting mixture of the earth and sweet spices from the dishes she served them every day. There was an additional aroma of flowers, but perhaps he was confusing his senses. Perhaps it was also visual memory of his mother surrounded by flowers, for she was an avid gardener even in the desert and their New Mexico home was always full of color.

But the sight and scent of flowers also reminded him of his mother's funeral, that horrible day. The abject grief his father displayed at the funeral was the only time Armando had seen his reserved father lose his composure, and in his pre-adolescent brain it was a frightening memory that became muddled with his own grief.

What was the life he had once known? Before? He was the youngest of the sons born to Javier and Kathy Jimenez. Armando had been born in the easy years of his parents' lives. His older brothers had arrived in the midst of the earlier, tougher years when Javier was finishing his PhD and working his way into a university post, living on a small salary in the beginning as he made his way up the tenure track. Kathy was spending long days between her work as an office manager in a public school and raising the children. Money and time were tight and demands were high in the early years of their marriage.

Javier and Kathy, who had met as undergrads, were devoted to each other and made a good team. Javier was cultured and introverted, Kathy outgoing. The older boys had no more than the usual misadventures as children and teenagers, and were about as well-adjusted as children could be even though their parents were busy working and could not afford much in the way of luxury.

When Javier began to relax into more job security, Kathy cut back her work hours to half time, and the couple was delighted to find themselves again expecting a child. The older boys were ten and twelve years old, in school most of the day, and Kathy could spend her nonworking time immersed in the delights of her last child, little Armando.

Armando, a somber baby with his father's dark eyes and hair, was like a play toy for his much older, fair-haired brothers, if he even registered at all in their lives. They were a self-contained unit, the two older ones, busy with school and friends. Armando was in essence an only child. And in the years of his father's rise to professorship, with all the long hours, it was Armando and his mother who kept each other company.

Javier had time later to berate himself for what he came to call his abandonment of his wife during those years.

He came to believe it was worse than it was. Guilt will do that. He was devoted to his career, and even though he was highly regarded in his department, he always felt he had to strive extra hard to make up for his humble origins.

Javier was happy when Kathy could cut back her working hours and devote herself to little Armando. He realized only later that he had failed to give Armando the attention the boy would have loved. His little son, the one who resembled him the most, was Kathy's little boy, her reward for all her hard work, just as Javier's academic success was rewarding him for his long struggle. Javier carried this realization as a shameful truth, shared with no one.

It became a sad story. Kathy became ill, one of those nightmares, a diagnosis of devastating proportions. Kathy protected Armando from any of the details, although he was now ten years old. For a long time he knew something had changed in the gentle attention he had experienced from her all his life. She was sometimes sharp with him for reasons he could not understand, not seeing the pain she was in or the worry in her eyes. No one told him much. No one listened to him much, but then again, he was a quiet boy and did not seek out others with his questions.

Months went by, two years in fact, although in hindsight it always seemed faster than that to Javier. Try as she might, Kathy could not focus on Armando. She was often hospitalized, in pain, and heavily medicated. There was no loving final farewell conversation with her son. No wisdom shared to guide the lost boy, twelve years old when she finally gave up the fight. There was just an open wound, a big hole. Armando's reality was turned upside down and he was left to his own immature imagining, trying to survive.

Javier was too caught up in his own misery to be an adequate single parent to his young son, especially while juggling his job responsibilities and, soon after, dealing with the death of his own mother back in Arizona. Left largely to his own devices, spending too many hours alone, Armando did not do well. At first he was easy to overlook, being an inward-looking boy, and other than a few teachers who tried to raise their concerns, no one saw what was happening. Kathy's family was small and living far from New Mexico. And Javier's family, nowhere around. Kathy and Javier's two oldest sons were off living their own lives, saddened by their mother's death but soon back into their budding careers.

Armando suffered quietly. At first sullen and depressed, as he entered high school he continued to underachieve, miss classes, and attract peers who gave him a sense of belonging to a group of sorts. His teen years involved a series of run-ins with the school and even some brushes with the law. At first he avoided the worst maladjusted behaviors, some inner sense of caution perhaps, but as he got older he began to take more chances. Javier finally became quite concerned. Armando had at last caught his father's attention.

Armando didn't think he needed his father's attention. He carried inside him a deep, dark hurt, a pain that first burned as an anger at himself. He never told anyone his deepest secret, which was that he was convinced he had caused his mother to die. He had been angry one day, frustrated about something long forgotten, and had shouted horrible things at his beloved mother. It had not caused nearly the pain that the boy imagined all these years later. Whatever it was that Armando had shouted at her in a childish temper she had most likely forgotten quickly, but soon after this, she began to be ill, and Armando was convinced that he was at fault, that his ugly words had killed her.

For several years he hated himself the way only a child can. He felt unworthy. Then as teenage hormones began to kick in, bits of this anger began to flare out at others here and there, and then more frequently.

Meanwhile in the years after Kathy's death, followed a year or so later by his mother's, Javier began to search for his father. It gave the lonely man some sense of purpose in his unhappy life. Work was distracting and challenging but did not erase the ache that consumed his daily living. Looking for his own father gave Javier something upon which to focus besides his loneliness. Coincidentally, Javier's search altered his relationship with Armando.

The two were living in the family home, but it was an uneasy existence. Gone was the warmth that once prevailed, where order and beauty thrived. The house now echoed in its emptiness. The garden became overgrown with weeds and the spices in the pantry grew stale. Now stacks of takeout food containers filled the recycling bins. The troubled boy and his grieving father lived a hollow existence in an unloved house.

One chilly New Mexico night, Javier slumped into his chair in the living room. Armando was home, and eating a piece of pizza while sitting on the sofa. Javier poured himself a glass of whiskey and closed his eyes. Then without warning, he began to talk. Maybe he was talking to his wife. Maybe to himself. Maybe in desperation he was actually talking to Armando. Armando stiffened and almost walked away, but he stayed where he was.

I realize that I have not been a very good father to you, Armando. I regret that. I should have been more involved. You see, I had no positive role models in my family life. I had to strike out on my own. My mother did love me in her own way. But she did not have high aspirations for me. I don't know if she had any expectations at all. She was protective of her children when pushed to it, but overall, she let us raise ourselves. And whether I did well in school or not didn't seem to matter much to her. She was a nice woman, most people liked her. But that was it. She lived day to day. Didn't plan ahead. Didn't dream big dreams.

"But what I really didn't have in my life was a father. I have never called anyone Daddy, Dad, Papa, Father, ever in my life. Not once, Armando. Not once."

Javier opened his eyes finally and looked at his son, who was not looking at him, but the boy's grim face was listening, even if reluctantly. Javier sighed.

"I know that having someone to call Dad is only the beginning. I do know that. But it represents something that is the biggest absence in my life. Over the years I have not let myself spend much time thinking about this loss. I have worked hard to make a good life, and I am very grateful to have a profession that satisfies my intellect and pays the bills. I have pushed aside the fact that I do not know my father's name, no face, no identity. No father. Like I sprang out of nowhere."

Again, Armando said nothing, but Javier could hear his breathing from across the room.

"When I met your mom, I convinced myself that I did not need a father. Kathy also felt like me, that we didn't need anything or anyone else but each other. We would be a complete family, just the two of us and our children."

Javier gave a gulp and choked out. "Oh God, how did I let her slip away. How did I let her leave me?"

Armando was extremely uncomfortable with his father's open grief. He had only seen it once, and that was at the funeral. Armando wanted to leave the room but before he could do so, he surprised himself by blurting out.

"I'm the one who killed her, Papa. I yelled at her and told her she was a bitch. I had never heard that word until that week in school, and I wanted to say the worst thing I could say because I was mad at her." Now Armando's voice was the one shaking. "I don't even remember why I was mad at her, but I yelled at her. I said terrible things to her and then she got sick and died. I killed her."

Javier stared at his son. He didn't know what to say. He was unprepared, and so he missed the opportunity to assure Armando that he in no way had killed his mother. Surely Armando was old enough to know better. Instead

Javier just gave a rational explanation, which did not remove Armando's deep level of guilt.

"Don't be silly, Armando. Your mother died of pancreatic cancer. I thought you knew that."

Armando, ashamed of his childish admission, swallowed his tears and sat with his head hanging down.

Finally, to lighten the loaded emotions hanging in the air, he asked his dad a question.

"So why can't you find out who your father is?"

"It is not an easy task, Armando, but that is exactly what I am trying to do. My mother, your grandmother, died before she could tell me who he was. That is the unfortunate part. I am distressed with myself that I did not try to get Mama to tell me sooner. I had convinced myself it was not important, that I was tough enough to make my way through life on my own. I was born a long time ago, just after World War II, and records weren't as easy to access as they are now. But I will not give up. Sometimes I think if I had had a father, I would have known how to be a better father to you. Or maybe I just need someone else to call family, now that your mother is gone."

Armando had no words to explain the emotions that raged through him every day, and especially not this evening. But he understood loneliness and emptiness when he encountered it, and to hear it and see it in his own reserved and professional father was both unnerving and reassuring.

That evening subtly shifted something. Armando continued to get in trouble in small ways, but never anything too serious. For a while he attended a community college and joined the wrestling team, where he was considered a natural. It was one of the first times since he was a boy that he was encouraged in any activity. He also played around with a jazz band at the same college. But in the end, he was not stable enough to keep up with his coursework, and he never did graduate.

Javier continued to teach, but he spent more and more time wondering about his past and trying to track down his birth father, with no real success at first. At home, the father and son lived a more companionable life together.

Armando inquired from time to time about Javier's hunt for his father. One day he even offered, "Dad, if you find your father, I'd have a grandfather."

Javier jerked a bit at that, realizing his search had been completely self-centered. He had never considered what this would mean to his son.

"Armando, you do have a grandfather in Montana, your mother's father."

"Oh really?" Armando snapped. I met him once when Mom took me to Montana to visit him. He didn't like me. He said I looked like my father, like you. And other than at Mama's funeral, I never saw him again.

"How come her father didn't like you, Papa?" Armando had never before asked.

"He was not fond of Mexican-Americans, Armando," Javier replied with this understatement, forcing himself to remember the past. "When your mom married me in college, he was very angry and would not come to our wedding.

He never did get over our marriage. In fact, I am not sure he is still alive. We haven't kept in touch since . . . " And Javier didn't finish the sentence.

Armando's pain was curiously diffused by the new hurt he now felt vicariously for his dad. His dad had lost his father before he even knew his name. He, Armando, had lost his mother after she was embedded into his very being as his source of happiness. Somehow taking on his father's loss helped Armando deal with the loss of his mother. Javier didn't understand what was happening inside his son but he was grateful to have an ally in his quest. In welcoming Armando's company into his life, Javier ignored the anger just beneath the surface.

The sense of injustice Armando felt burned deeply, and his envy for others who had not felt his pain, or his father's pain, was strong and ready to burst.

Twenty-Four

Rex had not sat down in the dentist's chair yet when he received Derrick's call, and he rushed back to his office, where Mateo was pacing to and fro, staring out the window, then pacing some more. When Mateo had hurried into the church office five minutes earlier, Derrick had asked no questions, provided a cup of coffee, and shut the office door for Mateo's privacy.

Mateo had the presence of mind to consider his mom and his aunts, and what they would do or think if they were visited by the two strangers. He wondered when he should let them know. But he needed guidance, couldn't make any more decisions yet. He just hoped for the best, hoped the startling claim would be disproved, despite the men's conviction and whatever evidence they claimed to possess. It disturbed him how much they had seemed to know about his family.

When Rex entered his office, he saw the young man moving back and forth across the small room, caught in his own thoughts so powerfully that he did not look up until Rex shut the door. Mateo rubbed his palm across his eyes roughly. Rex put his hands on Mateo's shoulders and gently eased him into a chair and pulled his own chair close.

"Tell me what's going on."

"It's too much. Can't be true. Don't know what to do." He sputtered to a stop and it took him another moment to be able to tell Rex about the visitors and their story. When he had finished, Rex took a big breath and let it out slowly.

"That's a shock, all right." Rex considered and then added, "When did you tell them to be here?"

"4:00."

"Okay we have about ten minutes, not much time. We're going to need legal help, of course."

Mateo nodded. "I figured that too, but I needed to get them away from Grand Pedro and needed to stall for time. I just couldn't think of what else to do. I just couldn't let them bother my grandpa. Not now."

"Of course, Mateo. You were thinking pretty clearly given the surprise of the situation. But we do need to start thinking of legal counsel. Does your family has an attorney?"

Mateo laughed, "My dad's an attorney, but somehow I don't see him coming to the rescue here. He hasn't set foot in Pine Junction in fourteen years. I mean he might help us out, but I wouldn't count on it."

And then Mateo remembered. "Aunt Maria's partner Rosemary is an attorney." And then he said with a note of hope in his voice, "She's a family law attorney!"

"Ah, that's a good thought, Mateo. Yes, I met her at the hospital that night and liked her. We talked for awhile and she seems steady. I think we are going to need that kind of help. Plus, while she is connected to the family, she is not so enmeshed that it would complicate things. Okay, I will ask Derrick to call her, and of course we need to bring your mom and your aunts into this ASAP, but we are running out of time right now, unless . . . "

" . . . unless they don't show up." Mateo finished Rex's thought. Then he laughed, "And maybe I imagined this whole scene and I need to start writing fiction or something."

Rex smiled. "Your literary career would be a lot easier to deal with than this situation!"

At that moment the telephone rang. Both of them jumped at the sound. Rex picked it up and listened to Derrick telling him that two men were there to see him, a Mr. Jimenez and his son.

"Make them comfortable in the Deacon's and Elder's room Derrick, and we'll join them in a couple of minutes. And Derrick, please track down Rosemary Silva, Maria Sanchez's partner, and ask her to call Mateo or myself as soon as she can. We may need her help with a legal matter. Thanks."

Mateo started to stand up but Rex put a hand on his shoulder. "Mateo, I find it very helpful to take a quiet moment of prayer before a potentially difficult meeting or encounter."

Rex closed his eyes, and as Mateo watched him, a transformation came over the minister's face as it settled into neutrality. Mateo closed his eyes too, but found he was as tight as a steel band. He heard Rex's voice and felt his hand on his shoulder. "Mateo, take a deep breath. Just start slowly, and let it out. Then do it again, and try to make it slower and deeper this time. Just let go for a moment. Let go of any need to conquer the world right now. Let go of the defensiveness that is bottled up in you. Just breathe it out."

Mateo's first deep breath came out sounding like a choking man, but the second and third breath were smoother. He kept his eyes closed another moment, and Rex's hand on his shoulder stayed steady.

"Mateo, we need to hear these folks out. We must surrender any thoughts of either defeating an enemy or of running away from this problem. Let's go learn more because that's the only way to figure out what to do about it. You're strong enough inside to do this. I'll be with you."

Rex paused and then with a squeeze on Mateo's shoulder, he moved to open the door and said softly, "Life sure does bring us some interesting situations."

TWENTY-FIVE

bout the time Javier introduced himself to Mateo, Cecilia opened her kitchen door to her friend. Vic came in with two purple irises in one hand, and a music disc in the other. Cecilia welcomed him in the vague manner with which she had faced the world since her mother's death. She had brushed her hair (lovely, lovely hair, Vic had always thought) and put on an attractive shirt, the first time she had made any effort in her dress for some months. Vic noticed, and approved.

He presented her with a new CD of the Faure Requiem.

"Oh," and she sighed. "It's so beautiful. I have to hear it right now." Cecilia immediately put the music on, and then crumpled gracefully onto the sofa that sat under the big window in her kitchen, one of this old house's finer features: a huge room to cook, eat, and live in.

A great kitchen it is, thought Vic, who lived his own simple life between a bare apartment in town and his headquarters in the church choir room. He knew that people considered him rather eccentric, but with Cecilia he felt understood. They rarely talked of personal matters. They talked of music, of books, of philosophy, of gardens, of places they would like to travel, although neither left town with any frequency. What they did not talk about was their own lives, their history, their deepest thoughts and desires. They most certainly did not talk about love, or loss, or pain, or hope. Cecilia, who with others could not stop talking about war and injustice, rarely mentioned her political concerns with Vic. It was not necessary. He met a different sort of need in her, and it was unblemished, oddly full of trust, despite lacking in openness.

They had traveled so deeply into each other's souls, without much intimate knowledge about each other's lives, that there was almost an abhorrence within each of them to tread where it was too tender, in fear, perhaps, of collapsing the whole exquisite bubble of their friendship.

Vic had been in love with Cecilia from the first day he saw her. He acknowledged that to himself. But when he met her she was newly married, newly arrived back in her home town, and soon was a mother to Mateo and then Rowan. Vic had deep scruples about violating that wedding bond, and so he became very adept at relegating his feelings for Cecilia to a more spiritual place for fourteen years. No one knew or even suspected his powerful affection for the young Mrs. Schumacher, town librarian, wife of the new attorney, mother of two bright little boys, and daughter of the prominent Pedro and Victoria Sanchez. And when Cecilia's marriage ended so abruptly in 1991, Vic had become so used to the status of the relationship that he was never able to convince himself to come out of his comfortable place of love-from-afar. It was too ingrained a pattern in his life.

No one seemed to question what Vic Dalloway's sexual feelings might be, or why he seemed so monastic. Perhaps they just felt he was married to his music. Perhaps they thought he was gay, but not able to come out of the closet. But for the most part, no one gave Vic's sexual orientation or lifestyle any consideration at all. He played a role that was irreplaceable and comfortable to others, and his very eccentricities made him a one-dimensional character to the bulk of the community both in his own church and in Pine Junction as a whole. Vic knew he had created this persona, this role, for himself, for better or worse. Sometimes he wondered if he was becoming an old man before his time. Other times he found it to be a wonderful protective shield, keeping him insulated from dealing with his own powerful emotions and any possible gossip. And when this all threatened to overwhelm him, there was always the thrill of filling the Casavant organ pipes with enormous vibrating sound to help him release his pent-up passions.

The brutality of words still rang in Cecilia's mind when she thought of being in a relationship, and since her divorce she had avoided all efforts to involve herself in dating, much less a relationship. Over the last decade, with both of her boys gone from her home, Cecilia lived a life that ran very parallel with Vic's.

During fourteen years, and then fourteen more years, of love from afar, which started as any normal sexual attraction for Vic, there were no flirtations. No courting.

No overtures. No relationship talk. But there was an ever deeper mystical convergence of two talented and flawed people, Cecilia and Vic, their time together vital but pure.

In the second week of Victoria's passing, the two sought the comfort of each other's company once again. It was like a hundred other times for them, yet different because of Cecilia's grieving. Vic offered to make their tea since Cecilia was totally absorbed in the Faure. He selected her favorite tea pot, and picked a rich Darjeeling black tea from her tea drawer. When he brought her the pot and cups on a tray, he saw that unchecked tears ran down both cheeks, wetting her blouse. Vic noticed that her buttons were undone, just the top two, but he found his face flushing and heart rushing like a school boy.

He quickly put down the tray and sat down next to her, handing her the napkin he had brought with the tea. She took it and clutched it in her hands, but did not wipe her face. Vic reached out tentatively and with his finger, brushed a tear from her cheek. She turned her eyes on him, those beautiful brown eyes that had so captivated him almost thirty years ago. Her broken heart seemed to have opened up finally. She couldn't stop crying, and he took her face in his hands, wiping her tears gently in the pointless effort to stop them from flowing.

Vic found himself kissing her, first her salty face and eyes, and finally her lips. He met no resistance, and soon she was reciprocating with gasps and hiccups which were pure music to Vic's ears.

The Faure played on and on, repeating, while the two silently consented, then insisted. Vic and Cecilia took off their clothes. The physical impact on Vic of seeing Cecilia's body being revealed, not in a seductive inch by inch scene as he had sometimes allowed himself to fantasize, but now with such pressing urgency, made him vibrate, shaken and exhilarated. Seeing her nipples appear, pinker than he had imagined, and her brown curls in the V of her thighs, his whole body responded with a lurch. Yet for some reason it was the innocent view of her belly button that made him treasure those fast seconds the most. That simple sight of her navel reduced him to a most basic state of enormous hunger and protection both, so vulnerable and so personal it was. Such a strange thing to turn him on so powerfully, he thought fleetingly.

Cecilia felt her own nakedness more than she saw Vic's. Once released from the covering of her clothes, her skin seemed to hum with a layer of nerves she had not known existed, like someone was running a feather lightly over all her skin. At this moment she had the sensation that her arms were powerful, sensuous, and her hands capable of both stroking and grabbing. Her breasts felt full and full of life. The center of her physical self, deep and fierce within her womb, her vagina, her inner thighs, experienced a whirling fluid-like sensation that pulled at connection. Her ever-churning mind was quiet now. Her body was taking charge and doing what it wanted to do. Vic could have spent longer soaking in the sight of all of her, but with a fierceness Cecilia reached for him, not wanting to be apart for even that short time.

Blessedly, neither of them were thinking. The big old sofa held them together and in turn they held each other in desire, yet also protectively. They pressed their bodies together as if to draw sustenance from each other, and the touch of bare skin electrified them both.

Vic held Cecilia's breasts and buried his face in their fullness. Decades of monk-like existence fueled a passion for the real, the here, the now and the sensuality of this moment with the woman he thought he would never touch. He would never forget the feel of her skin or the sight of her.

And she was overcome with the sensation of being touched by this man whom she trusted so well. Time was suspended. Was it ten minutes or ten hours? No matter. She would always remember his hands and the heat of adrenalin when his body pressed on her, and he would not forget how she fiercely pulled him into her, and how much she asked of him and wanted him. A brief eternity elapsed before they shuddered to a peaceful quiet. Then she lay with her head on his chest, her eyes finally dry. She listened to the sound of his heart beating under the warm mat of soft graying hair where her cheek and ear rested. He stroked her head in a way that was meant for a long relationship. They were at perfect peace, yet they knew that their lives were irrevocably changed.

"It's so right," murmured one of them.

Later when they eventually got up, their talk was minimal but their comfort level was fine. They walked out to the back porch and sat on the bottom step together, Vic holding a cigarette he really didn't want, and Cecilia closing her eyes in contentment. As if it was totally natural, Vic asked her, "Were your tears for your mother, or for something else?"

Although they had never spoken of hurts or sorrows, past or present, Cecilia very calmly told him the story of why, besides the shock of losing her mother, her sorrow was so great. She told him what she had never told a soul, what she had been hiding in her body and mind for so many years, and she told him of her current dilemma and how she wrestled with what to do.

It was a surprise to Vic, and yet, as he absorbed what Cecilia said, it was no insurmountable monstrosity, nothing to ruin the joy in his heart, and her revelation in no way diminished her in his eyes. He shoved the un-smoked cigarette into his pocket and took her hand in his long, musical fingers and stroked it, admiring the lines of a lifetime of living. She too stared at her hand in his, and wondered why she had spoken the unspeakable, and why she felt so peaceful about it all. They sat quietly, just being together, letting the words she had said hang there between them, shared now, no longer damning her, no longer hiding her from him.

Finally Vic spoke gently, in no hurry, just as if it were time to speak these words. "This is something you must share with Mateo, and that will not be easy."

"Do you think he'll ever talk to me again?"

"Let's give him more credit than that. But it won't be easy for either of you. That's a given."

"I've always intended to keep it to myself. Until Dane showed up here, I really planned on keeping it here only." With that she pressed her hand onto her heart and kept it there.

"How's that worked for you so far?"

"It's broken me," Cecilia finally answered. "My heart's been broken so long that I've gotten used to it."

She continued, "But I wanted to protect Mateo. That's all. And now? Is it too late?"

"You'll figure out what to do. That son of yours is a very fine young man, if you haven't noticed."

Vic stroked Cecilia's hair. "By the way, Ceci, when did Dane come to see you?"

"Three, four months ago or so, well, no, I know exactly. It was January 15th, Mateo's birthday. Uncanny. He can't have known the date."

To be sitting on her back porch, talking together about matters so deeply personal was feeling absolutely natural to Vic and Cecilia, and at the same time, they both were aware how much had changed in just a few hours.

Neither of them wanted to move when they heard the phone ring inside. Cecilia wanted to extend this moment forever. She did not want reality to interfere. He was of the same mind, but he reluctantly suggested that she answer it in case her father needed her.

"What if it's Dane?" she managed to say quietly, voicing her worst fears. It was the reason her heart froze every time the phone rang following his January visit.

"If it's him, I'll be right here for you," Vic whispered, matching her voice without realizing he was doing so. "I'm always right here for you, Ceci. You don't have to do this alone anymore, and . . . " he paused as if in discovery, ". . . neither do I."

TWENTY-SIX

D r. Javier Jimenez sat at the round table in the Deacon and Elder's room, a room where Pedro and Victoria had often chaired meetings. He sat with great composure, at least at first glance. If one looked closely a slight twitching around his left eye lid might be noticed, but it was almost imperceptible. By contrast his son Armando sat on a chair next to him, half on and half off, hunched over with elbows on his knees, fingers wrapped tightly in his hair. And so the two sat, waiting the few minutes before Rex and Mateo entered the room, followed by Derrick with the coffee cups and carafe.

Both Jimenez men stood up when the local men came through the door, Javier by carefully cultivated manners and Armando out of nervous energy.

"Mr. Jimenez, I'm Reverend Randall." Rex nodded to both men but stretched his hand out first to the elder who shook his hand calmly. Armando also took Rex's hand briefly after noting the clerical collar that Rex had slipped on. He rarely wore it, saving it for hospital chaplain calls or when he felt a little reminder of his pastoral calling might be helpful.

Mateo just nodded at both men and sat down at the table. The others followed his example, with Derrick leaving the coffee and telling Rex as he left the room, "I have some phone calls to make. Is there anything else you need me for?"

Rex thanked him and asked him to interrupt if he had any information to share. Derrick nodded, somehow understanding the situation.

"Well, gentlemen, Mateo has given me an idea of the startling information you delivered this afternoon. But why don't you tell us more of your story. And I'm sure you don't mind if I take some notes. It helps me remember details."

Armando stirred restlessly in his chair and Mateo felt a cloud of anger coloring the air around the young Jimenez. Mateo focused his eyes on the father who took a sip of coffee and then began to talk in a well-modulated voice. Mateo did not want to hear any of it, but he found himself drawn to the voice and the story Javier told, and eventually even to the man himself, despite the barrier of distrust the last few hours had brought to him.

"I was born in Phoenix, Arizona, in June of 1947. My mother Celina Jimenez was a single mother. I was the oldest but over the years many more half brothers and sisters joined our family. None of their fathers stayed long enough to make more than a fleeting impression. My mother was a good-hearted woman who made poor choices in men.

"From the beginning, she told me that my own father had died in the war, World War II that is. And this is what

I grew up believing. I had few male role models in my life. The principal at my public school took an interest in me, as did our next door neighbor. Mr. Reyes's influence was positive, but our neighbor turned out to be a sex offender. He preferred the boys in our family, but also abused the girls. When my mother found out, she attacked him with a butcher knife. He died, but when the circumstances were brought to light, thanks to his relieved wife testifying, my mother was released."

Javier spoke these horrifying words with a matter-of-fact tone, and paused only long enough to drink some coffee. The room was silent around him. Even Armando seemed to have fallen into the spell of his father's story. From the look on Armando's face, Rex considered that this was probably new information to the son.

"I share all these stark and morbid details not to be a sensationalist, but rather to try to explain what has driven me to this day and this place."

No one interrupted.

"Fortunately, as I said, my school principal was exactly the man he appeared to be, although I learned early never to blindly trust anyone. My life experience had not given me human trust as a legacy. Mr. Reyes encouraged my natural interest in learning, and between my good grades and involvement in music I was able to get scholarships to attend college."

"However, to back track, when I was in junior high school, I finally realized that World War II ended in 1945. I wondered how my father could have died in the war if I was conceived in mid 1946. After thinking about this for months I finally approached my mother one day and asked her this question. Her response was to slap me across the face, hard enough to bloody my nose. My mother had never hit me before. Say what you would about my family life, and my mother's choices, she had never raised a hand to any of us. We had been hurt enough by others, but not her. So I was completely stunned by her response. I never asked her again about my father, but from that day on, I knew that my father had not died in the war."

Again, Javier paused, and again, no one interrupted.

"I was able to put these thoughts aside, and being young, I simply focused on improving my own life, to create myself in a proper image. Feeling that I was on my own, I educated and reeducated myself. My true love had been music, but I needed to be practical. So I majored in mathematics and decided I felt at home in the academic world. I kept studying and finally finished my PhD in Mathematics. I teach at the University of New Mexico."

He opened his portfolio and showed papers inside, although he did not pull them out. "I have all this background information documented, and I would imagine you will want to look at this at some point." He looked at Mateo when he said this, and Mateo just nodded.

"I have had a good career. I like teaching and I find the research and theories of mathematics to be both stimulating and relaxing. They seem to help me deal with my past and the holes in my life. Miraculously, I had the good fortune to find a kind and supportive wife and we had three healthy sons. Armando is my youngest. My older sons have not been interested in my quest to locate my father, which I finally began some years ago."

For the first time he showed some emotion in his storytelling. "My wife Kathy passed away ten years ago, very young. It was about that time that I began to feel compelled to pursue the mystery of my father."

"And then there was the death of my mother. She was a victim of a lifetime of hard work as a housekeeper as well as her own excesses, I am afraid. Finally her body could not hold up anymore, and she died of complications from diabetes soon after my dear Kathy died."

He again needed to stop, just for a few seconds as his face tightened, but then he resumed. "It was a rough time, but again, I am only relating this because I feel I must fully disclosure why I am so motivated to meet my father. When my mother was very ill, I would sit up with her in the late hours. She was drifting off to sleep one night, and then she told me, 'Javier, I never told you about your father.' "

"Naturally I listened carefully, holding my breath because I thought finally, finally, she would tell me more."

"But all she said was this, 'Your father was a very handsome man, and so smart. Oh, he was so sad but very kind to me that night. No one knew about us. I kept it a secret.' "

"I begged her to tell me who he was, tell me about him, asking her if my father knew about me, knew that she was pregnant with me. And all she said, and I could scarcely hear her because she was falling into a coma-like sleep. 'No, he never knew. He had just come home from Germany. The war was over then. But he didn't stay, he left Phoenix the next day . . . .' And then she added, 'His family moved away too.' "

"I stayed with her all night and into the next day, but during the short periods she came into consciousness, she was not able to answer my questions, and then she slipped away, died before she could tell me more. I searched her belongings but never found a single bit of evidence. Even my birth certificate gives no father's name."

Javier took a handkerchief out of his pocket and wiped a subtle sheen of perspiration off his upper lip. The room held his story in continued silence.

Finally he spoke again. "From the day my mother died, searching for my father became a priority for me. At first it was just an all-consuming mental preoccupation, but in time I began to pursue this quest more actively. I never dreamed how long it would take, but finally I came up with the name Pedro Sanchez after going back to my home town. One night in a local bar, an old man, rather inebriated, made a lewd comment about my mother. I almost punched him, until I realized he might be helpful. And this unpleasant incident led to a remarkable encounter with another man, an old man who not only had known my mother very well but had also met my father just one time. Your father, he told me, is named Pedro Sanchez. There are many men named Pedro Sanchez in Arizona as you can imagine, but this man also knew the details of my mother's affair, rather her one-night stand, with the man who was my father. This gentleman most certainly was the only person who gained my mother's confidence, the only one she ever told. But he moved away soon after my birth and only returned to Phoenix many years later.

"With a name I was on my way."

Javier looked at Mateo and Rex, and finally at Armando. "Armando has taken a real interest in this search, and he carries some of the strong emotions I have learned to quell. Do not let my equanimity deceive you, however. I am passionate about this search, and firmly intend to complete it."

Yet again silence reigned around the table. Mateo had no clue how to articulate his churning distrust that contrasted sharply with his unwilling sympathetic reactions to Javier's story. He did not know what he should say. Rex also waited. He had a feeling that Javier had one more last thought.

"I do not want to be disappointed again. My mother died before she could reveal her secret, and I do not want any more deaths to stop me in my tracks and leave me fatherless. I am 58 years old, and Pedro Sanchez, my father, is a good twenty years older than me. Time is of the essence."

TWENTY-SEVEN

T he atmosphere in the room following Javier's long story was layered on top of the quiet that happens in a small town. When finally there was something to hear, it was a small airplane droning overhead, an annoying backdrop to the thoughts running inside the minds of each of the four men around the table. Javier was composed, seemingly willing to wait for a response. Even Armando seemed to have been hypnotized by his father's voice, and neither spoke nor moved. Rex was carefully considering his next words.

Mateo remained sitting, staring at the shiny silver communion cups on the shelf across from him. Despite the unreal nature of the events unfolding, and his intense desire to make the whole scene disappear, he felt drawn to the man and his story. Had he heard this same story from someone at his coffee shop, he would have found it utterly compelling. He would have been fully sympathetic with the storyteller. He would have hoped for the best for the man searching for his father. Mateo caught himself when he remembered that this was his grandfather they were talking about. His family. His own flesh and blood. And the need to protect the old man, protect his grandmother's memory and sense of honor, and his competitive dislike for the younger Jimenez, all came rushing back to him. He looked at Rex for some help.

Rex finally spoke.

"Dr. Jimenez, thank you for sharing such a profound personal story. However as you can imagine, this is an incredible shock to me as Pedro Sanchez's pastor, and certainly to his grandson. And the remainder of his family is not yet aware of what you are bringing to us. To the best of my knowledge, and I think Mateo's as well . . . " At this he looked at Mateo . . . "we had absolutely no inkling of the possibility that Mr. Sanchez may have fathered a son prior to his coming to Pine Junction. As to whether his three daughters have had any knowledge or even hints of this possibility, we'll find out, but please remember that they are all reeling over the unexpected death of their mother. And, of course, Mr. Sanchez himself is in a fragile state right now, between his loss and his own medical conditions."

Rex sipped from his coffee, now grown cool, as he considered his next words. Armando started to speak, but Rex held up his hand and the young man's voice subsided.

"I hear that you have a sense of urgency in your quest. And while I cannot speak for Mr. Sanchez's family, I respect your feeling. However I ask you to also think of this family and in particular Mr. Sanchez himself, and be prepared to give everyone space and time to proceed. First and foremost, the family must be given an opportunity to check out your story. As you yourself said, there are thousands of men named Pedro Sanchez."

And again, Rex silenced the indignant Armando.

"But should your information and your story be proven true, we still need to proceed with careful consideration for a healthy end result for Mr. Sanchez and his family, and in the long run, this will also be in your best interest as well."

Before the two visitors could reply, the phone on the table buzzed and picking it up, the minister listened a few minutes to Derrick. Rex jotted a note and then looked up.

"The rest of family has been notified that something is up and is sending legal counsel to take a look at your documentation, Dr. Jimenez. Are you comfortable leaving the paperwork with me here at the church? I can suggest some restaurants in Amherst for your dinner. I can also give you references for hotel rooms."

For the first time Javier looked unsure of himself and asked for a moment of privacy with his son. Rex and Mateo got up and left the room.

"Let us know when you are ready," Rex said before he shut the door.

Mateo, Derrick and Rex sat around Derrick's desk. Mateo again found himself unable to speak, afraid that if he did, it would be an angry rant. Rex gave him a sympathetic pat on the back, "Hang in there my friend. "

Derrick spoke up then. "I don't know exactly what is going on, but I have a bit of the drift, and it seems to me that it could be rather unproductive if the three sisters arrive when the gentlemen are still here. Perhaps we should let Rosemary handle the visitors, and have the sisters meet elsewhere?"

"Wise thought, Derrick. Mateo, could you get your aunts settled at your house while we try to get Rosemary here? I'll do my best to get them to leave their paperwork and find a hotel, in the opposite direction from Pine Crest Village, just to make certain they don't go back to drop in on Pedro."

"I'll try. How do I tell this story though? What if they lose it? My mom is already not so stable." Mateo's voice trailed off as he considered the possible reactions of his mother and his aunts. He was not at all sure he could manage to keep them from going into full attack mode in denial and protection of their Papa. And he wasn't sure he wouldn't be inclined to join them. Then he thought again of the nature of Javier Jimenez's story and its emotional impact, and he wondered what to think.

"I'll join you if I think it's wise to leave our visitors, Mateo, but I think my place is here right now." Rex looked at Derrick, and Derrick quickly affirmed the unspoken question.

"I'd be happy to join you Mateo, I mean if you don't think I'd be intruding."

Mateo snorted, "Well, I can see that there is nothing you don't know working at your desk here, so I think you've proven yourself trustworthy. Besides, are there any secrets in a small town?" He thought for a moment and laughed again, bitterly this time. "Well, that's a stupid cliché, because clearly there are many secrets in a small town, and especially in my family!

"So yeah, Derrick, come with me. I could use the support, particularly someone who can have some detachment. I mean, it isn't your family. Your family is probably all sane and boring with no closets of skeletons."

Derrick simply rolled his eyes.

Mateo questioned Rex, "Do you suppose I should call in Rowan to keep him updated on this craziness?"

"If you think he would be helpful, give him a call. If it makes it more difficult for you to think right now, then wait until tomorrow. That's my advice."

The door opened and Javier stepped out and into the front office. Armando was behind him.

"I understand that I need to meet with your family's attorney, Mateo," Javier addressed the young man. "Do you know when he may arrive?"

"She's on her way from Amherst now," Derrick answered since he had talked to Rosemary himself. "Maybe an hour."

"We'll wait then," Javier spoke firmly. Rex nodded. Armando sulked, pulling up his hood and looking more like a young teenager than a man of twenty-three.

Mateo found himself glaring at the younger man, surprised once again at the intense reaction he had to this stranger. This anger was foreign to him. In fact, the escalating adrenalin that rushed over him whenever Armando was around scared Mateo as much as the potential threat to his grandfather's integrity and well-being. He could picture himself as the protector of his grandfather. That was a role, although new to him, that was at least a comfortable fit with his view of himself as a man and grandson. It was in a sense heroic, as ridiculous as that would have seemed just a week ago. By contrast the tidal wave of hatred towards Armando did not make Mateo feel like the man he thought he was. These feelings were too out of control. He did not trust himself.

He was also daunted by the prospect of presenting the story to his mother and two aunts. Since returning to Pine Junction, Mateo had seen himself as the rational family member, with the three sisters behaving in ways that to his youthful eyes seemed complicated and unproductive. His assumption of superior competence caused him to feel burdened by an illusion that he alone could save his family. But tonight he was feeling scared, and he thought he could not show this to his mother and aunts.

As he walked home with his new friend Derrick, Mateo did not yet know that wisdom can emerge out of mistakes, and resiliency from vulnerability.

TWENTY-EIGHT

T he porch light was on above Cecilia's door when they arrived. As witness to the staggering events of the day, Mateo had not thought about food or drink for hours. But the smells of garlic and cumin wafted out to greet the two men. Cecilia and Vic were in the kitchen. Mateo stood in the kitchen doorway bewildered to see his mother and Vic moving easily with each other as they put noodles into the steaming pan on the stove and stirred something that smelled wonderful.

Cecilia came over and gave him a full hug and kiss. "Matty. I understand that you've had quite a day. You'll tell us all about it soon. But first, you must be hungry. Some goulash for you? Derrick, so glad you came. How about you? Hungry?"

Vic poured each of them a glass of red wine with a casual flare, as natural as if he had spent years in this kitchen cooking and drinking with the Schumachers, and Mateo and Derrick found themselves sitting at the kitchen table with a savory looking plate of lamb and vegetables on their plates. Surprisingly, Mateo found himself hungry, and he put the mystery of Vic's presence aside for later consideration. He was also surprised his mother was not bombarding him with questions, but was comforted by her solicitous caretaking, finding himself slightly less alone.

Before they were finished, Olivia and Julia rushed in the front door bringing a charge to the atmosphere, but, by this point, Mateo felt calmer and more ready to broach the crisis.

"Oh my God, Ceci, what is going on? How's Papa? We only heard a bit over the phone. We almost got a ticket getting over here, but Julia was able to talk the cop out of it."

Julia interjected, "An old friend from high school, new sheriff now. He sat behind me in algebra and I used to help him. I called my cards in just now."

Cecilia put her arm around Olivia. "Matty is the one who knows what's going on, and he's going to explain what this is all about. Are you two hungry? Want something to drink?"

Olivia shook her head, too preoccupied. Julia grabbed the plate of food that Vic quickly made for her and started to sit down by Mateo. But Cecilia motioned for them to all go into the living room, and grabbing two more wine bottles and some glasses, led the way. After sitting down, Mateo looked around. "This has been a day that I could never have imagined and it's still unfolding. But let's wait until everyone is here. It would be best to go through this step by step all together."

"Brad won't be home until 11:00." Olivia explained, "But I suppose we should wait for Maria so you don't have to start all over again."

Julia couldn't resist. "Matty, did I hear the message correctly? There's someone claiming that Grandpa is his father?"

Mateo nodded. "Yes, that's the long and short of it. But let me call Maria and see where she is."

Maria and Rosemary were close at hand. Mateo instructed Maria to come to the house and Rosemary to head to the church to meet Rex. Then Rex called and said he had persuaded Javier and Armando to go out for a dinner break, but they would not leave their paperwork unattended.

Waiting was difficult. Vic sat fiddling at the piano, the rest simply sat. Olivia looked as if she would burst, but Cecilia seemed to be in a bubble of serenity despite the questions that loomed over the room. Mateo simply could not imagine what had come over his mom, but it took a mental back seat as he turned over Javier Jimenez's story. Visions of his Grand Pedro kept coming to the forefront of his mind, and he wanted to call out to him, "Is it true?"

They heard the sound of a car on the gravel driveway through the piano notes, and Vic stopped playing. They all listened to the car door slam, then the car drive away. Maria walked in the door, glanced at the expectant faces, and as though beginning one of her lectures, said crisply, "It looks like we're all ready to discover yet another new thing about our family. Matty, are you the one with the information?" She headed towards an unoccupied corner of the sofa, and folded her lean body onto the cushions as she reached for the wine bottle.

For the first time Mateo really looked at the women of his family. Maria, strong, logical, resourceful, her life wasn't defined by the multitude of tempestuous relationships she had outlasted. It was a new thought to cross Mateo's mind. Here, in his eldest aunt, was a cornerstone of clear-headed leadership. Then he looked at his mom's younger sister. Olivia was known in the family legend as being over-emotional, reactionary. Yet as he looked at Olivia with her daughter Julia perched on the arm of her chair, he saw a face full of anxiety, but also great kindness. He recognized her love and trust in him, and also her love for her parents. Finally he met his mother's eyes, and she gave him a reassuring nod. It was such a small gesture, but it restored his shaken confidence both in her and in himself, and so he began to tell the story of all that had occurred that day.

TWENTY-NINE

It was almost 9:00 before Javier's car drove back up to the church, so Rosemary Silva had sufficient time to be briefed by Rex on the events of the day. Rex apologized for not being able to persuade Dr. Jimenez to leave his paperwork behind for her to peruse.

"Rex, if Dr. Jimenez is telling the truth, it is reasonable that he would be concerned that his paperwork might be discarded or misused in his absence. And if he's not on the up and up, then he doesn't want to share more than he has to. It sounds like you handled the earlier meeting very well. And Mateo too was able to think on his feet quite nicely. Boy, it must have been an incredible jolt to him! He's very close to his grandfather, from all the family stories I've heard."

She thought a moment. "Tell me something, Rex. And I know you can't divulge confidential confessionals, so to speak. But can you tell me if, in your opinion, this claim has any basis in fact whatsoever?"

"I've been wracking my memory and I can't shed any helpful light," Rex replied. "I'm as surprised as anyone." Rex paused to reflect on what he had just said and then continued. "However, I'm perhaps less surprised than many people would be. I've been a pastor for many years now, and my surprise at shocking news like this is tempered by all that I have seen and heard."

Rosemary nodded. "I can believe that, Rex. This has an element of emotionality for me just because it's my partner's family, but in my work, I've seen things that seem incredible turn out to be true."

She made some notes to herself, and then mused, "It's interesting that Dr. Jimenez arrives in person, without even an advance letter, and that he goes straight to Pedro's apartment, especially since he was apparently aware of the very recent death of Pedro's wife. It seems so . . . " she fished for the right word.

" . . . so unprofessional."

"Yes."

"And that's bothered me too, especially since Jimenez, Senior that is, presents himself as very rational, controlled, sophisticated . . . . Oh, he did give me his card." Rex pulled it out of his pocket. He looked at it for the first time. "This card would seem to confirm that he is a mathematics professor at the University of New Mexico."

Rosemary reached for the card and made a quick check on her laptop. Within a few minutes she spoke. "Well, this looks legit, unless he is forging someone else's identity." She laughed. "It would've been simple if he wasn't who he said he was." And she laughed again more ruefully. "I'm not using my legal mind right now. Here I'm wanting a certain result instead of just looking at the facts. Must be thinking of Maria and the family. And dear Pedro."

Rex looked at her sympathetically. "Yes, it's hard not to love this family, even though secrets seem to keep popping out."

"So, Rex, tell me about the son, let's see, Armando Jimenez. I'll trace him, make sure he doesn't have a record or something."

"Resentful, hot-headed, well, just pissed off, to put it in un-clerical language. Troubled, or covering for some pain. But I can tell you one thing - there's bad blood between him and Mateo. It's palpable. This is a whole new side of Mateo and I think it's distressing to him, too. I thought it would be good to separate the two young men for a while."

"Tell me," Rosemary asked, "do you think we have anything to fear for Pedro's safety?"

Rex immediately replied, "Oh no," recollecting Javier's stoic matter-of-fact summation of his difficult life story and his subsequent quest to find his father. But the minister paused as Armando's edginess came back to his mind. "Well, the young man is another story. I can't figure what part of this story disturbs him so greatly. His father seems to have control over Armando's actions, hopefully . . . . I'm surprised that the father brought his son along with him on this sensitive mission."

"Well, what motivates people? In many situations it's money, but Pedro has none to speak of, nor does the rest of the family. And sometimes it's power, but again, that's not an issue here. So if it's about lost connections, finding one's family, whether Dr. Jimenez is on the right track or not, it can be pretty overpowering, and even a very stable person does not always behave logically."

Rex turned in his chair restlessly, glancing at the clock on the wall, saying, "I wonder how Mateo is managing with the family at the house?" And then he added, "I sure wish those two men could get back. Dinner should not have taken this long."

Rosemary wasn't feeling good about this either, but she tried to calm Rex and herself both. "Maybe he decided he should contact his own attorney after all."

Before Rex could answer her, they heard a sound at the door and Javier walked in. He still carried himself with professional aplomb, but he looked tired.

Rex introduced Rosemary to Javier and invited them to all go sit down in his office. He looked back as he waved the two into his inner office and asked, "Is Armando still in the car? Shall we wait for him?"

"He went to find a place to buy some cigarettes. Don't worry, he will not smoke in the church."

Rex was uneasy, but just said, "I'll leave the outside door open so he can find his way back in here. The Stop and Shop at the corner sells cigarettes."

The three went inside Rex's office, and the night sky outside his never-curtained window was pitch black. Dozens of moths threw their bodies against those windows, thudding with suicidal force in an effort to gain a oneness with the light.

"Dr. Jimenez, Reverend Randall has filled me in on the information you provided this afternoon. He has also

related what Mr. Schumacher told him about the afternoon encounter out at Pine Crest Village, Mr. Sanchez's
home. Before we go any further, I'm wondering if you have
legal counsel representing you, or whether you're representing yourself?"

"I have not felt it necessary to have legal counsel. I have
nothing to hide and hope to be treated with respect."

"Thank you, Dr. Jimenez. I've no reason to doubt your
sincerity, but my own experience unfortunately includes
more than a few erroneous and unscrupulous claims. So,
I'll ask you to be patient. And I hope you also have some
sensitivity as to the bombshell you've dropped on this
family."

To this Javier bowed his head slightly. "I am mindful
of the delicate timing of my arrival. However," and here
he seemed to bristle, ". . . in light of my lifetime of being fatherless, I also think I have a claim on emotional
trauma."

Before Rosemary could respond, he continued his mono-
logue and it appeared he was talking to himself. "I am sure
that I have finally solved the fundamental question in my
life which has been defined by being fatherless. I trusted, because my mother told me so, that my father was dead. And,
while it was lonely, when I was a small boy I could at least
fantasize he had been a hero, dying in an unknown World
War II battlefield. But the shock of coming to understand as
a youth that my father had not died a heroic death in war,
well . . . " Javier looked steadily at the brightly-colored ministerial stole that hung from a hanger on Rex's doorway, " . . .

that was deadly to me. As hard as it is to be fatherless, my early illusion gave me a respected story to hold next to my pillow while growing from childhood to my adolescence. But, then that security was ripped away from me by the slap of my mother's hand. From that time forward, I knew I was fathered by a great mysterious unknown. I sometimes thought of my father as a famous and wealthy man who was not aware of me, but, if only I could find him, he would embrace me with great fanfare."

Javier gave a bitter smile at this reflection, and still inwardly focused, he continued. "And other times, in despair, I thought of my father as cruel, even an evil man, who knew of me, but did not care enough to find me. I felt cast off. In time, I knew that the truth was probably between the two extremes of my teenage imaginations, yet emotional scars do not become more sophisticated. They can only be temporarily covered, in my case by academic success and becoming a father myself, inventing that role as I went. My life looks successful. I am held in high esteem by my colleagues. My two oldest sons are accomplished. But it is Armando, my youngest . . . "

At that he stopped, realizing for the first time that he had been extremely forthcoming to strangers and possible adversaries. Surprised at himself, he stopped talking. In unison, all three people in the room turned and looked towards the door, where they saw and heard nothing.

Rex had a sinking feeling. He turned to Javier and probed aggressively. "Your son. He's not just getting cigarettes, is he? He's gone to confront Pedro. Right?"

"I hope not." Javier again looked futilely towards the empty doorway as if he could beam his son back by his side. "But I fear he might try."

His face constricted. "I should not have brought him along. But he was so insistent and he is the only person who has cared. I can see he has carried the pain of my childhood into his own life and is too angry. My other sons have no taint of loss. They are living normal lives. I made it happen for them, but I could not make it happen for Armando."

"You may be quite right in your theories, Mr. Jimenez," Rex said, "but right now I'm far more concerned about Mr. Sanchez than with your parenting." He grabbed the phone and called Cecilia's house while standing up and slipping on his jacket with his other hand.

THIRTY

ecilia answered the phone when Rex called. The sensual euphoria of her day, topped off by the news Mateo was sharing, had pushed aside her worries about receiving phone calls. She listened while Rex explained his fears. She said little but nodded frequently, adding a quiet, "Yes," in agreement with Rex. When she hung up, she quickly motioned her sisters into the hallway where she shared with them Rex's concerns that Armando may have driven to Pine Crest Village to find Pedro.

Then she lowered her voice, "But Rex advises that we should be careful about how we discuss this because he is concerned that Mateo might do something precipitous. He'll call Pine Crest Village right now and ask them to be extra vigilant for Papa, and he and Rosemary are heading over there now with this man. Rex says that the father is the one who can keep his son from confronting Papa."

Cecilia looked at her sisters for help. "What do you think? Shall we head over ourselves? How do we keep Mateo out of it? I could tell he was very threatened by this young man."

Maria grabbed her sweater. "Why don't you let me check in with Rosemary. You try to stay relaxed and ask Matty some more questions about what happened. Think of something." She headed for the door, then stopped. "Damn, Rosemary has our car. Can I borrow one of yours?"

They were scrambling, looking for their car keys when they heard the front door shut, and soon a car door slammed, once and then twice, followed by the engine rev of the old Volvo, and finally tires churning in the gravel driveway as the car sped off into the street.

Derrick and Vic sat in conversation in the living room, oblivious to any further crisis until they saw the faces of all three women in the doorway. When Maria demanded, "Where did they go?" they all looked around but the two were nowhere in evidence.

A grim and pumped-up Mateo sat in the passenger seat next to his cousin. Julia had insisted upon driving when she saw an agitated Mateo dash to the door after they both overheard their mothers' hallway conversation. Julia's hands gripped the steering wheel of the old Volvo and they sped through the woods down the road that curved to Lakewood. Mateo's sense of danger was contagious, and she drove faster than she had ever before dared. She had no idea what Mateo would do, but she knew that they needed to reach their grandfather as soon as possible.

Mateo himself did not have a clear plan, yet he had never felt so single-minded in his life. He must get to his grandfather. He was certain of Armando's hatred, and the threat towards his grandfather felt imminent. It was the only picture in his mind, galvanizing him to action with every fiber of his being. All semblance of the laid-back barista was gone. Would Catherine have recognized him at this moment if she had been present? What would she have made of the fierce expression on his face?

Arriving within a hundred yards of their destination, out of the corner of his vision Mateo saw a car parked by the woods near Pine Crest Village. Staring deep into the woods, Mateo thought he made out the faint movement of light, a flashlight. Was he imagining it?

It was not his imagination. Armando had somewhat earlier approached the front doors of the peaceful establishment, intent on confronting the old man with the truth that burned inside him. The truth that would solve all his father's grief and leave Armando as the hero. It was a childish notion, but Armando held it close to his heart. The time had come for this truth to be unveiled. But when he walked up to the big glass entry doors, they were locked for the evening. A sign instructed evening guests to ring the bell and wait for admittance. Inside, Armando could see two women sitting at a front desk chatting. They didn't notice him outside and he was confident he could easily overpower them, but then he noticed a burly night custodian emptying garbage just down the hallway. Armando stopped, uncertain. He was strong and a skilled wrestler but, even in his agitated state he had to concede that the commotion any encounter would cause would thwart his plans.

Armando retreated into the shadows to reconsider, his intent still strong, but he needed another entry point. Surely this facility had a back or side entrance, and he set off to find a new strategy. He fully expected to find a back door to enter with little disturbance, but if not, he would try a window. He went back to the car to get a flashlight and screwdriver, and then decided to move his father's car out of full view, finding a place just off the road to make it less conspicuous and give him an easy exit if needed. He moved stealthily. His mission would put to rest his father's lifetime of suffering, and thus his own. Armando felt sure his mother would be proud of him, and that was his guiding light.

THIRTY-ONE

I nside his apartment, Pedro was lying in bed, hoping that if he pretended to fall asleep, he might actually reach that safe blank zone of unconsciousness for at least a few hours before he woke again to find Tori's side of the bed empty. At the front desk, the night receptionist and Tina sat and talked about their families and movies and any subject they could think of to pass the time. Tina was usually home by now, but after Mateo's warning call, she had phoned her boyfriend to say she needed to stay late. He asked if she wanted him to come down and keep her company, but she did not want to draw more attention to whatever was bothering Mateo.

So while Tina chattered with one part of her attention about low carb diets as opposed to low fat diets, the back of her mind was mulling over what in the world was going on in Mr. Sanchez's family.

Unnoticed by the attendants, Julia and Mateo pulled up to the front circular drive of the retirement home. Mateo jumped out and for the first time, Julia asked him what he was going to do.

"I'll go around the back just to check things out. You can go in the front door and make sure things are smooth. Whatever you do, don't alarm Grand Pedro."

"Mateo, be careful. Do you really think Armando is around here? Why would anyone want to hurt our grand-pa?" Now that they had arrived her voice sounded tremulous, in real contrast to her competence during the fast drive.

Mateo reached back into the car and squeezed her arm. "I'm probably over-reacting, Jul. I'll see you in just a minute after I swing around the back side of the building. Don't worry."

As he spoke, he wondered how he could lie so easily. His instincts were on full alert, and he knew he would find Armando somewhere. If he had been thinking more clearly, he might have wondered how much of his certainty was his imagination fueled by his dislike for the other man. He may also have wondered why he felt so unnerved by Armando. But for now he behaved like a soldier on patrol. He set off, leaving the car behind and soon disappeared in the darkness behind the building. Julia watched him a moment, started to walk into the front office, but then she stopped, turned in the direction Mateo had disappeared and followed her cousin into the night.

At first Mateo could see little behind the long single-story building. The residents were all sleeping, or like Pedro, lying awake wishing for sleep to descend, therefore, the lights were out in the rooms. One spotlight shone from its place on the corner of the building, but it was directed out into the woods so the area along the windows was in dark shadows. There was no moonlight. Mateo stood a second to get his night vision. Behind him, Julia stopped in her tracks too.

Mateo made a mental note of where his grandfather's apartment would be located, counting windows, and glancing out to the woods that ran around the perimeter of the long building. "Two, four, six, yes, there it is," he thought. The eighth window down the hall was his grandparent's unit, and he started walking in that direction.

In that moment Julia saw movement, and without a second thought screamed out, "Mateo, watch out behind you!!"

Mateo whirled around towards the woods and was immediately grabbed around his neck from behind. Caught by surprise, Mateo was at a disadvantage, but responding from instinct he grabbed his attacker and flipped him to the ground. The two rolled in the wet grass, throwing punches when able, but mostly it was a do-or-die wrestling match. Mateo felt the other's muscles and body in contact with his own. It was like one body, only the body was hurting itself, as punches made contact with bone and cartilage. Both noses were ripped and slammed, and pain roared through Mateo's brain. They clawed and grasped at each other, squeezing breath out of the conjoined thrashing body, like Siamese twins locked in a self-hating battle, determined to destroy. Mateo had never been a team sport player, and although in good shape from biking, had not been trained in any one sport. His opponent was, however.

He soon had the upper hand, although Mateo fought with fury.

Julia ran towards the struggling men with a large stick in her two hands, but they whirled around so quickly and it was so dark that she feared she might smash the wrong man. Her shouts alerted the family members who had driven up to the front of the Village, and provided a distraction that allowed Mateo to slip loose and jump upright, but only for a moment. Armando seized him and threw his body weight against Mateo, hurling him to the ground again where Mateo's head hit a curb, and the fight instantly left his body.

He lay completely still. Julia pulled her phone out to use as a flashlight, and then screamed. Armando sat on his haunches, breathing hard, shirt torn, blood coming from his nose, staring out of his already swollen eyes at Mateo. Then the phone light went off. It was this moment of darkness Julia remembered afterwards. Before she rushed to Mateo's body. Before Armando swore and tried to run away. Before the family careened around the corner.

Now it was Olivia's flashlight that caught the horrible scene: her own daughter hovering over a man who could hardly be recognized. A bloodied, wild-eyed stranger was squatting on the ground and then tried to run, Derrick tackled him, the young stranger crumpling and holding his arm in pain. Cecilia rushed to Mateo, and Vic called for help.

Within a minute, Rex and Rosemary arrived with Javier, and Tina ran out with the night supervisor to see about the commotion. So many people gathered now. At this point Armando stopped trying to flee. His father sat next to him, Javier holding a steady hand on his son's arm, the one not broken. Derrick crouched on the other side, discouraging Armando from any thought of renewing his flight.

Rex checked on Mateo and assured the shaking Cecilia that he was breathing. After an endless wait the emergency responders were guided around to this normally quiet lawn. Tina remembered her duties and reluctantly took her shocked eyes off Mateo's pulverized face and went inside to check on Pedro. She found him sound asleep. What a blessing, she thought. As a matter of fact, no one in the entire residence woke up. A gift of poor hearing, Tina reflected. When the paramedics arrived, not even the nosiest gossip stirred from sleep. Ambulances were not unusual at a senior living facility, so the neighbors driving by that night said a little prayer for aged bodies, and kept right on their way. They would hear what happened in the next days, as various versions of the story swept through Pine Junction and beyond.

As the hours passed that night, besides the seniors in their beds at Pine Crest Village, there was another who was out cold. In the hospital near the University, Mateo Schumacher rested, unconscious.

THIRTY-TWO

In the weeks that followed the assault, as Mateo lay in a coma, Cecilia did not go to work. But she began going to the library at all hours of the night, not turning the lights on but letting the glow of the outdoor street lamp guide her as she drifted around the familiar space. She had discovered that she could sooth herself by walking the wooden floor in her bare feet. She was past caring what anyone thought of her. Her heart lay in that hospital bed with her son.

While the specialists gave a prediction that Mateo would awaken, no one really knew for sure. His brain scans looked hopeful, but every case was different, the doctors explained. As his grandmother Victoria would have said briskly, "Proof's in the pudding." And only when and if Mateo did wake up would they begin to get an idea of his prognosis for full recovery. Meanwhile Cecilia slipped out to the library at night to pace back and forth, back and forth. Rowan, who had come home to see his brother the night of the crisis, spent most nights at the hospital, but there was often someone else in the house, which was a comfort most of the time, but sometimes Cecilia wanted to be alone in her disbelief. She felt scorched now, but at some level that pain made her more alive than the years when her heart was numb and hollow.

However, when morning came, she became again the strong maternal presence at the hospital, the advocate, watching for minor details in Mateo's care that the busy staff might miss. She took copious notes when the doctor made his rounds. She consulted daily with the nurses and specialists, and spent hours reading about brain injury. She helped do the passive rehab exercises for Mateo's legs and arms. And she sat and waited by his bed. Only at night would she go home, replaced by friends and family who would take turns sitting the night hours with Mateo so he was never alone.

Catherine spent hours with Mateo too, curled up in the chair, sometimes sneaking in to lie by his side on the bed, held in by the guardrail, entering a strange state of being present to the young man she now knew she loved. She sang for him, softly, to not disturb others in the hospital. She talked to him and held his hand. She was distraught, but she also was hopeful, and clung to the words that most encouraged optimism. Frequently she had to go back to the City for rehearsals. She had passed her first round of auditions for the esteemed Tapestry String Quartet, and while her inclination was to let it go, just focus on Mateo, everyone convinced her that Mateo would want her to pursue this the biggest opportunity of her musical life. So she put the miles on her dad's car, driving back and forth between her loves: music and Mateo. Somehow she managed to practice and prepare. Later she would wonder how she did it, fighting the forces of sleepiness on the drives while keeping a spirit of hope.

Besides Catherine, the visiting contingent was large, and even Warren came once or twice to watch over his son, despite his discomfort being around the Sanchez family.

One evening, as Vic and Cecilia sat at dinner in her kitchen (Rowan having gone to the hospital for the night shift and Catherine having driven back to a rehearsal), Vic without preamble, asked Cecilia, "What about Dane Faber? Are you going to call him about Mateo? Let him know?"

Cecilia found it both unnerving and relieving how Vic always seemed to get to the core of things, somehow without bringing out any defensiveness within her. It was a new experience, one she was not familiar with.

As she sat with Vic, Cecilia replayed the horror of that night, seeing her beautiful son lying on the ground bloody and unresponsive with his assailant wounded nearby. On that terrible night, she had looked across Mateo's bloody head and caught the sorrowful eye of Javier Jimenez for just an instant, as Javier sat holding his own son's injured body.

Because of that single silent visual exchange, Cecilia had, despite her protective mother tiger instincts, been unable to sustain a lasting hatred for the Jimenez boy. She was focused only on Mateo and also to a degree on Rowan, who had arrived in Pine Junction and stayed. She left the legal matters to others. She was assured that the system was working its process. Armando was recovering from his injuries, chief of which were a broken arm and nose, as well as fractured ribs. He had been charged with assault and battery, held in jail even after his arraignment because the local judge was not convinced that this out-of-towner might not flee. The raging emotions that had possessed Armando seemed to have vaporized. What the legal outcome would be was unknown, although a trial and prison were all very possible. Pedro had been told that Mateo had had an accident and was in the hospital. As he had lost interest in following the news since Victoria's death, Pedro had not read the story of the assault in the newspaper or seen it on television. And not even the most talkative of residents told him the full story, kept away by the fog that hung around Pedro night and day.

Pedro visited his grandson at the hospital, and for the second time in a month, he sat by a bedside and wept. To the grandfather, the family continually emphasized the doctor's hopes for Mateo's good recovery, although as each day went by without consciousness, their worry increased.

As of yet, Pedro had also not been told of Javier Jimenez's search for his father. Of course this withholding was dishonoring to Pedro, once the family's strong patriarch, but when the sisters contemplated the stress of such traumatic news, both the yet-unproven news of Javier's claim and the news of how Mateo suffered his injury, they agreed that it was best to say nothing. So the old man spent his days mourning his wife, worrying about his grandson, and feeling the effect of his Parkinson's disease advance.

Mateo's hoped-for recovery put everything in perspective, even Dane Faber. Cecilia, looked calmly back at Vic and answered his question about Dane. "Yes. I left him a message last night. Although it seems to me he might have heard about it."

Vic nodded. "Yes, I thought about that myself, halfway expecting he would just show up. Maybe he won't come even when you let him know, but at least you know you did the decent thing by contacting him."

Cecilia agreed, although it had taken her two weeks to bring herself to make that call. After weeks and months of avoiding Dane's calls, now she was calling him. Ironic.

She squeezed Vic's hand, and then stood up, still holding on to him. "Rowan'll be at the hospital all night, and Catherine's gone back to the City. Will you come hold me? I think I need you more than I need dinner right now."

The relationship between these two with such complex pasts continued to unfold with satisfaction, and there existed for both of them a tremendous relief to have someone to talk to, and also, at times, the comfort of not needing to talk at all.

THIRTY-THREE

T he day had been full of visitors for Mateo, now three weeks into his comatose state. Julia, Rex, Derrick and Maria had been in. Tiny and Leticia brought more flowers from their garden and stayed for awhile, Tiny's massive hands hanging uselessly on his knees and Leticia's face haggard with worry. Cecilia updated each visitor, but there was nothing new to report.

Just before she left, Cecilia talked with the man who had become her favorite nurse. Henry was a tall broad-shouldered man of American-Indian descent. His strength allowed him to move Mateo's body easily, but his tenderness made Cecilia see he was as gentle as she had been with Mateo when he was a baby. She watched him clean up messes and change IVs with an elegance in his movements. She never tried to explain the comfort she felt in Henry's presence. He simply represented strength and kindness.

As Cecilia readied herself to go for the day, Rowan entered and the three of them stood by Mateo's still form, mother and brother both fiercely wishing for Mateo to open his eyes, say something, or even squeeze their hands. Henry, who had been changing an IV bag, watched them and then said in his unhurried voice, "Keep talking to him. I've been seeing Mateo in my dreams lately. He's been talking to me, not with words, but showing me things he's seen. He's smiling at me. The dream is a happy one, Mrs. Schumacher."

Cecilia stared at Henry. He had never said such a thing before. He had followed the protocol of a good nurse, kind and capable, but never going out on a limb. She was desperate though, like a mother who has not heard from her child for a very long time and then encounters someone who mentions that they just spent time with that very son or daughter.

But all she said was, "Henry, I have dreams too, but I've been frustrated because I can't dream of Mateo. I want to. I want to feel him near me, as close as I can, but my dreams are too strange and scrambled. I can't tell what they mean."

"Don't worry, Mrs. Schumacher. Mateo's close to you. His showing himself to me only means that my mind is clearer and less full of the love you have for him."

Cecilia fell silent, calmed.

Rowan listened to all of this with interest mingled with skepticism. Rowan was new to this business of relationships. His life had been turned upside down three weeks ago when he got the call about Mateo's injury. As seen by many people in Pine Junction, Rowan appeared to be self centered and detached. At age twenty-five he was beginning a career in the pressured world of a stockbroker and took pride in his early success, indulging in the perks of that success.

Rowan had been a sweet-natured boy of eleven, already with a cut-and-dried personality enthused with interests such as sports and mechanics, when the familiar pattern of his life was shattered by his parent's sudden divorce. To deal with his new unsettled life, he focused on those things that seemed permanent to him, things that distracted him from the uncertainties he now lived with. He craved doing things that seemed never-changing and light-hearted, and he took care of himself by spending his time with his friends whose families seemed more normal than his own. It kept him from being confused by the feelings of hatred mixed with love he felt for both parents. Just out of old loyalties to his father, he let more of his anger go towards his mother, effectively punishing her by going away to boarding school. Spending the formative teenage years in the company of other boys with little parental interaction advanced the alienation from his family. He found it easier to see his father because they had things to talk about that were in keeping with his interests. But his relationship with his mother, in early childhood so natural and animated, became uncomfortable and began to disappear completely under small talk. Cecilia had a sense that she let him slip away, just as she felt about Mateo at times, but she had no words to explain the divorce to her boys, and was unable to muster the energy to remain a strong presence in her sons' lives. Later, when she felt stronger, it seemed too late.

On the night of Mateo and Armando's violent encounter, Rowan received a phone call from his mother telling him about Mateo's fight and injuries. Her message was so difficult to understand, in the midst of her sobs, that Rex Randall took the phone and gave Rowan the unbelievable facts. And even in Rex's articulate summary, there was a sense of disbelief so strong that Rowan made the minister repeat his words several times. Rex patiently restated the message. Rowan thanked him for the call and then hung up, too stunned to move for a full fifteen minutes, staring blankly at the television screen.

Rowan finally looked around his apartment as if waking up from a dream, hit the remote's mute button, picked up his phone and called his dad. Warren had received a similar call from Cecelia a short time before and was in his car on the way to the hospital. Warren confirmed the message. All Rowan could keep saying was, "Mateo? It can't be. Not Matty."

Warren acknowledged the unlikely nature of the event but said he had confirmed it with the hospital, so it was true. Something had happened and Mateo was in serious condition, so he was on his way to check it out.

Warren made no suggestion as to what Rowan should do. In some way, Rowan was hoping that his dad would give him some guidance, but there was none forthcoming. He was on his own to decide how to respond. He started to the refrigerator to grab a beer when he had a sudden memory. He and Mateo as boys, locked in a knock-down battle over a stupid toy from the cereal box. It was rare for the boys to have such a fight. The three-year age difference usually kept the competitiveness to a minimum, and Mateo's personality did not make him inclined to be aggressive. But this time it had been different.

It was a plastic harmonica that had come in the cereal box. Rowan had no real interest in musical instruments. If it had been a toy car, he would have claimed it and there would have been no protest from Mateo. But this harmonica was something Mateo had his eye on and immediately grabbed. Rowan fought furiously for it. He really didn't want it, but it became intensely important that he have it at that moment, and for once Mateo was standing in his way. The two boys became entangled in a battle of arms and legs and teeth and elbows as Rowan fought to take the toy out of Mateo's clenched fist. The battle ended when Rowan banged his head on the refrigerator, which just happened to be in the way of their wrestling match. Their mom ran into the kitchen in time to see her two little boys tumbling in fierce combat on the floor and to witness Rowan's head smack hard against the door of the old white fridge. Magnets went flying along with the drawings and lists and photographs they held in place. Both boys stopped struggling at the crack of Rowan's head, Rowan because he was physically stunned and Mateo because he was scared of his uncontrolled actions and how he might have hurt his little brother.

Rowan stopped now with this memory, hand on his sleek stainless-steel double-sized refrigerator. He didn't remember how old he and Mateo had been at the time of that fight. Old enough so there could be a degree of physical parity despite the three year age difference, but young enough so that the plastic harmonica was considered worthy of combat. And other than sulking and crying a bit after he recovered from his head thunking, Rowan didn't think about the incident again, until this moment, twenty years later. He stood there in his kitchen, still clinging to the refrigerator handle, remembering that long-ago sensation of losing all control and concern for personal safety as he fought fiercely with his brother. He realized that he had never seen Mateo lose his laid-back sensibilities again since that day. But now Mateo was in the hospital, seemingly after a physical altercation with another man.

What had come over his brother? Rowan shook his head as if to clear his thoughts. He finally let go of the refrigerator door handle, without opening it. He walked back into the living room. The big screen kept sending bright colored movement into the dark corners of the room. Rowan turned it off and grabbed his jacket, his phone, his wallet and keys, and walked out the door. Soon his BMW was speeding towards his brother Mateo, and with a mix of fear and curiosity, he pushed his foot down faster than normal on the accelerator.

THIRTY-FOUR

If you were measuring time, it had been three weeks now. Many lives were put on hold over three weeks; all the people central to Mateo's life were frozen in place, and even the peripheral acquaintances were left holding their breath.

Rex was certainly coming to quite a different impression of Rowan after seeing the younger brother night after night in the hospital with Mateo, providing companionship to Cecilia, learning to talk to the doctors and nurses, and even, on some occasions, reaching out physically to hold his brother's hand, or touch his shoulder.

As for trying to get on with one's life in the midst of crisis, Catherine did the best she could. While she appeared spirited, her heartbreak was like a terrible surprise that she kept revisiting with regularity. She knew that Mateo would want her to keep her music going. And then the next moment she would doubt that knowledge. She felt so torn. What if he woke up when she was back in the City? It was likely because she had to go back for days at a time. What if, horrible thought, Mateo would die and she was not there with him? What if? She had always been able to lose herself in her music, but it was sheer work these days. She tried to develop an attitude that she was pursuing her life for them both, for their future relationship when surely he would wake up and be the same Mateo she had fallen in love with. And so she drove back and forth, city to hospital, certainty to doubt, and back again.

The only two people who simply gave up their lives to be there for Mateo were Cecilia and Rowan, mother and brother. That Cecilia would do so was not surprising. Regardless of Mateo's age, she was his mother. It was Rowan, however, who surprised everyone. He told his employers that he was going to be taking an unknown amount of time off work. A leave. Warren advised him strongly not to do so, that he was too new in his company to take an extended leave. His workmates and friends, while trying to be sympathetic, also tried to talk Rowan out of what many saw as an ill-advised move and kept trying to draw him back into his former life. But from the moment he stood by his brother's bed and looked at Mateo's immobile face and body, Rowan felt something shift. He was uncomfortable trying to explain to anyone what was motivating his decision, but he stubbornly held his ground. His mother felt herself fortified by Rowan's presence. She alone did not question why he was doing this. At this point, she just accepted his continued presence with gratitude.

Three weeks into Mateo's coma, Cecilia left for the night, still pondering Henry's comments about seeing Mateo in his dreams. Rowan settled into his chair and paged through a sports magazine without much interest.

Rowan had come to look forward, in a bizarre sort of way, to these evenings at the hospital. It would sound macabre if he ever tried to explain this, but he could not remember ever feeling so meditative and timeless. He also had never felt so close to his brother. Of course he was worried. But Rowan also felt relaxed and comfortable in the hospital atmosphere, the long quiet hours interrupted by a flurry of staff activity, some nurses more contained and some more boisterous even in the midnight shift hours. Angels of mercy they were, these nurses. That is how Rowan came to view the men and women who attended his brother and gave Rowan friendly greetings. They seemed to accept that he was there night after night, that it was natural that he inhabited their night-shift world. Rowan admired their skilled care of his brother's body, their careful monitoring of those physical things that needed measuring, and their equal skill at measuring those intangible levels of a patient's emotional well-being. In the night time, the doctors were not around, and it was only the nurses who floated into the almost dark rooms, lit only by the necessary monitors and blinking IV machines. Rowan felt strangely at home and content, even in the midst of his family's anguish.

On this particular night though, Rowan was beginning to feel the physical strain of all the nights in the hospital. His attempts to sleep during the day at his mom's home were often disorienting. He drank the soda he had brought with him and settled into the chair by Mateo's bed. For the first time in his three-week vigil, Rowan decided to make use of its reclining feature, and despite the caffeine, he soon drifted off. When the nurse came in to take Mateo's vitals soon before 11:00 p.m., she found Rowan in a heavy sleep. With an affectionate gesture she covered him with a blanket. Then she hurried out to continue her rounds down the hallway. Rowan slept on and on into the dark hours.

The nursing staff was short that night. Two nurses and an aide had come down with the flu, and replacements were not able to come on duty. This left the remaining staff to work extra hard to cover the needs of the unit. With the nurses involved in patient care, the desk was empty at midnight when Dane Faber entered the hallway, looked around for some help, and not finding any, went to the room number Cecilia had left on his answering machine for his son's hospital bed.

THIRTY-FIVE

Later, Mateo would vaguely remember the strange sensations of his coma. He went through a time where he was thrashing around with a backdrop of hurting. But then it changed. He became enveloped in gentle liquid pastels, with mute yet comforting faces drifting in and out of his visual field. Often there was music, too. Music that he couldn't identify, couldn't hear with clarity. Music that was elusive, dancing out of his hearing just when he thought he had brought it into focus. He lived during that unmeasured time as if he were under water, swimming like a fish, drifting through water effortlessly, with those distant faces somehow giving him a reassuring sense of belonging. Somewhere. Someplace. He was not in despair. He was not agitated. He was peaceful, yet not completely at rest. He began to find himself swimming with more powerful movement. Eventually, the faces became more distinct. Details and differences emerged, but still he did not have words for any of this. He felt no need to have words for anything. But he was very interested in those faces. He paid attention, and the more he paid attention, the clearer they became. First one and then another, sometimes more than one at a time. Sometimes many. He scrutinized the faces, with interest, with intelligence, like a new born baby will do. He wasn't trying to figure it out, but he was very interested. Yet his eyes never opened.

And so it went, time unmarked by hours or days to him, until one moment when all was quiet except for beeps and the quiet padding of footsteps, Mateo saw a face, and saw it with open eyes. The face he looked at was not alarming. Two pairs of eyes looked at each other, with understanding if not recognition. The look held. It held for one minute, two, three and more. Finally the aware one, the man who knew the story, said to the one emerging from a deep watery zone, "Mateo."

The young man's face relaxed, and before his tired eyes blinked a few times, finally closing, he responded with some relief, "Yes."

THIRTY-SIX

When Dane entered the hospital room he saw a young man asleep in the recliner next to the bed. Dane gauged that he was in a very deep sleep, so he next looked at the figure on the bed. It was Mateo, that he knew. His face was imprinted in Dane's memory from the one photo he had seen, a news article he researched showing Mateo in a short-lived Brooklyn band. He could see the physical resemblance to himself. Cecilia had told him that much when they had talked ever so briefly months ago, before she became so unsettled that she refused to take his calls or see him. He had backed off, not wanting to distress her, hoping that in time she would come around to his request. In the meantime, he had a music gig that took him away for several weeks. He had returned home to New York that very afternoon, heard Cecilia's phone message of a week earlier, and left immediately to drive to see Mateo, all the while cursing himself for stubbornly refusing to get a cell phone. It was late when he arrived at the hospital. Much to his surprise, there were no security guards to question him, no locked doors, and not even a nurse at the nurse's station to stop him. So, here he was. In the room.

Dane looked at Mateo a long time, sensing a kinship although he rationally knew it was wishful thinking. He had to admit that if Mateo had not been unconscious at this moment that the young man might be angry and have no desire to meet him. He knew that his presence here would be very unwelcome by most. He wondered who the sleeping fellow might be. Friend? Brother? Lover? He didn't know enough about Mateo to wager guesses about his life. He just knew that ever since January when he found out that he had fathered a son with Cecilia almost thirty years ago, he needed to try to make a connection regardless of the obstacles.

This knowledge had come about through a chance encounter in far-off Seattle. That such monumental news could be revealed by chance astonished Dane. Should one's life's direction teeter so precariously on a casual bit of conversation? One night four or five months ago, while playing at a club in Seattle, he had run into a singer from those long-ago days at the Franklin Club, an old acquaintance who had also known Cecilia. After Dane finished his last set, and in the course of their alcohol-enhanced conversation, the singer made several comments about old times that led Dane to a dawning realization. Sobering quickly, he pushed more questions on the woman. "I might have a child," was all he could think about on his flight home.

Soon after he got back home, Dane had driven to Pine Junction from his home in New York. When he approached

Cecilia's door last January, he had so startled Cecilia that she looked like she was seeing a ghost. With a rush of feelings, Dane stood a few feet away from the woman who had bewitched him back in 1976 when she was working as a waitress to pay for library school and he was playing in a band at the same club. During their short conversation on her porch, in the total surprise of seeing Dane and hearing his theory, Cecilia had confirmed his paternity before telling him to leave. Dane stood his ground and demanded why she had never told him about Mateo. He told her that he wanted to meet his son and get to know him, to be in his life. She became more distraught the longer he talked and first begged him - and then ordered him - to leave town. He agreed to go for the moment, but promised that he would contact her soon. Frightened for her secret, she had not taken his phone calls or any others over the next months.

After Cecilia sent him away, Dane had made one stop at the Pine Junction pharmacy to pick up some aspirin because a headache was growing and he had a long drive in front of him after his fruitless visit to Pine Junction. A man with a beard said hello while Dane was waiting for the clerk to direct him to the headache remedies. The gregarious stranger introduced himself to Dane, and so the surprised Dane had introduced himself in return. When the man said he was the minister of the local Congregational church, Dane had a flash of memory that Cecilia had once told him she grew up attending a Congregational Church. On impulse, obsessed with his new sense of fatherhood, Dane asked the minister if he knew how Mateo Schumacher was doing. That was perhaps unwise of Dane to have asked, but he couldn't help himself. The minister seemed puzzled and commented that Mateo lived out of town now. The clerk returned with Dane's medications, and already concerned that he had gone too far with his questioning, Dane excused himself and started his drive home.

Now he stood in the hospital room with Mateo. This was the culmination of months of churning feelings since that night in Seattle, ranging from disbelief to acceptance, from acceptance but feeling that he should just let things be, to a surge of desire to connect to his son. His son! And now he found himself here with Mateo, in this room, along with a sleeping young man in the chair who might wake up in a protective furor or blow the whistle on the slack hospital security. Neither prospect seemed like a good introduction to his son. Dane knew that he should retreat right back out the door of room #406, and, if he got caught in the hallways, claim confusion and hopefully smile his way out of trouble. Yet he was more bemused by the situation than alarmed; this was certainly not the way he had envisioned trying to enter his son's life for the first time.

Perhaps Dane was picking up some of the same peaceful atmosphere that had melted Rowan's high-powered, easily-distracted mind. Was it the subdued hospital night atmosphere, or was it something about being in Mateo's comatose presence? For whatever reason, Dane sat down in the second chair in the room to look at Mateo and study him carefully. It felt like an unfair advantage to be able to so leisurely take stock of an unconscious man. But this was the situation, so Dane sat quite still and let his gaze rest on Mateo's face to absorb the sight of this man, his son. Dane wondered if life was delivering a cruel joke to take his son away from him just when he had learned of his existence. Yet, for some reason, Dane didn't feel angry.

An hour into this gentle but intense connection between birth-father and son, Mateo opened his eyes for the first time since his altercation with Armando. His eyes took some time to focus but they were locked in on Dane's own gently penetrating look. Dane did not feel the need to talk or explain, but finally he breathed out slowly, as if to relish the saying, "Mateo." It was not a question or a demand. It was just a naming, as if after such a long time away from reality, Mateo might like to be reminded of his identity. It was a statement that this stranger knew who he was.

After Mateo's "Yes," his whole body relaxed and his eyes closed. Dane knew he should leave. He hoped he would be back, but for the moment he let go of needing to know how things would work out. He had a deep satisfaction in his heart right now. The rest would work out in time. Quietly he pulled out a card from his pocket and a pen. He wrote a brief note and left it on the hospital tray table where the unknown sleeping friend had left his phone.

Then Dane Faber slipped out of the room and managed to leave the hospital, seeing only one aide, who was so tired after a long shift that she never gave Dane a second glance as they exited the elevator together. When Dane walked out the front door, the security guard had his back turned and never saw him leave. "Perhaps I am invisible," Dane thought.

PART TWO

Conversations While Waiting

THIRTY-SEVEN

ROWAN AND MATEO

Rowan woke up suddenly with a grunt, and before his eyes were fully functioning, he reached out blindly for his phone on the hospital tray. As he picked it up, Dane's card dropped to the floor, un-noticed by Rowan. He checked his messages and the time, 3:14 a.m. Standing up, he stretched and then stood beside his brother's bed. He felt comfortable in this spot by now, with none of the shock he'd felt the first few days. His new calmness was hard to put into words, even to himself, so Rowan found himself talking to fewer people who knew him from his regular life. Those who visited Mateo's bed in a parade of concern were all profoundly affected by the experience, so Rowan found himself more comfortable with the Pine Junction visitors than his more prosaic colleagues and bar mates.

"Well, bro, kind of a quiet night tonight. I just had the weirdest dream. It was you and me, at that cabin that Dad and Mom took us to when we were in elementary school. Remember, up at the lake?

"It was a damn good spot for fishing. That was one thing we all liked to do, all four us, remember? Fishing. We caught lake salmon and trout. I caught the first one of the day, which made me fucking proud. Can't believe how I danced around, trying to make you feel bad, I guess. Little brother showing off."

"Well, so me and you were on the boat alone, in my dream, I mean, not in real life. And then a bunch of stuff happened."

Rowan stopped, remembering his dream. He kept talking to his unconscious brother.

"In the dream, I pushed you over the side of the boat. I don't remember why. But I'm real clear that I pushed you over."

Rowan stood there in the dark, watching the little beeps light up the instruments around the bed.

"So, you went over the side, Mateo, and it was a real deep lake. Now I know we can swim - Dad and Mom always made sure we could swim, but in my dream we couldn't. So I was scared, and then just as you went over, you grabbed me, and I was down in the water, too. Fucking cold it was, even in my dream, wow! I was going to drown, that was clear. I panicked, but then you were beside me in the water, and we were like fish swimming in the water, and then I wasn't afraid. And somehow we could breathe under the water. That part seemed to last a long time, but who knows with dreams, right?"

Rowan came back to the present, back to his brother's still figure lying under the covers, lifting the blanket gently with each slow but steady breath.

"So then guess what happened, Mateo?" Rowan almost seemed to expect Mateo to respond with a "What?" He gave a pause before finishing. "You pushed me out of the water, and back into the boat. You saved my life, brother."

Rowan stood there absorbing it all, the dream, his strange new lifestyle, and his brother's unresponsive body in front of him.

"Hey Matty, when you wake up, I owe you a beer. What a guy! Your stupid little brother pushes you into the water and you pull me in after you, but then you decide to rescue me. Crazy. This is all crazy. You gotta wake up so you can tell me what's going on with you."

Rowan paused. Then added, "You will wake up, Mateo, won't you? You gotta wake up. Please."

With this beseeching plea Rowan wiped his eyes, looking around as if there was someone lurking in the room to see his tears.

Thirty-Eight

PEDRO AND VICTORIA

Tina finished picking up the accoutrements of Pedro's shave and bath and headed for the door with her usual cheery farewell. Before she left the room, Pedro called to her.

"Tina, please bring me Tori's urn."

Tina went to the shelf, and with two hands carefully picked up the simple but elegant pot that stored Victoria Sanchez's remains. She had performed this ritual several times since Victoria's death. She placed it gently in front of Pedro in the middle of the coffee table and asked if he needed anything more.

"No, my dear, I just need to have a little talk with my wife."

"All right, but I will check back in an hour to see if you need anything more. And don't forget, someone is picking you up to go visit Mateo this afternoon."

As if he could forget. It was the highlight of Pedro's days, those afternoons when he would go keep Mateo company, sitting by his silent grandson as long as he had the energy to do so. The door closed behind Tina, and Pedro sat for many minutes, hands on his knees, with his arms twitching frequently. His eyes stayed on the glossy black vessel in front of him. Finally he sighed deeply.

"So, Tori, here we are. We haven't even had a chance to give you the memorial service you deserve with this terrible accident of Mateo's. I miss that boy so much. Here he just came back into our lives, was here just long enough for us to remember what a light he is in our life, and then first you leave me and then he had this terrible accident. Now he just lies there in the bed."

Pedro sat silently before he continued his lament.

"Seems crazy. He fell and hit his head is what they tell me. That just doesn't sound like Mateo. That boy is as graceful and coordinated as they come. Remember how his dad and the coaches always wanted him to get into sports, soccer first, then baseball, then wrestling? But he wouldn't. And for such an easygoing guy, he sure could be stubborn."

Pedro choked as he thought of his grandson. "Oh, I know what you would say to me now, Tori, 'Pull yourself together, Pedro. Show some perseverance. You're falling apart and that's not what our family does. We're strong.'"

Pedro snorted, suddenly angry, "Well, Tori, I'm sorry. I'm tired of being strong. I'm not as tough as you after all, you with your Lessing stiff upper lip. I always thought I was weak if I let my memories come out to haunt me. But I can't keep them hidden anymore. And you, look what happened to you when you kept everything bottled up inside of you."

Pedro sat mulling over these thoughts for a minute and then he addressed the urn once again. "Ever since I met you, Tori, I thought I had to behave like you wanted me to act. That was how I blended in to this town. And, if I'm honest, I admit it was my choice to work so hard to be accepted here. I wanted that. But by God, Tori, I was not part of this town to begin with. I'm a poor Mexican-American kid. My upbringing was different from yours, different from Pine Junction. To try to forget my family's terrible story, I turned my back on my whole culture and that was wrong. Wrong! My family was messy, mean, always drunk, in fact it was a miserable life . . . but it was my life. It happened. And . . . and . . . what I have denied is that there were good people in my world like my blessed neighbors, the Gonzales family, and, oh I am so ashamed, there were my innocent brothers and sisters, and I turned my back on them all."

Pedro was breathing hard now, and words tumbled out of his mouth, but the silent Victoria did not speak back.

"Maybe it's just that I'm getting old, or maybe it's all this change, this loss, but I know I've made an enormous mistake trying to bury my past. It's part of me."

Pedro tried to rise to his feet, and he shook with the effort of standing and whispering hoarsely, which felt to him like shouting.

"It's part of me, Tori, it's who I am . . . the way I was. And I think I need to go home!"

Pedro fell back into his old chair and repeated, more quietly now but with some resolve, "Yes, as soon as Mateo's better, I'll go back and take him with me to visit my home. I'm sorry, Tori, I love you but I need to go without you. I don't think it would suit you."

By this point, Pedro was drained physically and closed his eyes. He felt peaceful. He whispered his prayer one more time, "Mateo, you'll wake up, won't you? Please, dear God, let him wake up soon." Then he fell into the most satisfying sleep he had experienced since before Tori had left him.

THIRTY-NINE

VIC AND CECILIA

Vic picked up the phone, too sleepy to check who was calling. He hoped it was Cecilia, and it was. The only thing better than a middle-of-the-night phone call from her would have been a call from anyone with good news about Mateo. After years of bachelor living, set in his own ways, with a lack of responsibility to anyone but the Casavant and the choir, Vic was making a remarkable transition to having someone to care about, someone whose needs often interrupted his life, particularly at this traumatic time. Vic felt like he had been in preparation for this relationship all his life. If he had had the time to think about it, he might have taken some pleasure in the shock many people experienced to find him in an active relationship with Cecilia Schumacher.

But these days Vic had no interest in seeing Pine Junction's surprise at the dismantling of his stereotyped image. He was too busy enjoying his physical and spiritual love for Cecilia and supporting her during this crisis.

"Hello."

"Ah, Vic, I know I woke you up, once again. I'm so sorry."

"Let's go over this again, Ceci. You never need to apologize. You having trouble sleeping? Anything new about Mateo?"

"Thanks, Vic. I don't know how I would keep my sanity without you. Yes, no. I can't sleep, so what else is new? But nothing new about Mateo . . . although . . . " Her voice trailed off.

Vic just waited. And Cecilia continued.

"This just shows how ready I am for anything, anything at all." She laughed sheepishly, but with the expectant and warm silence from Vic, she said more.

"You know the nurse named Henry? The one who is so good with Matty? I think he was one of Papa's students in high school maybe ten years ago, now that I think of it. You remember seeing him? The big guy with the braid? Well, he was in with Mateo right before I left about 5:00. Rowan had just come in for the night, and I was leaving, and Henry was going off shift . . . Sorry, I know too many details.

"Henry said something that shouldn't mean anything, but somehow it seemed like a sign. Oh, I don't know. Nothing rational in all of this. And Henry strikes me as very rational, and yet with something deep about him. And I am probably reading too much into it, given his

Indian background, making him out to be someone who can have special insights, so wrong of me, but yet . . . "

Vic listened patiently .

"So, Vic, right before he left, he was standing there with us, the three of us, and we were communing with Mateo, like we do. Henry encouraged us to keep talking to Mateo, as if we would stop, and then he said that he had a dream about Mateo. In fact, he said many dreams, and that they were happy dreams and that Mateo was showing him things in his dream, but not talking to him."

"Sounds like not only what Henry said, but how he said it, has had a big impact on you, Ceci." Vic himself was not sure how much credence to put on the nurse's dream life.

"Vic, I believe in dreams, and yet I am trying to be sensible." Her laugh was self-deprecating. "What could it mean? Does it mean that Mateo is going to come back to us, or does it mean that we should just all accept that Mateo will not wake up but that he is happy? "The gulp that escaped her ripped Vic's heart.

"We just don't know, Ceci,, sweetheart. I'm hanging onto the neurologist's high expectations that Mateo will come out of the coma, but of course we don't know when, and, what." He started to reference that they didn't know what kind of brain damage might have occurred, but figured he didn't need to state the obvious.

Cecilia's voice came out like a whisper, "Oh, Vic, during the day I'm so strong and business-like, but when night comes I'm so scared. What if he doesn't wake up, Vic? What if he doesn't wake up?"

Vic wiped the tear that had come to his eye, unseen by Cecilia, and could only answer this, "Do you want some company right now? I can come."

Cecilia hesitated for a moment. She really did want his company, but then she regrouped, "Thanks, Vic, just makes me feel good to be able to reach out to you in the middle of the night. You have a big day tomorrow, with the organ repair and all, so get some sleep and call me when the man leaves. Love you. Goodnight."

FORTY

ROSEMARY AND JAVIER

"**M**y search moved from fantasy to reality with the name I was given in the bar that day."

Javier sat across the desk from Rosemary in her law office. His face showed the weariness accumulated in the days following Armando's assault on Mateo, but his speech was as precise as ever. Rosemary sighed inwardly and told herself to be patient. There would be no rushing this man and she needed to find out if his claim was legitimate or if he had come to the wrong conclusion. His sincerity was not in doubt, but only a fact-check would prove his insistence that he was the son of Pine Junction's Pedro Sanchez.

"After Tomas Garcia - he is the old friend of my mother Celina - gave me the name Pedro Sanchez, I went to the local high school and spent an afternoon looking at old school yearbooks and newspapers for that pre-war period and the early 1940s. I found several younger boys named

Pedro Sanchez but there was a photograph of one 1942 senior that stopped me short. I thought I was looking at my own son, Armando. My reaction was involuntary, the resemblance uncanny. I think you will see it, too."

Javier pulled out a photocopy of a high school yearbook page, dated six months after Pearl Harbor. He laid it on the desk between them. Rosemary peered at it with interest. In her six year relationship with Maria, she had never seen a photo from this time period of Pedro's life. She wanted to be skeptical but she could see that the look in the dark eyes and the set of the handsome face in the old black and white photograph looked like a serious young version of the Pedro she knew. She steeled herself to not take this as evidence of anything, especially not the paternity issue in question.

Javier continued. "I was able to find military documents for a Pedro Sanchez during the Second World War, showing the date of enlistment, place of service, and date of his honorable discharge. Of course it also showed his home town, and his next of kin, a Ramon Sanchez. I went to the local Catholic church and a sympathetic priest helped me find records of a Sanchez family and baptismal listings for the younger the children, but not Pedro, who was apparently baptized in Mexico. And, here, the 1930 census record shows the family living in the same town with several children including Pedro."

As he spoke, Javier pulled out these documents and lay the copies on Rosemary's desk.

"I wanted to work faster than I could do in my limited free time from the university so I hired a private detective to see if he could track down any family members that may have stayed or returned to this part of Arizona. That was an expensive and time-consuming task especially having to go back and forth across the border into Mexico. But finally there was success. A younger brother of Pedro's, a Juan Sanchez, was located in Flagstaff and, although he was reluctant to speak to me, and seemed to be reclusive and disturbed, he did tell me that his older brother Pedro had returned after the war for only one day, then walked away and never contacted the family again. Juan Sanchez either did not know or was not willing to tell me more. No other family members could be located. The trail went cold at that point."

Javier took a methodical sip from the water glass Rosemary had provided him. She wondered if he was always so contained, or whether his life had given him no option but to cultivate this persona.

"I was in despair then. I had no proof of relationship. It was at this low point that I got a call from the bartender at the same Phoenix bar where I met Tomas Garcia years earlier. Sadly, the old man was very ill and near death, but he was adamant that his nephew, the bartender, find me and give me this message: 'One more thing your mother told me about Pedro. He was heading to Kansas to attend college.' It wasn't much, but it opened a door to continue my search.

"I went to the office of vital statistics and found that through the GI bill Pedro had gone to Wichita State. It didn't take long to find a Pedro Sanchez who had attended the year immediately before and after my birth, making the timing seem correct. I also learned he earned a teaching credential. The college of teaching had a newsletter with an article about its graduates and their plans. There was one sentence about Pedro, stating he was headed to New York to look for a teaching job. So I found myself venturing north of my native South West. I started looking up everything I could on professional organizations and it was in some archival work on teachers unions that I came across his name, or the name of a Pedro Sanchez. I found out that a Pedro Sanchez was a very active leader in regional union activities for a number of years. I went to the New York Times and the public libraries of Boston and New York and kept searching for more.

"In one newsletter I saw a photograph that matched the young photo I had seen from his high school yearbook." Javier pulled out more papers to add to the pile on the desk. "I kept looking. You must realize this has all taken years to research. I discovered that this same Pedro Sanchez had done graduate work at Columbia. And then I found his home town was in Massachusetts, a small town called Pine Junction.

"I also came across many references to his community service, documented in the local newspaper. He and his wife were active members of this community, that is clear." Javier stopped and reflected. "When I was discovering all of this, it seemed so distant from our home town in Arizona, a world away. But the common bond was that he and I were both teachers. I felt there would be no bad surprises or disappointments when we finally met."

Rosemary wasn't sure if Javier saw the irony in his last statement.

Finally Javier pulled out a copy of Victoria's obituary from the Amherst newspaper. He looked at Victoria's photo sadly. "I am sorry I did not get to meet Mrs. Sanchez. It seems her death was very unexpected."

Rosemary just nodded, keeping her own counsel at this point. She let Javier conclude his own story, impressed with his diligent searching yet realizing that what he had produced, while strong, was more circumstantial than evidential or scientific. Javier seemed to read her mind.

"I had to stop myself from rushing here on the next plane, but I first went back to the reluctant brother in Flagstaff and convinced him to go to the medical clinic with me and give a swab for DNA testing. I am sure you are familiar with how this works, Ms Silva. Juan Sanchez and I were exactly the match you would expect for an uncle. Short of a DNA sample from Pedro himself, this is almost undisputable evidence."

With this last page set squarely in front of Rosemary, Javier had only one more thing to add.

"If you need more proof I would ask my father to submit to a DNA test as well, or perhaps you can get the necessary samples from his doctor. For myself, I do not need any additional proof. One look at Mateo and Armando and you can see they are cousins."

Rosemary stifled her annoyance at Javier's slide from his calm recitation into his sensational reference to the two young men. She was glad that it was she who was gathering this information, not any one of the Sanchez sisters who at this tender juncture would have reacted with anger to Javier's last comment.

Still, she conceded that Javier's paper trail leading to Pedro in Pine Junction was impressive. And given his long search and the drama of the recent days, he might be excused for occasionally slipping out of his academic demeanor and becoming maudlin. For now she just bundled up her copies of Javier's papers, turned off the tape recorder, stood up and told Javier that she would call him when she had had time to scrutinize the evidence.

A week later Rosemary picked up her phone to make that call."Dr. Jimenez?"

"Yes."

"This is Rosemary Silva. I'd like to talk to you about the paternity claim you've made regarding Pedro Sanchez. Is this a good time?"

"Of course. I am on my way to the jail to see Armando but I can talk first."

"Dr. Jimenez, we've done a check of your claim. I have two things to tell you. First, rather than bother Mr. Sanchez, his daughter Maria volunteered to submit to DNA testing. The results show a positive match to yours, and your paperwork also checks out positively, all indicating that Pedro Sanchez of Pine Junction is most likely your father."

She could hear the man's muffled exclamation, then the even reply. "Thank you for informing me of your conclusion, Ms. Silva. And what else did you want to tell me?"

"We want some reassurance that you'll work with Mr. Sanchez's daughters to proceed cautiously. I don't need to tell you what a stressful time this is for the family, caused by the manner in which you brought your claim to Pine Junction and certainly by the actions of your son."

To this Javier nodded, unseen by Rosemary, and then acknowledged, "Ms. Silva, I am regretting many decisions I made in the last weeks before this terrible occurrence. I understand that no amount of wishing on my part can erase the fact that a young man is lying in a hospital in a coma for weeks now, and that my son is facing criminal proceedings. Two young lives damaged severely, if not destroyed. I make no excuses, but I would like to make amends if possible. And yet, I have not given up my quest to meet my father."

Rosemary's response was business-like. "I'm hoping you have a sense of the time and challenges ahead of you and the Sanchez family to work towards reconciliation on the scale that's needed. Only then can your desired contact, much less family assimilation, happen."

"I have thought of that. At times it seems insurmountable to me, yet I cannot see going back to my life without having tried." He paused and then in a voice that sounded less sure of himself he asked, "What do you think? Do you feel the family, the sisters . . . my sisters . . . do you think they will be open to even meeting me, maybe even someday accepting me?"

There was something about this change in his normal demeanor that softened Rosemary's professional reserve and her loyalty to the Sanchez family. She took a moment to gather her thoughts before replying.

"Realize what they're dealing with. First their dad's illness, then their mom's death, followed by your arrival with shocking news and then tragedy for their beloved Mateo at the hands of your son. It's hard to absorb that it could be their nephew who has put Mateo in such a serious state, where no one at this point knows if he'll ever be the same. These are huge issues to overcome, even for the most generous of families. You must give it time."

Javier grasped at what straws he could. "Thank you for your assessment, and I do see that it makes sense. I will take whatever glimmer of hope I can find, and pray that someday I can give my apologies in person to the whole family, and that I might meet my father."

Rosemary ended the conversation by getting an agreement from Javier not to contact Pedro until further notice. Certainly there would be a restraining order against Armando once he was released. The family would meet in court, no doubt, but in the meantime all thoughts were on Mateo's wellbeing.

Before she hung up, Javier asked one more thing. "Do you think that poor young man will wake up?"

Rosemary found herself bristling, "So your son won't be convicted of manslaughter?"

Javier flinched but hung in the conversation to say, "I can see how that must look like my first concern, but no, I do want only for Mateo to have a full recovery, not just for my own conscience, or my son's legal troubles, or so I have a better chance of meeting my father. There is more. I was impressed to see how protective and attached he was to his grandfather, and I want him to live, and live well. I want him to live even if I am never in the picture again."

It was a huge admission, and he knew for the first time that it was true, a turning point in Javier Jimenez's long self-focused quest to find his father.

FORTY-ONE

JAVIER AND ARMANDO

Meanwhile, an Assault and Battery charge was made against Armando Jimenez at the arraignment, held once Armando had had his broken arm set and his other injuries assessed. It had taken some time and two attorneys to finally convince the judge to set bail because the local judge questioned whether Armando remained a threat.

Javier walked stiffly through the unfamiliar environment of the county jail where Armando had been held awaiting his bail. In the past, Javier had sat through truancy hearings and suspension meetings for his youngest son and taken more than a few phone calls from authorities, but he had never seen his son in confinement. The arraignment had been terribly unnerving, and the preliminary hearing and probable trial were looming yet in the future. The whole atmosphere in the jail dismayed Javier, and he thought how hard he had worked to not go the route that led some of his impoverished childhood friends to such harsh places. And now his son was here.

But the sense of failure Javier felt being inside the jail was topped by numbness; he was shocked by the course of events he had unwittingly unleashed. That his son had caused great bodily harm to his own cousin was an unrelenting nightmare for Javier, and his heart ached to see his son's injuries as well. The same thought kept washing through his mind: two young lives perhaps destroyed forever. And over what? Javier remained convinced that there was nothing wrong with his quest to find his father. It had started so purely, fueled by his emotional void. And Armando had been the only one who encouraged him to pursue the search. Javier had been comforted by Armando's interest. But it had all gone so wrong. Javier couldn't stop blaming himself.

He passed the security clearance, flinched as the heavy doors clanked shut behind him, and entered the room where Armando was waiting for him. Armando jumped up eagerly like a fourth grader, and then winced with his sore ribs. For a second, Javier allowed himself to remember his son as a school boy, full of excitement about everything. He and his wife had thought it would always be that way for the boy. But now Kathy was gone. Oh, how much Armando had suffered at the death of his mother. Here in this bleak jail visiting room, a smile lit up Armando's face and the young man looked like he might fall into his father's embrace, broken arm and all. Armando then stiffened, perhaps to retain his gruff facade in front of other prisoners. His arm was in a cast and his face remained bruised and swollen.

Underneath his tough exterior, Armando now knew that his father was his only fan. At this critical time, what he was receiving from his dad was unconditional love, and this made Armando's guilt over what he had done all the more acute. He could still muster up some indignation over how Pedro Sanchez had abandoned Javier all those years ago, and he could still taste the remains of the blazing rush of jealousy that had overtaken him the instance he first saw Mateo. Mateo was the chosen one, the one who had been given the kingdom. That is what had raised Armando's hatred. But now, in the aftermath, these bitter emotions lay in tatters.

From the moment he sat on the ground that dark night and looked at the unmoving body of his adversary, the anger had drained out of Armando. Now he was empty and scared. He suddenly cared very much about having a future, somewhere away from this place where the men behind bars strutted their bravado to protect their own fear. Armando had been in trouble more than a few times, but he had never been imprisoned; the reality, and the prospect of more, changed everything.

"Papa," Armando said.

"Mijo," Is all Javier could manage to reply, both reverting to Armando's childhood. Javier gave his son an awkward hug, which he could feel being received with gratitude before being pushed away.

Looking around, they found a table in the corner to sit down and talk. Javier explained that bail had finally been set and Armando would soon be able to go home with him to wait for further legal proceedings. There was also a restraining order against Armando to stay away from the Sanchez and Schumacher family members.

Armando nodded and looked around the room, before asking the question on his mind. "So, how is he?"

"Still in a coma, from what I heard from the family's attorney today." Javier added, almost to himself, "It has been so many days now."

Armando stared straight ahead and said nothing more. Javier could see the emotions washing over Armando's eyes, and a slight tremble in his lips. Otherwise, he looked stoic. He thought back to putting Armando to bed as a little child, and watching his face as he fell asleep. He sighed. There had not been enough of those bedtimes.

Armando looked at his father and asked, "What're you thinking, Papa? Tell me. And in fact, why don't you just tell me off. I know I deserve it. I've ruined my life and yours, and his too." He dropped his head so that Javier could barely hear his mumble. "What'd Mama say about me?"

"She would simply love you, Armando, of course. And what am I thinking right now? I am thinking that we are in a damn big mess but although this is a terrible place, because you are here, I wouldn't be anywhere else in the world. If you are here, then I would rather be here than on a yacht off Baja sipping champagne. I am here with you, Armando."

"How can you not be angry at me? Don't you hate me?"

"I did not say I wasn't angry at you. I did not say it will be easy to do what we have to do to rectify this mess. Yes, you screwed up badly, but I need to take responsibility for setting us up to fail. I was too eager, and I became lost in my own needs. I have not been the wise father I would like to be. So, no excuses for me, and no excuses for you. We have a long road ahead of us. I will be honest, sometimes my head spins when I try to wrap my mind around all the things we need to do."

"I really want to get out of here, Papa, but I am scared I will have to come back to prison for a long time."

"You may be back, but let's take it one day at a time. Right now the biggest wish we need to have is that Mateo recovers consciousness. And we need to hope that for his sake, but it would be better for you, too. I hired a different attorney. That first one didn't represent you very well, but this new man, Powers is his name, was able to get the judge to let you out on bail so you can get out by tonight."

Javier passed on the greetings from Armando's older brothers, neither of whom, despite Javier's pleas to them, apparently had the motivation to come north to visit their brother in jail. They had given up on their brother. Javier grew quiet. There was nothing more to say, but so much to consider. The father and son sat side by side.

The conversations of the other inmates rose louder as the visiting room filled up with visitors. The "motherfuckers" flew fast and loud across the room, and Javier looked sadly at the visiting children who didn't blink when their fathers and mothers peppered their talk with profanity. And each curse made Armando uncomfortable for his father. For the first time, he felt grateful for his father's carefully-crafted lifestyle. It had given his family more opportunities to choose their paths, and right now Armando was in great need of an opportunity.

FORTY-TWO

CATHERINE AND REX

On the evening before Dane Faber made his late night visit to the hospital, Catherine stopped by the church to see Rex before making the drive back to New York. She was grateful for her father's willingness to keep loaning her his car. In fact, her father had been exceptionally accommodating. Whether he had been impressed with the young man Mateo or just wanted his daughter to navigate through this agonizing time in her life, he was making it as easy for Catherine as possible.

"Reverend Randall. Did you leave me a message?" Catherine knocked on Rex's office. Rex was still in his office working on the Sunday order of worship and invited her in.

"Call me Rex if you'd like."

"Okay, I'll try. I have sort of a hierarchical inbred reaction to priests and preachers," Catherine confessed. "You know, I really am not churchy at all, but I am Italian and my mom is definitely religious. I grew up in Catholic schools and, well, maybe that is why I'm not religious today." She laughed a little nervously.

Rex smiled at her to help her relax, but in his mind he was wondering how many times he had heard that phrase, "I'm really not religious at all, but . . . . " He understood.

"How're you doing, Catherine? These weeks have been very trying for you. Just worrying about Mateo alone as we're doing here in Pine Junction would be hard enough, but you are going back and forth, trying to live your daily life. I hope you're taking care of yourself. Are you on your way to or from the hospital?"

Catherine sighed. "Home, back to the City. I spent two nights here with Cecilia, spending as much time in the hospital as I could, but now I need to get back. I have my final audition for Tapestry in two days, maybe the biggest audition of my life, and I hope I can concentrate enough. And then I think to myself, why does any of this matter? Shouldn't I just be sitting by Mateo's bed all the time? What kind of girlfriend am I, running back and forth? Why does my music or career matter one bit in light of his life?"

Catherine sat silently staring without seeing out the window. Rex didn't try to answer all her questions right away, knowing some were rhetorical and some were ones only she could answer. He just took a clean cup from his drawer and poured her a cup of coffee from his thermos.

"Derrick left it for me knowing I was working late tonight. Here."

Catherine took it gratefully. "I miss Mateo. He made the best coffee and brought it to me in bed." She started crying, not hysterically, but just softly and steadily, staring not at Rex, but beyond. Rex handed her the tissue box. There really were no words. They all missed Mateo, and Catherine probably the most. She had known him only a short time, but he was her present and her future.

Finally Catherine sniffed and calmed. "I don't mean to say that the only reason I miss Mateo is because he makes good coffee. You know?"

Rex nodded. "Of course I know. It is the little things that hit us hard. For instance, I still remember how my wife always removed the advertisements in the paper before she handed it to me because she knew it annoyed me to have to pull them out. Of course I could have done it myself, but it was a small act of love, and I remember it even though it comprised only a minute fraction in our long relationship, and wasn't really important at all."

Rex sat thinking of old times, and Catherine now looked right at him. "You aren't together anymore?"

"My wife died several years ago, Catherine, before I came to Pine Junction. It was a good marriage, loving and authentic, and I miss her very much."

"I'm sorry. Rex, why do these things happen? Why did Mateo and that guy get in a fight? Oh, I understand why it happened, that Mateo wanted to stop him from approaching his grandpa, but you know what I mean. Why did it happen? Why does any of the bad shit that happens anywhere happen?"

Rex laughed, but he quickly said, "Catherine, I'm not laughing at you, believe me. I'm laughing because it is such a big subject and a timeless one. And I believe you need to get on the road before it gets too late and I have a liturgy to write yet tonight. Someday you and I will have that conversation. I hate clichés and I refuse to give you any, theological or secular. For now you need to hang fast to your love for Mateo, and remember that he is surrounded by people who care for him and who sweep you up in their embrace as well. You can know that you are pursuing the music that Mateo loves and that he's proud of your talent and always hopes for your future to be strong."

He continued, "When Mateo wakes up, you'll get a phone call, probably from all of us, but I promise I'll call you right away. We'll tell him that you are making music and will come the minute you can. We'll tell him that you love him. He needs you, Catherine, and the way he needs you is to stay on the course you started and to take each day as it comes. He'll get a lot of different kinds of support from his mother, family, doctors, friends, but what he needs from you is to be yourself, strong, loving and beautiful. Don't spend too much time dwelling on the sad whys. That is my advice, although I'm more than willing to indulge you in a good theological discussion on the meaning of life and its joys and sorrows. Terrible unexplainable things happen, Catherine; I can tell you that from personal experience as well as from all the years of being a pastor. My opinion? No point wrestling with the why, unless there is a way to change things for the future. What you need is the resiliency to say, 'Okay, it happened, so how do I go on? What do I do now? I'm not alone.' But mostly, Catherine, don't lose your joy in life. Pursue joy as a tribute to Mateo. That's why you must keep making music. Do you see?"

Catherine's shoulders lost their tense scrunch. She rose, put down her coffee cup, and Rex stood up too and received a spontaneous embrace from the young woman. "Thanks. And I am so sorry that your wife died. I want to know all about her, next time, okay? Meanwhile, what was her name?"

"Beth."

Catherine nodded and softly repeated, as if in responsive prayer, "Beth."

As she walked out of the office, she stated, with no question in her tone. "I believe Mateo will wake up, and then we'll take things one step at a time."

Rex called after her, "Best of luck on your audition, or is it 'break a leg' for music auditions, too?" But she was gone, singing to herself, buzzed on the coffee as she pulled her dad's car out onto the now-familiar road home. For the first time she did not feel like she was wrenching herself away from Mateo's side as the miles grew between them.

FORTY-THREE

MARIA, OLIVIA, CECILIA

M aria pulled the lasagna out of the oven and placed it on the table. Around the table were her sisters and Rosemary. The four women made an attempt to eat, but for the most part they moved the food around on their plates and drank their wine. Maria realized it had been a long time since the sisters had sat together at a meal. In fact, she was having trouble thinking of when. In the past, family meals involved their mother and father at their family home, with Pedro and Victoria doing a well-practiced dance in the kitchen to produce yet another perfect family dinner. Their parents dominated the kitchen and their efficiency pushed the sisters out, without any words spoken.

Over their lifetime, the routine of those family meals became normal to the sisters and was also accepted over the years by their boyfriends, partners, husbands, and friends, who found the Sanchez house to be full of good music, conversation, and delicious food and drink. From the time they were young, the grandchildren also took this for granted, each finding their role in the family, Mateo by playing guitar and in animated discussions with his grandfather. Julia followed her grandmother around her garden and was the only one who found her place in the kitchen with Victoria. Before his parent's divorce, Rowan either brought friends along or kept close to his dad Warren to talk sports.

Neither Maria nor her sisters spoke aloud of their family history over this night's dinner, but they understood how those family dinners lay irrevocably in the past. Tonight there was a subdued atmosphere and no one tried to pretend that everything was okay. It clearly was not. But Cecilia did have a moment of grace where she looked around the table at the three other faces and found herself grateful that she was part of something bigger than herself. She didn't think she could bear it if she was all alone with the fear and uncertainty that boiled around her. Even Vic as a new partner in her life could not take the place of sisters, she realized, and she also realized that she had always taken Maria and Olivia for granted.

Seeing Cecilia's misty eyes, Olivia patted her hand, and Maria filled up Cecilia's wine glass, which was already fairly full. Still the gesture was comforting, and Cecilia appreciated it.

Maria gave up trying to eat, and put her fork down. "We need to talk about Mother's memorial service. Shall we just put it off indefinitely? Hold off until Mateo regains consciousness? Or just wait. . . ."

Olivia glanced at Cecilia. "I think Ceci should call it."

Maria nodded, "That's what I was thinking. But then I was with Papa the other day, and it occurred to me that he seems very spaced out, and, while that is probably to be expected, the Parkinson's symptoms seem more pronounced. I was just wondering if holding Mother's service might be a settling ritual for him. Then again, Papa is so close to Mateo that perhaps now wouldn't be the right time for the memorial service."

She shrugged. "I just think we should talk about it. This is the most traumatic time ever in our family life. While we've had a few dramas in the past, each one of us in our separate lives . . . " Maria gave a wry grimace." . . . Right now I feel we're hurting together, and I don't think I could stand to have alienation among the three of us."

Both Olivia and Cecilia nodded. Cecilia spoke, "I admit I'm completely preoccupied with Matty now. And I know you're all backing me up one hundred percent. I'm really glad because otherwise I'd be incredibly lonely. But I don't know if I could give Mother's memorial service a fair shake right now."

Finally Olivia suggested that they ask their father what he wanted to do. "We should ask him, and follow his lead. And Ceci, you might just go through the motions right now, but that's okay because we can do another service a year from now, like a one year honoring."

With that settled, Olivia and Cecilia began to eat, but Maria looked at Rosemary, who had been silent.

Maria cleared her throat and blurted out. "There's something Rosemary needs to tell us."

Three sets of eyes turned to Rosemary.

"As you know, I've been looking into Javier Jimenez's claim that your father is actually his father, too."

Cecilia felt a sick feeling in her gut, her heart reaching out back to the hospital room as if even now she needed to protect her son from the mention of the men who caused his injury.

Rosemary forced herself to go on. "It's not a frivolous claim. There's every evidence to believe that Javier Jimenez is indeed your father's son. His paperwork checks out, and . . ." she darted a look at her partner, ". . Maria did a DNA test and there's a strong link to Javier."

As the finality of what she said sank in to the sisters, there was first a silence, and then their eyes swiveled to Maria.

"Why did you do that, Maria? When? Why didn't you tell us?"

"How much can be told from a sibling's DNA anyway?"

"How will we talk to Papa about this?"

"Did Papa have any idea about this?"

And, finally, Cecilia said the thought that no one wanted to touch. "This means, of course, that Mr. Jimenez is our brother, our half-brother. And that monster is our nephew, Mateo's cousin even."

"It makes me feel sick." Maria spoke from her gut.

After an hour of venting their various reactions, the four women moved from the table to lay on the sofa and easy chairs in Maria's book-lined living room.

"I didn't mean to call that other young man a monster."

"Well, it's understandable, Ceci. He hurt your son. Now he'll go on trial, yes, and maybe face prison, but at least he's walking around."

"Thanks for your back-up, Livia," Cecilia covered her face with her hands. "But you know, I've been thinking and thinking, and in fact that's all I do at night. Instead of sleeping, I think and think and think."

"Honey, you've been doing that all your life. " Maria put her arms around Cecilia's shoulders to lighten her words. "How about Vic. Helping any?"

The whole town knew about Vic and Cecilia within a matter of days, but the staggering astonishment of this news, which would normally have been discussed with great delight all over town, had been over-shadowed by the more momentous reality of Mateo's battered condition. Even the sisters had not had time to dwell on Cecilia's new relationship.

Cecelia blushed a little, but replied honestly, "I don't know what I would do without him, and the physical connection really helps. Still, I spend way too many hours thinking, and fretting, and now, with Mateo in the hospital, agonizing.

"But like I was saying, I've been thinking about Armando. I need to use his name, because otherwise I see him as a monster. And I'm thinking that it's just like in Iraq. By demonizing the enemy it's easier to hate them. And, of course, Armando - see I can say his name - is the enemy, right? He hurt my son. He hurt our Matty. At first I could have killed him with my bare hands. I have to admit that, so it's good that he was in custody. Honestly. I'm not proud of that thought, but that's what I was feeling. And now I ask myself, in my darkest moments, will Mateo wake up? Will he be normal if and when he does wake up? And then I hate that boy Armando all the more."

She paused.

"But you see, I know what that gets me, when I feel that way: angry and angrier. I want justice. No, I find myself wanting more than justice, I want blood. Then I feel so unbelievably churned up inside that I can't go and sit with Mateo and channel love and healing to him, to draw him back into our world. I can't help but feel that my own culpability is also at fault here. My own secrets. And now we find that Papa had a secret too. And we know that Mother kept her sickness secret, for whatever reason."

And here Cecilia paused a moment, guiltily remembering that she had yet to share with her sisters her knowledge of her mother's journals, nor had she opened up her secret about Dane Faber. There would be a good time soon, surely. For now she simply did not have the energy. She was too drained to formulate the words or engage in follow-up questions. She gathered her thoughts. "I suppose we all have good and bad reasons to keep secrets, but in the end, they hurt us. I'm learning that the hard way."

Cecilia took a shuddering breath before going on. The other three women felt the sand shifting but the rock beneath holding firm.

"I can't sit by Matty's bedside and hold these angry thoughts about Armando Jimenez, nor his father. It's impossible to be present for Mateo when I have so much hatred in my heart. I keep thinking I should be able to do both, be a strong champion for my son and still keep the fire of hatred in my heart for the one who hurt him. But I can't. Two incompatible states."

They sat awhile longer absorbing Cecilia's words. Finally Olivia mused aloud. "I haven't said anything because it sounded so flakey and I thought I was getting overly emotional given all that has happened. But when I'm in the hospital room with Mateo, I keep feeling this sense of serenity or . . . . " She fished for the right word to finish her thought.

Maria tried to help. "Tranquility? Strength?"

"Maybe the word is compassion," offered Cecilia. "I feel it myself, and it's soothing the Mother Tiger in me. Of course those first days I was enraged and that was because I was really scared. And I don't know why I don't feel quite so scared now. There's every reason to be. But somehow it seems that Mateo's helping me. He's trying to help me, the old worry wart."

"I'm exhausted," Maria finally interjected. "We have a plan." She looked at her sisters kindly, but ever the eldest, she went on. "We'll talk to Papa about whether he wants Mother's memorial service now or later. And we have Javier

Jimenez's news to further absorb, which isn't going to happen overnight. Plus we need to figure out how and when to let Papa know about Javier. And Ceci, you and Mateo, and Rowan too, bless his heart, have our love and support. Let's talk tomorrow after work, but for now, I have a class to teach tomorrow morning and Rosemary has about ten appointments before noon, so we are going to either kick you two out or get out the blankets. What'll it be? Stay or go?"

PART THREE

Surfacing

FORTY-FOUR

Cecilia arrived early at the hospital room, greeting Rowan with a kiss. He looked exactly as if he had spent the night in the chair next to a bed. Yet because he was young, or perhaps because something more subtle had come over her youngest son, Cecilia thought Rowan looked adorably handsome and content. At some point Cecilia wanted to give her youngest son more thought, but for now, she was just thankful to have him around. He had not yet shared with her anything about his job status, and she vaguely wondered how he could spend so much time away from work. But in light of Mateo's life-and-death quagmire, she never pressed the subject with Rowan. Now she just tousled Rowan's hair and asked about the night.

"No visitors, but I got a couple calls from some of Mateo's friends, and another text from his work. They had to hire someone else to fill in for him since he's been gone so long, but his boss will give Mateo his job back when he gets better."

Rowan spoke with great confidence, which Cecilia appreciated. Sometimes, just for a few moments, she wanted to be twenty-five again, just for the sheer optimism she thought she remembered in her early twenties. But then again, she could immediately recall her own great doubts and the confusing issues of her twenties. Shuddering, she put that thought away.

"Okay, love, go get some sleep. There is leftover lasagna in the fridge from Auntie Maria. I won't bother you with phone calls unless there is something important. And if you want to take tonight off, Julia and Olivia volunteered to spend the night. Olivia doesn't have to teach tomorrow."

"I'll see. I'm hungry, so the lasagna will taste great for breakfast."

When he left, Cecilia carefully straightened out Mateo's sheets, and gently brushed his hair. She kissed his forehead, then straightened up the hospital tray table, amazed that, even in a coma, her son could have a messy room. As she tucked some items into the hanging garbage bag, her eyes spotted a small card on the floor. She started to drop it in the garbage and then stopped when she saw the logo on the business card. It took her another couple of seconds before she could bring herself to turn it over and read what was hand printed on the back.

He had been here. There was no other explanation. No one else she knew would be carrying business cards from the Franklin Club.

She read the note three times and then ran out into the hallway hoping to find Henry or one of her other favorite nurses or even Dr. Patel, the neurologist. Often he started his rounds early. She did not find the doctor but asked the nursing station to request that he come to Mateo's room as soon as he arrived. As she headed back to Mateo's room she spotted Henry starting his morning shift.

"Henry!"

He whirled around, caught off guard by her wild eyes. "Good morning Mrs. Schumacher. Can I help you?"

Cecilia looked at his steady eyes for a moment, not sure what to say. Finally she blurted out. "Mateo, Mateo opened his eyes last night, and he smiled at someone."

Henry looked at her and then drew her into Mateo's room. "Did Rowan see something?" he asked.

"No, and I don't get it. Rowan said there were no visitors last night, but, but, well look . . . . " She pushed the card in front of Henry and he read the unsigned message written in neat capital printing on the back of the card.

"Who wrote this? Where did this note come from?"

"I found it on the floor, was going to throw it away, and then I read it." She stared at Henry. "Oh dear, Henry, I know you have a million things to do here at the beginning of your shift. I shouldn't take your time."

"Who wrote this note, Mrs. Schumacher?"

"I know who wrote it. I do. But I cannot believe he was here, and that Rowan didn't see him. And I didn't think visitors could come in the hospital in the middle of the night."

She continued, "But the really important thing is what it says. Do you think it could be true? Do you think Mateo woke up? Mateo doesn't seem any different this morning from yesterday, but no one would play a horrible trick on us like this. He wouldn't do that, nobody would."

Cecilia grabbed Mateo's hand and urgently called his name.

Henry was a little confused over who "he" was but realized he was not going to get a name out of Mateo's mother at this point, either because she didn't want to tell or because she was so flustered she couldn't answer his question. So he walked over to Mateo's bedside and checked his vital signs, all the while observing him closely. Cecilia hovered from the other side of the bed.

As Henry worked, pulse, blood pressure, changing an IV bag, starting his exercises, Cecilia thought he worked more roughly, with a little stronger touch this morning than she had observed before. All the while the nurse talked to Mateo in a conversational voice and began humming a song, popular about ten years ago, the name of which escaped her. It crossed her mind that Henry and Mateo had been in high school around the same time.

Cecilia watched her son's face intently and gave out a loud gasp, "Mateo!" Henry looked at Cecilia and then back at Mateo. They had both seen his eyes twitch and flutter. Cecilia held her breath and Henry continued his ministrations with his sure hands and his voice continued to hum the song.

In that moment Cecilia saw the miracle she had prayed for. Mateo's eyes opened and he looked at her, working to focus, but she felt a moment of connection. Then Mateo flicked his gaze over to Henry, and Mateo smiled his familiar grin.

He smiled.

Henry kept singing the old song, almost bawdy-like now, and the smile stayed on Mateo's face. And it was at that moment that Dr. Patel walked into the room.

What a sight he saw. Cecilia Schumacher stood perfectly silent as she watched her son's face, her body shaking and her hands both clutching Mateo's hand. Before the doctor's eyes, she dropped over the bed, resting her head on Mateo's shoulder. Henry, with his long black hair tied into a braid, was massaging Dr. Patel's comatose young patient, all the while singing an old pop song which Dr. Patel vaguely remembered. It really was a stupid song, as Dr. Patel recalled, and it sounded even more ridiculous coming from the mouth of the normally serious Henry. Yet there was no denying that Mateo was looking over his mother's head, straight at Henry and grinning a lopsided smile.

"And to think," Dr. Patel said to himself, "that I almost called in sick today. I wouldn't have missed this for the world."

FORTY-FIVE

For several days now, Mateo had been paddling just below the line where the sky and the water met. It was a beautiful place to be, like snorkeling where one is buoyant and feeling both the cool water and the light of the sun. Always under the water, but looking up more and more.

He was not putting sensations into words at this point, no need. But it was a warm and comfortable place. He felt his body like he had not before when his existence was all about dreams. Now he felt his body from toes to fingers. He felt the water in his hair, long, much longer than he had ever grown it before; it was floating out behind him. His stomach was tickled by the underwater grasses and his back by ripples of the gentle waves. Creatures swam near him, keeping him company, sometimes brushing his legs or arms, but he had difficulty knowing what they were. It was not important; he admired their beautiful colors and felt the warm sunshine from above. He was drifting in and out of awareness, but every time he awoke, the lovely rocking of the water and the warm sunshine kept him secure and peaceful.

It had not always been that way. Before this time, he had been caught in raging waters, surging waves, where his vision was obscured, as he was tumbled roughly from side to side, and even upside down, head over heels. Loud noises hurt his ears, but the sounds made no sense to him. He had not been able to rest when embroiled in such turmoil, rammed this way and that. He felt pain as a backdrop, and had to swim as powerfully as he could to escape that turbulent undertow. It had taken all his strength, and, suspended in timelessness, he barely remembered it all. Only vague snippets.

It was much better now, so peaceful. While his existence was still a blur, it was tranquil, and he found himself looking up at the sunlight more often. He did not have awareness of words or speaking. But, oh, he could see such color, such light. And he was beginning to hear sounds infiltrating the water. Some sounds were like a dull rolling from above. But sometimes the sound was dancing like the colors, together in motion, the colors and the sound together, and it pleased him, and he wanted more. When it stopped he sunk down a little lower into the water to rest, suspended but with his head upward to the sunlight, and just below the surface now.

When the sound and the color began dancing again, this time he was so close to the surface that he was almost blinded by the light. Why was it so bright? He didn't know that he had opened his eyes. Before, open or closed had not mattered, he saw the same. But now his eyes came open and the light was blinding. He looked longer. He saw familiar.

He saw color. Then he heard the color-sound dance again and his eyes moved to the source. There he saw where the sound came from. And the sound was familiar again. It was a happy sound. Something deep inside made a connection. He smiled. He could feel that he was smiling. He was aware of familiar.

He was back, at least for the moment. He went back and forth for a while, needing to retreat to his lovely undersea world for spells of rest. But he never went deeply down again, and he came up more and more to breathe air, which he now knew he needed. He saw more familiar. He did not know the words. He was silent for a very long time. But he was connecting the pieces slowly, one by one. In the meantime, the air felt good to breathe, and more and more pieces were fitting together. The music was happy. Soon he began to move, or at least be aware that he was moving his real body. It hurt, but it seemed to be familiar, and he longed for the familiar.

FORTY-SIX

To Cecilia now, time rushed like a wild fire; like a flame fanned by wind, the news of Mateo's awakening spread from the hospital across Pine Junction, and of course to Catherine in her music room in New York. Whereas the three weeks of Mateo's coma had seemed endless to his mother, now life seemed to speed up almost faster than she could fathom.

First, Dr. Patel met with the family. Excited himself about his young patient's awakening, he also wanted to caution the family about what this new reality might look like. He knew he needed to keep them from having their hopes dashed if Mateo's recovery was not instantaneous and complete, but at the same time their positive energy would be essential for Mateo as he regained consciousness.

If he maintained consciousness, the doctor reminded himself, as well as Cecilia and the rest of the family. They had finally pulled themselves from Mateo's room, leaving him in the hands of the nurses, and moved to a small visitor room down the hall. The doctor explained that while he had always expected that Mateo had a great chance of regaining consciousness, it was possible that what they had just seen might be a momentary recovery and his condition might not progress any further. And although he predicted most if not all skills would come back to Mateo, they still needed to know that they would have a lot to contend with.

"First of all, Mateo's body has been lying there for three weeks and it's astonishing how much strength can be lost in three short weeks of inactivity. I'm sure you have noticed that he is not as muscular as he was, and he's lost weight. Then we need to consider his sense of equilibrium. He'll need to learn to walk again. While we've done brain scans, we still have to learn if he has any other impairment from the head injury."

He looked around the group to see if they were following what he was saying. Except for Cecilia, who looked only half-present, the rest were carefully listening and some were taking notes.

"So there'll be physical challenges to overcome. But he is young and healthy, so my hope is that it is only a matter of time and practice."

"We also don't know what might happen with speech. So far this morning we have not heard him say anything. He also hasn't talked during his coma. Some patients shout gibberish, and some speak normally but without recognition. Mateo may have to learn to speak again. The speech pathologists will work with him in rehab, but you all can be very helpful to him. You need to know that he may become agitated and upset if he cannot communicate verbally as he did before. Was he a good conversationalist before the injury?"

The group gave a collective smile, as someone answered, "He certainly was!"

"Finally, we don't know if there has been other brain damage. Our scans look very encouraging, but he may have short term memory loss, or other memory loss or learning disability that may be temporary, or it may be long term, even permanent. Progress can almost always be achieved through therapy. But I must explain to you all that we don't know what to expect. Mateo may have frustrations, anger, and even personality changes."

The doctor looked around at the faces in the room. They looked deflated, not the thrilled folks who had entered the room ten minutes earlier, delirious with the news that Mateo had smiled and made eye contact.

"I apologize, but I need to prepare you that waking up from a coma is not like it is portrayed in the movies. You are not going to walk back into Mateo's room now and see him jump up and grab his guitar and play you the new song he wrote while he was in his coma."

The room remained silent, and Dr. Patel, feeling like he had certainly let the wind out of the collective sails, stood up and finished his comments.

"Now that I have prepared you for the worst, I want you all to put what I have said at the back of your minds to give you patience for the next part of the journey. Okay? But gather your energy so you can start your positive thinking and be open to how you can help Mateo, and his mother here." He nodded at Cecilia, who managed a weak smile. "And be creative in planning how you can serve as his community to help him take the steps he needs towards independence."

He shook Cecilia's hands, Rowan's, and on around the room, before opening the door and leaving. After the doctor left, they sat talking, except for Rowan, who restlessly needed to move. He and Julia left and began walking up and down the hallway. Rex had abruptly left a meeting at the church when he got the call, remembering to call Catherine as he had promised, although cautioning her to stay put until they had more news. She was heading into her final audition and Rex could only hope that she would not be too distracted.

Cecilia sat silently, hands clasping and unclasping in her lap. Vic came over and took her hand in his, but found a crumpled card in her sweaty palm. He asked if he could throw it away for her, starting to pull it out of her grip, but her sharp "No" caused everyone to stop talking and look at her.

Vic felt like he had been punched and backed away, causing Cecilia to grasp at him to pull him back towards her. "I'm sorry. I'm so sorry." Breathing was about the best she could manage. Just one breath in and another one out. Sometimes the one coming in her lungs was slow to come and the inhalation was jerky and her chest convulsed with a hiccup. No one in the room knew what to do. She opened her lips several times, but it was useless. She was voiceless.

Minutes passed. Her sisters figured it was the stress of all that happened that had rendered their sister mute, and it was no wonder, they thought, especially with the cautionary information they had just heard from the neurologist. Surely he could have picked a better time to dump all that negativity upon them.

Vic unloosened Cecilia's fingers from where they gripped his arm, and fetched her a drink of water. Cecilia swallowed, choking some, but it seemed to clear her head, and finally loosen her voice.

"Sorry. Vic. Everyone."

She looked at the faces around her, taking in their concern and puzzlement. Her shoulders firmed.

"There's something I need to share with you all, and I will soon. Please trust me, as crazy as this sounds. But now, it's all about Mateo. Dr. Patel was honest with us. He had to be. It took my excitement and dashed it around a bit, but that's my son in there, and I intend to see him through this and on to the other side. Mateo looked at me. I saw him smile."

She took another gulp of water from the flimsy paper cup. "You cannot imagine how much I appreciate everyone sticking with us."

Her thoughts went to Pedro. "How about Papa? I hate to get his hopes up too high."

"He needs something, Ceci." Olivia insisted. "I'll drive over to see Papa on my way back to school. I'll tell him that Mateo opened his eyes and smiled, and while we aren't sure what it means, it is our first positive sign. Just like all of us, Papa needs something to hold on to."

Rex laughed. "I went to see Pedro yesterday and he was as optimistic as Catherine and Rowan and Julia. Maybe the young and the old can share that kind of faith. He was making plans to take Mateo on a trip with him. Didn't tell me where, but he seemed quite resolute. In fact, he seemed as strong as I have seen him since your mother passed away."

FORTY-SEVEN

Rehabilitation therapy now became the focus of Mateo's life. The high drama in his life had happened in just a few minutes out behind Pine Crest Village. By comparison, these focused and hard-working weeks of rehab were not a colorful or dramatic story when viewed step by step. But the rehabilitation process, as Mateo and all those around him would later relate, was transformative on many levels. Being thrust into an unwanted circumstance and finding himself having to play by completely new parameters radically altered life patterns.

The family held Victoria's memorial service after Mateo was able to walk, slowly but independently, down the church aisle and sit between his grandfather and brother. Pedro looked stronger than he had in months. Vic played organ along with Catherine on the cello as she had promised, filling the church with the glorious music that Victoria had loved. The sisters spent the service and the reception focusing on their mother for the first time in weeks. In his memorial homily, Rex did his best to guide them all to recognize the extraordinary woman

Victoria had been and her enormous contribution to her family, her community, her teaching, and to the church. He also tried to illustrate the many layers of her complex life. Rex had admired Victoria a great deal, sternness and all, and he hoped to help her family to see her in a positive light, with good memories and high regard for their strong maternal heritage.

Present in the back of the church, slipping in almost unnoticed and leaving before the reception, was Warren Schumacher. He had been fond of Cecilia's mother and saw in her a pragmatic and dignified character. It was a style of living that he admired. He also wanted to get a look at his sons. He had kept a distance, only visiting the hospital for brief checks on Mateo's progress.

Rowan moved his things back into his mother's home, took over his old childhood bedroom, and spent his time helping his brother with rehab and exercises. In most people's eyes, this change in Rowan Schumacher was as miraculous as Mateo's recovery. But neither Cecilia nor Mateo, nor Rowan himself, spent much time being dumbfounded. It just was. As Rowan said, "Hey, I don't have a job right now anyway, so why don't I help out?" And it allowed Cecilia to finally get back to her library work. Surrounded by her familiar stacks of books, the sight and smell of her library served as a great healer for her. Her relationship with Vic continued to evolve at a gentle pace around the demands of work and caretaking, and it seemed to both of them that they had been intimate companions for as long as they could remember.

No one had yet talked to Pedro about Javier. After they absorbed the startling news that they had a half-brother, what had horrified Pedro's daughters the most had been the possibility that their father had known of Javier's birth, rejected his son, and walked away from his responsibilities. That was contrary to Pedro's character and they all hoped that Pedro had never known of Celina Jimenez's pregnancy.

Of course they should tell him, but it was not a simple matter to the sisters. Pedro was aging and in ill health. It felt disrespectful not to tell him immediately, but what would happen when he learned? He might bluff and deny, or be crushed and have his health degenerate further. Or, if he would want to meet Javier, and then at some point Pedro would need to find out about Armando's assault being the cause of Mateo's injury. When his daughters discussed what to do they found they were unable to come to consensus about how and when to finally lay out to their father the story of Javier Jimenez. For better or worse, at least for now they opted to protect their father.

Javier was very preoccupied. He was preparing for Armando's trial and resuming his own work. He honored his agreement to keep his distance from the family for a period of time. So he did not for the moment press his wish to meet his father. He worried a great deal that he might lose his chance if Pedro should pass away, but he could see no positive outcome from pushing.

Pedro was so wrapped up in Mateo's progress that he thought of little else. Mateo, Mateo, Mateo. That was his concern. Pedro had never sold Rowan short, as Victoria had done in her exasperation over the years. So once he left the hospital, Mateo found himself doing his rehabilitation with the doting support of his grandfather and the capable care of his brother. Rowan acted as therapist with drills and exercises. Pedro, brought over from his apartment, contentedly watched from the sideline. And on most days there could not have been a better environment in which to mend. Mateo understood how fortunate he was.

There were days, though, when Mateo felt so frustrated with his limitations that he lashed out at his new saint of a brother, and even at his beloved grandfather for whom he had been willing to give his life. On those bad days, Rowan quietly thanked Dr. Patel for warning them that this could happen. He would then leave Mateo alone for a while, and get Catherine on the phone if he could track her down. Or he would ask Henry to drop by the house. Somehow talking to Catherine or Henry would always restore Mateo's good humor. Rex Randall's calm presence was also soothing to Mateo.

Catherine had made the cut in her audition for the Tapestry. It was the culmination of years of discipline to see her passion so rewarded. It agonized Catherine to reach her dream on the very same night that Mateo re-entered consciousness. What would a good girlfriend do? Drop everything and rush to the side of her man and help him get through the stages of reentry, learning to walk, talk, and remember again? At times Catherine wanted to drop it all.

She felt guilt pressing down on her. But she knew something inside of her would die if she made that choice. Her light would become dim. Then within her mind, a voice would lecture her and say that she would rediscover a new kind of light, a new sense of purpose far more noble than playing the cello in the noted string quartet. She felt that she could rationalize either choice, debate it as if in court, defend either decision.

Soon after his reawakening, while she was agonizing over this, Catherine visited Mateo. He was not speaking much at that time, a strange thing to witness, given how easily they had conversed. Catherine watched Mateo working with his physical therapist and he was clearly making good progress, regaining balance, motor memory and strength. Even though his speech therapist told him what quick progress he was making in regaining his language skills, it was not fast enough for Mateo, and he was embarrassed for his girlfriend to witness his verbal and memory stumbles.

Now his therapy was over for the day. They sat next to each other on a sofa at the rehab hospital where he was spending a few weeks. No one else was there. Rowan had gone. Cecilia was at work. Mateo asked Catherine to tell him about the audition and her new life in Tapestry. Catherine began slowly, trying to downplay the whole process of her hopes, her nervousness. She did not mention her exhaustion in preparing for the biggest audition of her career while driving back and forth to visit Mateo as he lay in a coma.

Catherine soon forgot her caution and found she wanted to share with Mateo all the joys of this musical opportunity as well as all the fears about a crushing rejection. And she sparkled as she spoke of how it felt to get the professional acceptance from the renowned musicians. She talked on about the music they would be performing, the concert dates, the travel opportunities. As she was eloquently explaining the fine details of a new piece she was practicing, she suddenly stopped.

Mateo was watching her with bright eyes but she began to backtrack and tone down her exuberant voice until Mateo stopped her.

"Catherine, this is amazing. I'm proud of you."

He went on deliberately. "You must do it."

Catherine made an attempt to placate the voice in her head that told her to do her duty and not be selfish. "Oh, Matty, I could wait to audition for another group in a year or so and be available to help you." She was proud that she could make that sentence come out of her mouth, given what it would cost her.

But Mateo was shaking his head violently. "No. No. No. Catherine this is your . . . your . . . time," he finally said, not being able to find the word he wanted.

Catherine began to cry. "But I love you. I want to help you get back to your old self. And I would be a terrible person not to devote myself to your care." Then the very words that had been running through her mind for days now. "I feel like I'm abandoning you."

Mateo smiled and said, slowly. "I love you too. Hey, look around, I have lots of help." He squeezed her hand. "If I need you for this work, I'll call you to come and get me." He laughed. "What I want, for us, is for you to make your music. That's what will make me happy. Okay, babe?"

She managed a nod. It was never easy for Catherine in the months to come. But when she dropped into the notes in front of her and placed her bow on the strings, she did it for both of them.

FORTY-EIGHT

When people asked Mateo what the whole experience of being in a coma had been like for him, he found himself tongue-tied, and somewhat violated. It was so private, so hard to explain, so complicated to him. So on this subject, Mateo closed down. Consequently his friends and family learned to only deal with the task at hand each day. Mateo did not remember the actual attack and the moment he suffered his concussion.

Cecilia was suspended in time, suspended in her layers of issues. When should they introduce Pedro to his son Javier? And how should they introduce Armando to Pedro and have her poor Papa learn: one, that he had a son, two, that he had an additional grandson (actually three), and, finally, that this new grandson had assaulted his adored grandson Mateo? How do you take on such a task? Fretting about all of this allowed her to push aside what to do about Dane Faber, and when and what to tell Mateo. She didn't know if she was letting the days go by as a necessary act of patience or whether it was a coward's act of avoidance. Cecilia did not want to get back into the pattern of keeping secrets, but the habit was hard to break.

In his ignorance, Pedro seemed most engaged in the afternoons when he could sit around with Rowan and Mateo, watching the exercises and exchanges between the two brothers. By contrast, Pedro seemed a little lost in a larger crowd. He found these days that when he tried to grasp the enormity of all that happened recently that he felt slow and old. But when he dealt with one aspect of his life at a time, he felt more energized. Rowan and Mateo became his life right now, and he threw his thinking into them, abandoning many of his former interests. He felt confident that when Mateo was back to his former condition, his dream of a trip to Arizona with his grandson would happen. While the details of this trip were entirely missing in his vision, the trip itself had become his guiding light.

Rowan saw the emotions going through Mateo's day in ever-changing colors: struggle, confusion, but also wonder and delight. Rowan had a quiet confidence, and Mateo was able to rely on Rowan as he could never have relied on anyone else. Mateo would have beaten himself up at what he was doing to Catherine's career if she had sacrificed it for his immediate care. He would have chafed under the loving care of his mother because it would have been so complex. No one else could do what Rowan was doing and do it with the clarity and lack of complication. Rowan's care for his brother was the perfect mix of detachment and connection.

For his part, Rowan had never enjoyed himself so much in his life. It was not that he was happy for Mateo's predicament. It was more that for the first time Rowan felt needed, and felt that he was discovering new skills and satisfaction every day. He didn't yet know what this meant for his future. In fact, he didn't spend much time worrying about his future. Mateo gently ribbed him one day about what a good Zen practitioner Rowan was becoming. The former young mover and shaker considered this, agreeing that he was living his life very differently these days, giving up his job and his apartment.

Mateo told him. "Seems like you and I both have our lives all screwed up. I'm glad for your company. Let's figure out what is next for both of us once I get back to normal."

Quickly, Mateo scoffed at himself, "Normal, whatever that might be."

Rowan rolled his eyes in agreement.

For the time being that seemed to be enough said, enough understanding between the two brothers.

Early on, Mateo had periods when he would be back in that underwater place. While it would be some time before Mateo could describe this vision to even Rowan or his therapist, Rowan knew that, wherever it was that Mateo went, it was sometimes a good place and sometimes a place of struggle. A number of times Mateo had partially awakened in the middle of the night, shouting. Rowan always got up and checked on him, but rarely did more than let himself be seen, which seemed to help the troubling dreams dissipate. Mateo never said anything in the morning, and Rowan, for the time being, kept it to himself.

One night when Mateo woke up in the middle of the night, he felt close to knowing something. Something important. He got up from his bed, and this smooth mobility to get up without effort was not a skill he took for granted yet. He urinated a long splashing pee, and then, still puzzled by what he could not quite nail down, he went down the hall and knocked on Rowan's door.

"Rowan."

A long silence was followed by a sleepy, "Hey bro, what's up?"

"I need some help."

Rowan came to the door pulling on his tee shirt, looking more awake than he had sounded. "Yeah?"

"There is something that I cannot quite . . . " his voice drifted away, leaving his sentence undone as his mind wrestled with whatever it was.

Rowan looked at him and motioned down the hall to the stairs. "Can I make you some coffee?"

"Sure." Mateo was so preoccupied that he didn't even make a joke about the quality of Rowan's coffee-making.

Sitting in the living room, sunk into the facing sofas, the silence of the night was interrupted only by the little hums of the refrigerator and the clicking of the old fashioned clock Cecilia had brought from her childhood home. Rowan looked at Mateo's face. He was distant and then he was present, back and forth. Rowan was used to this, but tonight something seemed to be especially troubling his brother.

"Something bad happened," is how Mateo finally began. "Well, of course something bad happened," he responded to himself. "I was unconscious, so something bad happened. Duh. But I haven't known what happened, why I hit my head, but I'm feeling like it wasn't just that I fell down and hit my head."

He looked straight at Rowan. "You know, don't you?"

"Sure."

"You going to tell me?"

"Whenever you feel ready."

"Why shouldn't I know? After all it's my life."

"Well, frankly, do you realize that you have never asked?" He watched Mateo carefully and then continued, "We figured that you would let us know when you were ready"

"Of course I want to know!"

"Is this the right time?"

Mateo was breathing hard. He stared at Rowan with a fierceness that Rowan understood was about Mateo's need to figure things out, rather than anger directed at him.

Mateo nodded. "Something is in my dreams, but I just cannot see it. I think it's what I need to know, but I need some help."

"Mateo, do you remember meeting Armando and Javier Jimenez, and do you remember who they are?"

Mateo's stare became even more concentrated. He was looking at his brother, but he was also looking inward to his jumbled memory. Finally Mateo said, in a quiet voice, "I do, now. But, Rowan can you say it, just so I can know I'm correct? I feel so confused."

"Yeah. Javier Jimenez is a math professor from New Mexico. He came to town and shocked everyone by claiming that he is Grandpa Pedro's son. And he brought his own son with him, that's Armando. Mr. Jimenez is a really controlled sort of guy but Armando is a hot-head. Got a real anger issue, for whatever reason. Well, turns out it's true. This guy really is our grandpa's son from his old home town, right after World War II, right before Grandpa came to Pine Junction. No one knew about it, we think maybe not even Grandpa himself. No one has told Grandpa about it yet because of what happened next. Before we knew if any of this was true, Armando decided to go and confront Grandpa Pedro himself. When you got wind of this, you went crazy yourself to protect Grandpa. You went tearing over to the Pine Crest. Julia was with you. Armando jumped you out behind the apartment, and you . . . "

" . . . got in a fight. Oh yes, I remember now. We rolled on the ground. I fought him, Rowan. I've never done anything like that in my life. God, where did that come from? He was really strong, quick, but I think I hung in there pretty good. Then, nothing." He looked at Rowan. "Is that when I hit my head?"

Rowan nodded. "Yeah. Armando threw you down on some cement. Julia saw it happen when she caught up with you, but it was pretty dark. It all happened so quickly."

Mateo absorbed this all, mixing memory with sensation with new information. "Happened so quickly," he repeated, "and then everything changed." He was quiet. "Grand Pedro. A son? So bizarre."

He sat forward now, burying his head in his hands. Rowan didn't say anything, just sat across from him. The house was very still. Finally Mateo looked up. "I remember it now. I remember them showing up at Grand Pedro's place. And I remember how I felt inside. I was seething."

Mateo looked at his younger brother, almost beseeching him to understand. "Rowan, have you ever been so angry that your whole body shakes? You're so full of rage that you cannot control yourself, can't think?"

Rowan just laughed. "I have my stories." But he didn't elaborate.

After a moment, Rowan continued, "Armando jumped you. You guys struggled for awhile. You got knocked out. His arm and nose were broken in the fight. He's been charged with Assault and Battery because he put your life in danger. There'll be a trial but I'm not clear on whether you will have to give testimony or not, but don't worry about that now because it is months away. Javier Jimenez is temporarily staying away from the family, but wants to pursue his quest to meet Grandpa Pedro. This is a lot of information for one night. How ya doing? This could take awhile to sink in and for you to figure out how you'll live with it."

Rowan added. "Hope it was a good thing for me to tell you all this, and not leave it to your doc or even to Mom."

"No, you're the right one. That is why I woke you up in the middle of the night. Didn't want anyone else to help me figure it out. It's all making sense to me now. How could I have forgotten?"

"It's called traumatic brain injury, Mateo. You could've easily not remembered anything at all, ever. Like amnesia or worse. You could have even . . . "

"Died. Yeah, say it Rowan. I know everyone is thinking that. I see it in Mom's eyes even though she has been great about not smothering me. She's trying so hard. Sometimes I can feel it from Catherine, too. It's not pity I see from her, but a scared sort of look. And that kind of makes me scared. But I don't get that from you. Thanks, you know . . . for . . . for . . . I guess just for being here and not being weird about it all."

"Well, I can't tell you I wasn't afraid too when you were so out of it. I mean, you scared the shit out of us. But, somehow, I always felt so at ease in the hospital room, like I was just hanging out with my brother. Felt natural for reasons I can't explain in a million years, and when you woke up I wasn't surprised, and whatever it's taking to get you back to speed, no problem. Seems so natural. But still, I hope this news isn't going to freak you out or make you too angry."

"For the moment it's just a relief to have the pieces put together. It's all been so mysterious in my mind, like something really important was missing. I just feel relief, but, in case I start to go ballistic, I'll find you first and let you tackle me before someone else does. This Armando

guy, you say I broke his arm? Maybe I have some gump-
tion in me after all," Mateo laughed.

Rowan yawned hugely, and stood up. "Hey, even the
coffee is not doing it. Let's get some sleep. We can talk
about this some more in the morning, and if you get
even the slightest flash of anger, let me help you work it
through, or you can punch me before you go out and get
hurt again!"

FORTY-NINE

Maria found herself drawn to Pine Junction in those weeks after Mateo's awakening. She felt a sense of assurance when she could see her niece and nephews, see her sisters, check in with her father. It had become important to her; it was an urge that came from inside her heart, not a duty-driven task. One day in the cool early autumn, midday between her classes, she jumped in her car and drove to Cecilia's home. After finding no one at the door or in the house, Maria walked around the house into the back garden, and there she gave an involuntary cry. Her sister was on her knees, head down nestling into her arms on a large rock. Cecilia looked up when she heard Maria, and her smile immediately calmed Maria, who walked over to where her sister crouched.

"Tell me there is a good explanation for this scene," Maria laughed.

"Yes, I suppose once again I look a little touched, eh?" Cecilia gave an opened-hearted laugh that was contagious, and Maria joined in although she had no idea what was so funny.

"I was trying to get this rock up nearer the house, but it's heavier than I thought. I was just resting before giving it another heave."

"How far have you been rolling this thing?" Maria looked around the yard in wonderment.

"Back of that far tree is where I discovered it. Didn't think it would be such a task to move it."

"I'll help you, but may I ask why you are doing this?"

"Sure, it's to complete my shrine."

Maria shook her head. "I'm still in the dark, Ceci. What shrine? And why this rock? This thing is huge. Don't you have a wheelbarrow, or, better yet, a dolly?"

Cecilia laughed with delight. "A wheel barrow! What a great idea. I guess that is why we have older sisters. I never thought of that. Let me wheel it out."

The wheelbarrow was produced and Maria knelt down with Cecilia, glad she was wearing her dark pants and not her linen suit today, and together they were able to roll the stone into the wheelbarrow, and then, with great mutual effort, tilt it upright. As Cecilia pushed the wheelbarrow closer to the house she explained what she had been doing.

"I came home to meet the furnace man. I didn't want Rowan and Mateo to have to deal with him since they have a therapy appointment today. While I was waiting for the guy to arrive, I was walking around the house looking at the garden and saw my shrine. I realized that, with all that has happened, I had not visited it or kept it up since Mother died."

"Wait a minute, Ceci. Tell me about your shrine."

Cecilia and Maria lowered the wheelbarrow lip down in front of a large pile of stones that sat in front of a carved wooden statue of Saint Francis of Assisi and a concrete garden Buddha. A candle sat between the two saints, burnt past usefulness, its saucer flooded with rain water. Leaves covered the whole array, with some dried and drooping flowers in a brightly painted vase. Clearly the shrine had not been tended for some time. Cecilia pushed the heavy rock into place in the middle of the hundreds of small stones, ranging from pebble size to the size of a large potato, and she continued her explanation between grunts.

"On the first day of the invasion of Iraq, I felt so helpless that I found myself out here in the garden and holding a stone. I don't remember picking up the stone, but I was standing there shaking with anger, and I realized I was ready to throw the rock. It shook me to feel how livid I was, and how easy it would be to release my anger by destroying something."

Cecilia wiped her faced, smudging her cheeks with dirt, then brushed her hands together absent-mindedly to clear the dirt as she recalled the day.

"At that moment I glanced at my Saint Francis statue, the old carved wood saint someone had left behind in the garden when we first moved into this house. Saint Francis stopped me, almost like he had reached out his hand to hold my arm. The sight of him reminded me of all the peaceful and nurturing values that old saint represents.

I took my stone over to him and laid it at his feet. I didn't throw that stone, and, while my anger didn't go away, it did retreat a bit. Honest, Maria, I only threw one thing in the last few years. I threw a plate at Cheney's face on the news one night."

She looked at Maria, worried that she might have shocked her sister, but Maria was listening without judgment, so Cecilia continued.

"Not proud of that. I really lost control. I have had a rough time with this issue, but it would have been even worse without my shrine. Every day, every single day, Maria, even in the snow, I came out here to my shrine - see, it's a little sheltered from the worst of the snow piles - and placed a stone on the shrine to memorialize all the people who have died in this war."

Cecilia brushed away the leaves, picked up the old flowers, and took the spent candle to throw out. Saint Francis received a loving sweep of her hand, and the peaceful Buddha, too.

"But then Mother died. I was in such a state of disbelief that I forgot to come out to the shrine, and forgot to watch the news, and forgot to worry so much. Everything became localized, I suppose."

She stopped, as if not knowing what to say. "Then Vic entered my life, or reentered my life in a new way. And much of the hopelessness I had been feeling was shared, or it lessened, anyway."

She gulped, "And when Matty was hurt all thoughts of anything else in the world disappeared. All of me, every last drop of energy was focused on him. I don't know if that is good or bad, but it sure changed things for me. Pulled me out of a deep pit of despair and my sense of spinning desperate wheels."

Maria was listening intently. She involuntarily commented. "Isn't that paradoxical? When these horrible things happened in your personal life, it distracted you from the depressive slump about the horrible things happening in the world at large."

"I agree, it's weird. It is like after having walked through the hell of the last weeks and months, I feel more liberated than I have felt in many years. I still have some trauma, still more that hangs over me, believe me, but it's like something has been unleashed."

"So how is all of this connected to you hauling this huge stone? What's that all about, and why didn't you wait to have someone help you?"

"Ah, Maria, when I get these impulses I feel compelled to act immediately. See, I was walking around the garden waiting for the furnace guy, who by the way called to say he cannot come until tomorrow. And I realized I have not been in my garden for a long time. And I walked out behind that big tree there and saw this beautiful rock. Isn't it lovely?"

Cecilia ran her hands like a sculptor over the smooth top and the rough sides of the big rock, admiring the fine grains of color in the stone.

"Maria, I realized that I didn't need to keep bringing one stone a day, but that this massive stone could be part of my shrine to all the sorrow and injustice in this world. It could symbolize a recognition of secrets and shame and fear, too. All the things that torment us, us humans, including me."

For the first time she sensed that she was actually talking with Maria, so she continued. "This feeling has been coming over me the last few months, that my angst is not just about this miserable war, not just about the people who perpetrated all this violence, as wrong as I believe they are, but that it's about wrongness that is all around us, and even in all of us, not only the Dick Cheneys of the world."

Cecilia moved her hand to indicate those whom she meant to indict. "Oh no, Washington doesn't get away with what they have done, not in my book anyway. But there is so much more. And some of the ugly, stupid stuff is inside me and my life. And conversely, Maria, and here is where the redemption comes in, there is this incredible beauty in all of us too. The potential is like the most glorious symphony, the most splendid sunset. And it is all inside us. I suppose that sounds like a simple cliché, and I know that it is not a unique thought, but for me, in my complicated life, it is like a refreshing waterfall, a shower of cleansing. Perhaps even some healing I have badly needed."

Cecilia added, "It was in the hospital that this started coming to me, this unwinding. This vision. Being with Mateo when he was unconscious brought me such peace, even while I was worried beyond belief. The worst time of my life, and yet, why this sense of peace? Maybe it can be explained psychologically, but it makes very little logical sense to me, so I have to call it a spiritual awakening. That is my language for it, anyway."

Cecilia stood with her big sister beside her.

"The big rock? I am hopelessly symbolic. This big beautiful guy here . . ." and she lovingly patted the stone, ". . . represents all the strength of the sorrow and the joy in the world. Instead of feeling desperately sad about it all, I am starting to see the human condition as part of life. I don't want to just focus on stone after stone, death after death. I cannot do that anymore. It's like torture. No, I have to embrace it all, the suffering and the beauty, and just do what I can. That's what this stone represents to me."

Maria put her arm around Cecilia's shoulders, their eyes gazing at the unchanging faces of the Buddha and Saint Francis, and at the large, solid stone they had worked together to move.

There was no awkwardness in Maria's tone. "Ceci, you're beautiful, you know. All my life I have admired your beauty. Your physical beauty. I'll admit to some envy."

She brushed aside Cecilia's surprised protest. "No, that is the truth, and I've never told anyone that, not even my therapists or Rosemary. Yeah, yeah, I know I've done okay myself and turned a few heads, but you have something special. Of course, Papa and Mother never let us think we'd get anywhere on looks alone, so I know you and I didn't stake our lives on our appearance. And I don't know why this comes up to me now, when you are opening your heart to me. Because that's what's important, your heart and soul and fierce beliefs. But somehow in this moment, your physical beauty is even more accentuated by the goodness of your struggle. I'm not being very articulate here, Ceci. But . . . just trying to say something I've never said before. I'm so happy you are my sister. I love you."

Cecilia's eyes stayed on the shrine, and her voice was soft.

"Thanks Maria, that's the most wonderful thing anyone has ever said to me. Life's so short, so tenuous and transitory, yet there is powerful strength in us. I don't want to waste any more of my life in a holding pattern. I have screwed up so many times, Maria, but this moment right now standing here with you, will stay with me forever. I love you, too."

FIFTY

Yet, despite dawning wisdom, important issues were still unresolved. Not for the first time, Vic and Cecilia had a conversation about the subjects that were hanging in the air. Up to now, Vic had tried not to be overly pushy, but, he was convinced that Cecilia and all those around her could not keep going through their days with topics left unexplained. Something would blow up. They would lose all dignity and be left to do damage control.

He often slipped away from the church at lunch time to share a picnic with her in the park outside the library, or in the same old staff room where she had once brought her little boys. On a fine autumn day they were in the park.

"Vic, I don't think I can live like this much longer. All this withholding is eating me up inside."

"So why don't you just talk."

"Do you mean to Mateo, or to Papa?"

"Well, you tell me."

Cecilia did not have a reply, but chewed her sandwich wearily as if unable to decide. Vic contained his impatience.

"The way I see it, you have two people, both dear to you, your father and your son, who are deeply connected to each other, and for each there is some extremely important information that you are holding as a secret. Now, I know you don't want to continue this way, so, somehow you just have to take that leap off the cliff and speak to them."

"But I am so afraid of how it will affect them. And they are both so vulnerable right now. I keep thinking that there will be a right time, and I will think of just the right words, and," she hesitated and gave Vic a haunted look, "I don't want them to hate me. I don't want to lose them." She choked on these words and realized that she had uncovered the basis of her hesitation, this fear that she would lose her son, as well as her father, although for different reasons.

Vic held her hand tightly, frustrated himself, but understanding what this meant for her and why she was frozen. And the two sat for quite some time, lunch forgotten.

"Well, of course it is not going to be easy, Ceci. And you can't know the consequences ahead of time, but what is your choice? Haven't you seen by now where keeping secrets can leave you? Haven't you suffered enough? How in the world can you get on with your life if you don't get past this hurdle?"

Cecilia nodded, wordless.

"Listen, Ceci. Can you talk about your worst fears, maybe get them out for just you and me to hear?"

Breathing hard, she whispered, "For Papa, I am afraid that he might be so shocked that he could die, or, at least get far more ill. I'm afraid that he will see his whole life as collapsing and everything he and Mother worked to build as being a charade, of no worth, a lie. He's been so highly esteemed in Pine Junction. So many people admire him and put him on a pedestal. Does that come crashing down now?" She paused, considering this, and then added, "And on the other hand - and this sounds totally childish, and I would never tell anyone this but you - on the other hand, what if Papa is so happy with his new son and maybe he really wanted a son all along and all he got was three daughters, and maybe he will," her voice became even lower, "maybe he will love this son more than us daughters."

"Okay, I said it, and it sounds pathetic, but at least I got it out of me." Cecilia pulled her shoulders up and looked Vic in the eyes as if to dare him to mock her. "Okay, Vic Dalloway, tell me that is ridiculous, go ahead."

"Won't ever say that, Ceci. And in fact I am applauding because of how brave you had to be to admit that to me. I am honored with your trust in me."

Cecilia seemed lighter for the moment. "Well, it did feel good to have said that out loud. But does this mean that I have never grown up? How can I be so insecure?"

"Never mind beating yourself up for feeling very primal emotions, my dear. And just think how good it feels to have cut the impact of those terrible thoughts in two by sharing it with me! Don't you think, though, that you are not giving your father a chance to figure out his own reactions? He is responsible for his own reactions, his own life. You are being either too protective or too controlling, and either way it compromises your father's dignity, even if he is an older man in ill health and, yes, in grief. But while you are at it, how about dredging out the worst case scenario regarding Mateo? What is the worst thing that will happen if - no, when - you share with Mateo that his father is not Warren Schumacher, but that his father is Dane Faber, a man he doesn't know? What could happen, Ceci?"

At this spelling out of the dilemma, Cecilia froze. Her look at Vic was beseeching, as if imploring him to stop pushing her. But he didn't: he pressed her.

"Ceci, it isn't going to go away. What kind of disrespect are you doing to your son by withholding one of the most important pieces of information in his life? How is it going to get any easier? How can you not tell him, even if your worst fears come true?" Vic came close to walking away in frustration, but he stayed on the bench.

"I will lose him!" Cecilia almost shouted these words but he did not flinch nor look around to see if anyone on the street had noticed. He kept his eyes directed on hers, willing her to be strong, to face the worst.

"Cecilia, how can you go on in your life if you don't take this plunge? Damn it, Ceci. Would you rather let Mateo go on living this deception and you continue to live suspended between these secrets? It is not honoring who you are to live this way. You are hurting yourself, and maybe you can stumble along the rest of your life with that, but I know you too well, and I know that it is the hurting of Mateo that is killing you. And yes, you are right. You might lose him.

I can't guarantee you that you won't. In fact, I would guess that you will lose him for a time at least."

Vic ran his hand over his eyes, looking drained. "How much do you love your son?"

Cecilia had always walked away from facing her demons. But too much had happened. Vic was absolutely right. She thought with a pang how good it had been these few weeks to have Mateo around, his light-hearted banter, his easy affection, his energy. She could hardly get her next breath out thinking that this would be gone. First to have almost lost him to his New York life, and then to the head trauma, and now to certainly drive him away from her with the truth, both because the truth would be shattering, but even more because her withholding this truth from him his entire life had let him live with a lie. And all, she bitterly reflected, because she loved him so much. Then it hit her that she may have only wanted to protect herself. But she also knew that if she didn't speak of it soon, Dane Faber would lose patience and come and tell Mateo himself, and that would be even worse, even for the part of her that felt so cowardly. Oh, how had she gotten herself and her family in this mess?

She made one more attempt to convince herself that it could wait. Even as she spoke, though, she knew that neither she nor Vic believed it. "This is not a good time to talk to Mateo. How can he handle it? Surely it is too soon."

Vic just shrugged. "Nope, it's a terrible time, but it's the time you have been given. So what are you going to do? The longer you wait, the less chance you have to do it in a way that seems right to you. It will be taken out of your control. You know that, Ceci. And that makes me hurt so badly for you."

"And as for your father, what are you waiting for? Pedro's getting older, he may degenerate so that communication is harder for him. Do you really want to deprive him of the knowledge that he has a son he never knew about? What if you were in Javier's shoes? What if you had waited your whole life to find your father? I'm impressed with Javier's restraint right now, although of course his own son has put him in a delicate position. I think of him sometimes and feel sorry for his state of affairs. Do you see Javier as the enemy?"

"Yes and no, if I'm honest. My reaction is fraught with fluctuating emotions. What would I feel about Javier if my own Mateo hadn't been assaulted by his son and almost died?"

Cecilia gathered the picnic debris and automatically started tidying up the table. Somehow her gestures, so domestic, just made Vic's heart surge with affection for this woman.

"Hey, Cecilia, I'm sorry to push you so hard. Please know I do it because I love you. Is there any way you can believe that? I feel like I've beat you up."

"I know, Vic. Doesn't make it easy, but I like you caring enough to keep pushing and not backing off. I like that. I love that." Her eyes flashed. "But, you know, you're a real badger!"

They both smiled weakly, but Vic's reply was serious.

"It's about love. About love. And about believing in the future. Hope takes courage. And I know I don't have much room to talk about such things, but my eyes are opening on my own life right now, too. I'm convinced it is about how we love each other. Sometimes it's very difficult."

Cecilia gave Vic a weary but affectionate look. "I'm exhausted, Vic. I'm simply worn out."

"Tomorrow, something will be different. And I'm scared to death," Cecilia concluded.

It wasn't "tomorrow" when things changed, but it did not take much longer.

FIFTY-ONE

"**I** am Javier."

Pedro didn't hesitate, but opened his arms and pulled his son towards him. Although the embrace was initiated by Pedro, it was the startled Javier who supported his father in his own stronger arms until, at last, Pedro drew back and gripped Javier's biceps to hold himself up, wanting to both look and hold at the same time. Finally Javier lowered his father back onto the chair and sat down across from him, so they were eye-to-eye. Neither one spoke for quite some time, but after the welcoming hug, the pause was comfortable.

No one had anticipated this meeting, not this soon. After all the anguishing on the part of the fretful daughters about when and how to tell their Papa that he had a son, and the impossibility of visualizing this scene, it just slipped out one day. And it was Cecilia who let it slip.

She popped in one day to see her father. Not seeing him in the living room, she peeked into the bedroom. There was Pedro sitting on the bed with Victoria's journals spread all around him, mostly open. Pedro was reading and didn't notice Cecilia was standing in the doorway.

This gave her a brief time to prepare herself, but not enough to really know what to say. Pedro looked up, as if to further absorb what he was reading, and then saw her standing there.

He turned to the bed full of journals and waved his hands across them to encompass them all. He looked back at Cecilia as if to try to explain.

She walked to the bed and sat down next to him. "Mother's poems. Did you know about them before?"

"No." Pedro shook his head. "Never. I was looking for something in her drawer and found them. I'm asking myself, where was I all these years? How could I have missed knowing she wrote so much?"

"Some of these were written before you met her."

"Yes, but she wrote many of these after we were married. All these years. I didn't know."

"I never saw her writing either, Papa, nothing like this. I saw her correcting school papers and writing up notes for meetings, and articles for the newspaper. But nothing like this."

Pedro looked at Cecilia as it dawned on him that she was not surprised by journals now. She shared how she had come across them right after Victoria's death, but had not known how to talk to him about what she had found.

"Papa, I was so surprised to find them at all, much less read them. I loved it, to find out this hidden side of Mother, but I felt guilty too about reading them, and then I felt really angry at Mother, for hiding so much of herself from us, and for dying without talking to us more."

She looked at her father apprehensively, because never had she criticized one parent to the other. But he nodded and agreed with her. "Ceci, I'm having the same reaction. Your mother and I were so close, such a smooth tight unit, but now I have to wonder. Did we really know each other at all? And here," Pedro picked up one of the journals, "Did you read this one? I caused my Tori pain. She knew I was keeping things from her, and it hurt her, and perhaps that was the reason she was so bristly with other people. It always made me sad when I saw how she ragged at you girls, especially Maria. With me, Tori was always more gentle, but with you girls and others, sometimes she was so critical!"

"And to think I may have been the cause of that. Ah, my poor Tori." He looked dejected.

Knowing she was diving into uncharted territory, Cecilia took a plunge. "Papa, were there things you never told Mother?" She held her breath, shocked at her own audacity, and fully expecting her father to retreat or change the subject as he had done so often throughout the years whenever she had made the mistake of inquiring about sensitive subjects. As a child, she had always done so innocently, unintentionally, but this time she laid out her question with direct intention. It was frightening to her to break this unspoken barrier, but Pedro had opened the door just a crack. And this time, he too stepped across the threshold.

"Oh, Ceci, there's so much I never told anyone before. I had such sorrow and hardship in my life, before coming to Pine Junction. I had one desire and that was to leave it all behind, to remove myself physically," and here he touched his chest with his hand, hesitated before finishing his sentence, "from not just the geography of the painful memories, but also the people who lived in that world."

Cecilia was so dumfounded by her father's disclosure that before she could think she blurted out. "Papa, how could you leave your baby behind?"

Pedro didn't react as swiftly as he once had, because all his responses were slowed down by the progression of his disease, but he jolted and stared at Cecilia as if she had suddenly started speaking in tongues. Cecilia realized in an instant that her father was not reacting to her in fear as if threatened, but as if flabbergasted by her comments.

"What are you talking about?" Pedro's baffled voice questioned his daughter.

Cecilia looked at Pedro. She had backed herself into a corner and there was no way out of it but to talk to her father. There was no time to call Maria or Olivia and ask for a family meeting. No time for Rowan or Mateo to come and buffer the shocking story. No Rex or Vic to offer counsel. And no Victoria to run a buffer and keep the family life running with respectable stability. It was simply Cecilia and her father sitting on the middle of the bed, the secret journals of Victoria Lessing strewn about them, her life and soul messier than either of them had ever imagined. Perhaps just as messy as Pedro's and Cecilia's lives had been.

And so, without preamble, Cecilia told her Papa about Javier's appearance in Pine Junction soon after Victoria's death, how Mateo had sheltered his grandfather from hearing his claim, protecting Pedro in his grieving until the authenticity could be verified. And then she said the bold truth.

"Papa, I don't know how else to say this to you. Javier Jimenez is your son. He was born after you left your Arizona home. He always longed to meet his father. He found you. It's up to you whether you want to meet him. I thought when you said just now that you had hidden things from Mother, that you meant you'd never told her that you had a son in Arizona. But I can see that you're completely surprised."

How could he not be completely shocked to hear this news? But Pedro sat there reflectively. So, she sat with him, tempted to defend against the pause with further explanations, questions, details, but, taking a cue from her father, she kept her mouth shut and simply sat.

At last, "It was her, of course. That's the only possibility."

"Why didn't she tell me?" he considered further before looking at Cecilia.

"Ceci, I'm buffaloed! So much to think about, but only one thing is important. I must see him. I wish I could be more mobile myself. I'd jump into my car and go find him. Javier? A nice name. I don't want you to tell me anymore about him, Ceci. Just tell him I want to meet him. I'll learn to know him myself."

Pedro stood up as if he was going to run out the door, and his face was full of mission. As he took hold of the handles of his walker, he asked Cecilia, "Tell me only this much. Is he angry at me? That's all I want to know."

Cecilia thought about Armando, but replied truthfully. "No, Papa, Javier isn't angry at you, especially since he's convinced that you didn't know about him. He just wants to meet you."

Pedro nodded. "Good. And I want to meet him. I want to meet him as soon as possible. Neither one of us is getting any younger."

He bumped his way back to the living room and Cecilia followed him, leaving the journals scattered across the bed. He settled himself into his big chair, and only then looked sternly at his daughter.

"And when were you going to fill me in on this, Ceci? And how about Mateo, you say he knew about Javier? Was that right before his accident? He probably forgot with all that he has gone through, but Ceci, I'm perturbed at you and your sisters. Am I such a weak old man that you thought you had to hide this huge news from me? I'm insulted. It makes me feel disrespected. It's condescending."

His look at her held anger. Cecilia instinctively dropped her head, and shame made tears come to her eyes. All she could say is, "I'm so sorry. We didn't want you to be hurt, and yet it looks like we ended up hurting you in a different way. We've just been so worried." After a moment of self-awareness she added, "Me mostly. I've been the one who couldn't tell you, not Maria or Olivia. It's been me."

Pedro 's face softened and he reached out his hand to Cecilia. "I'm sure that you were only trying to protect me, looking out for my best interests, and I know I've been a basket case since your mother died. So I guess I brought this on myself, but for God's sake, I'm weak, grieving, and old, but I'm not stupid or dead."

The pain on Cecilia's face as he said this hit him, and he again reached out his hand for her, and she came and knelt down on the floor by his chair. She put her head on his shoulder and he stroked her hair as he had when she was a child. And, as he had when she was a child, he consoled her.

"Ceci, it's going to be okay. It's going to be okay. Don't worry."

And, amazingly, it was okay. Javier flew out the next day and spent two hours with his father that first visit. Pedro was adamant that no one else be present. Exactly what was said between the two men was never overheard or discussed. Javier promised Cecilia that he would not tell Pedro about the fight between Armando and Mateo just yet, but the father and son talked about everything else. Pedro listened to Javier avidly, question after question. Like a father is eager to hear about his son's first day of school, so he listened to his son's first fifty-eight years. Javier did not withhold the ugly side of his youth, and in Pedro he found a sympathetic ear. In time, Javier came to know of his father's early life. After more revealing, Pedro and Javier came to a mutual respect. Both had overcome many hardships and both had found good people just when they needed them. Both had worked hard to thrive, and both had paid a price.

Javier encouraged Pedro to share his early life with his daughters, not to try to shelter them. Pedro grimaced, but admitted it was time to let go of his past secrets.

Javier replied. "Why should they be secrets, anyway?" Then he finished by saying, "It is your life, some of it hard and ugly. But nonetheless, your life, and your daughters would want to know you in your wholeness."

After three days, Javier had to leave to return to his classes in New Mexico, and Pedro assured him that he would be visiting him in the Southwest soon. Javier looked unsure of this, glancing at Pedro's weakened body. But Pedro laughed and confidently asserted, "Mateo will come with me. You haven't had a chance to spend time with my grandson, but he's getting stronger every day and he'll go with me and take care of things. You'll love him, too. I'm ready to share some of my stories with Mateo, even if they are harsh. And then he can meet your sons and I can meet my other grandsons, too."

Javier did not have confidence that the future held hope for a good relationship between Armando and Mateo, but Pedro's blissful state of mind was encouraging, if not contagious. Javier and all three sisters felt that Mateo should be the one to talk to his grandfather about the cause of his coma, when Mateo was ready. A very big secret still hung out in the air. But everyone agreed that, ideally, it was Mateo's story to tell. Armando's trial date had been set for three months hence. By then, the story would be shared with Pedro.

FIFTY-TWO

The day after Javier left for home started out sunny, a perfect autumn day, and Pedro found himself restless indoors. When Mateo and Rowan arrived to visit, he almost begged them to take him outdoors for a walk, and they were happy to oblige. Rowan dropped Mateo and Pedro off at a park where Pedro could negotiate his walker without too much difficulty and enjoy the colors of the trees now transitioning with vividness from their summer green to winter bare. Rowan drove off to get the oil changed on his car and promised to be back in an hour. Rowan's BMW was the last vestige of his recent extravagant lifestyle, and, as it turned out, his most treasured possession. He fancied he might have to live in it soon, unless he stayed in his old bedroom at Cecilia's.

The weather looked promising. Ten minutes into their walk, however, clouds came in to cover the sun's deceptive warmth, and a wind with wintery overtones began to blow. The idyllic afternoon walk was abruptly altered, so the two turned back to the picnic table to wait for Rowan's return. It would be a wait, he told them when Mateo called, since the BMW was up on the rack being serviced.

The New England fall season had never failed to thrill Pedro all these years after his move to Pine Junction. However, he looked shaky now as he sat, his face still distinguished, but colored by age and experiences. He was trembling with the sudden chill in the wind, so Mateo took off his own jacket and put it around his grandfather's shoulders.

Pedro smiled at Mateo gratefully, and then calmly said what had been on his mind for some time now.

"Mateo, I would like to tell you about another Mateo. In fact, most likely the source of your own name."

Mateo could not have been more surprised. His eyebrows went up, but he nodded and encouraged his grandfather to go on.

"There is a great deal I need to tell you, Mateo. My girls too, yes, of course. But you, Mateo, you need to hear it first. I haven't shared much of my early life with you, so I don't know how easy this will be now, all at once, but bear with me, because it is important for to me to start."

"Grand Pedro, I don't know anything about your life before you came to Pine Junction."

Pedro nodded, and then seemed at a loss at how to begin, although he had rehearsed his memories into stories over the last nights in bed.

Mateo gently pressed. "Grand Pedro, what did you say about telling me about another Mateo?"

"Ah, yes. Mateo. Mateo Gonzales. My friend. Really, like my brother. We grew up next door neighbors. But there was one big difference between us." And here Pedro looked at the young man sitting across the table from him, and, as if taking courage to continue from his grandson's kind and curious eyes, he forged on.

"The difference was that my family was a mess. A wasted family, if you can even call it that. My father was a drunkard and abusive. My mother worked too hard, had too many babies, and then joined my father in his drinking. My most common memory of my mother was her lying half passed-out on the couch in our unkempt house. And my memory of my father is of him beating me and my sister. My memory of my younger brothers and sisters is of them hiding from his rage."

Pedro did not stop, not even when he saw the shock in his grandson's eyes. He had started and he needed to talk.

"I can't sugar coat it. There are stories too horrible to share yet. In time, I may be able to tell you more. But let me tell you my saving grace, my lifeline. It was Mateo's family, and this is why Mateo was like my brother. They were our neighbors, the Gonzales family. They embraced me into their home. Sometimes they took on my father to stop his abuse. They also gave me the nurturing that my mother was not able to provide. Señor and Señora Gonzales became my parents in fact, if not in birth. And Mateo was my best friend all through school. I could talk to you for hours about all the love and happiness I received from the Gonzales family. Let's just say, Matty, that they saved my life in more ways than you can imagine."

"Grand Pedro, you never told me about any of this."

"I know, Matty. I never told anyone."

"Grandma Tori?"

"Not even my Tori, no." And here Pedro looked stricken, but he relentlessly went on. "It's only one of my many sorrows, Matty. Only one of my many sins." And when Mateo started to protest on his behalf, Pedro held up his hand and continued, "My many sins of omission, Mateo, my boy. And my list is long. I only thought of saving myself, not of all the people I turned my back upon, or all the people whom I've hurt by holding my secrets too tightly."

Mateo had no clue how to respond. Finally he asked, more for his own ears than his grandfather's. "Why? It just doesn't sound like you, Grand Pedro."

"I have no real excuses, Matty. I guess I've been a coward. Many bad things happened that I wanted to forget and wipe out of my life, but I can see now what a coward I've been. No matter what horrors I experienced, it still didn't excuse my withholding, nor did it make the memories go away, not ultimately."

"What happened?" Mateo asked cautiously.

"She died, you know." Pedro's eyes held so much sadness that Mateo felt he aged himself ten years in just being present with his grandfather in that moment. "She killed herself, cut her wrists, after they hurt her so badly. I found her. In the bathtub, bleeding. So beautiful, so sweet and good. They hurt her so badly. Oh, how could anyone do that to a sixteen-year-old girl?"

Mateo, totally baffled as well as shocked, reached out and held his grandfather's hands, and quietly said, "Grand Pedro, who? Who got hurt, what happened?"

"They raped her. My father was too drunk to stop them, and they were his friends. They raped her, and beat her, and then she killed herself, the only honorable way she could imagine to lose the shame." Pedro spoke these horrifying words like he could not stop himself, and Mateo could only repeat part of his question.

"Grand Pedro, who?" Mateo was almost crying himself now.

"Maria." Pedro choked out her name.

"Maria?" Mateo shook his head. "Aunt Maria?" Mateo suddenly thought his grandfather was . . . what, confused? Having senility issues? Too overwhelmed by all that had happened recently? It didn't make sense.

"No," Pedro gasped out, "No, no, no, my sister Maria. My pretty little sister Maria."

Mateo tried to both absorb the story his grandfather was telling him and all its graphic horror, and to comfort his grandfather. He didn't ask more questions, but just leaned over the old picnic table and held Pedro's two hands in his and waited until the older man regained some composure.

"I didn't know you had any brothers or sisters, Grand Pedro."

Pedro picked up the story once again. "It was the night of my high school graduation, and the happiest and proudest day of my life became the worst day of my life. After she died, everything happened quickly - the war, the draft. I just didn't care anymore about anything, so Mateo and I didn't wait to be drafted, we enlisted together. All through the war years we were able to stay together. We were in Europe. It was all sort of a fog, the boredom, the cold, the heat, the fear, the whole damn experience. And I never got hurt, not even a blister." Here Pedro laughed bitterly. "I didn't particularly take cautions. I just walked through it all like I was untouchable."

Mateo asked, despite his fear of the answer, "And Mateo Gonzales?"

There was a long pause. "I lost him." Another silence. "Right near the end. Right in my arms he died. Shot, sniper. Just like that. My brother. My best friend. Died before we could say goodbye. The war was almost over. We had plans. Why couldn't he have made it just a little bit longer? Why? I have asked God that a million times.

"I visited his family only one time after I was discharged, when the war was over. I had to, of course, to tell them about Mateo's last minutes. But I couldn't go back to Phoenix again after that. I felt too guilty. Why was I alive and their son, their real son, dead? I walked away and never returned. Never called. Never wrote to any of them. I realize now, and in fact I realized even then, that they loved me and wanted to keep me in their lives. They expected to, and even if it was painful, I would have been a good reminder of their Mateo. They were not angry at me. They loved me, too. And my walking away meant they lost both Mateo and me. But I felt too guilty. And after what happened to Maria, I hated my parents so much that I left town and never went back."

"Of course, I did stop one place before I left town. And I now know that one stop created a son, and by not ever going back to visit my roots and to share my gratitude with the Gonzales family, and by not helping my younger brothers and sisters, I also missed my chance to learn that I had a son, Javier, and that poor boy had to go his whole life not knowing who his father was. See how many people I have hurt, Mateo?

"Mateo, I had lost the two people who meant the most to me to terrible violence, and I had survived years of war. I just wanted to create a happy life. And I got that. Here in Pine Junction, far away from my roots and far from the battlefields. I pushed all the past away from me, and sacrificed the past to have a present and a future; it was always worth it to me. But I hurt myself doing that. And I hurt the ones I loved by keeping secrets."

He looked straight at Mateo now. "I'm sorry, my dear boy, if I have overwhelmed you with a lifetime of stories, much of it so traumatic, here in this short thirty minutes. You and I have always had a special bond, and we would have even if your mother had not given you the name Mateo. But I have never shared any of the old stories with you, stories that for better or worse made me the man I am. Now I know it is time to do so, to open up and confess, share, and let the old pain scream out. I don't know whether to say, 'I'm sorry,' to you, or to say, 'Here is a horrendous part of your legacy, my dear grandson.'"

Mateo had no answer, so he didn't say anything for awhile. He was staggered, but then again, so many strange things had happened in the last months that he wasn't as shocked as he might once have been..

All he said now was, "Grand Pedro, I don't understand how I came to be named Mateo, though. Have you shared all of this with Mom?"

"No, Matty. As I said, not with anyone until I met Javier yesterday, and now with you. Please don't talk to your mother or anyone about this for the time being. I will share my story, of course. I can see that everyone who is in my life deserves to know my full story. But I have to do this in stages. I shared first with Javier because we both had rough beginnings, and I am responsible for his, and now, with you because, Mateo, I want you to come with me - well more appropriately I should ask, please take me to Arizona so I can visit my past and see if any of the Gonzales family are still around so I can give my belated gratitude to them. And it's time for me to track down my brothers and sisters and see if they will forgive me. I need you to help me make my atonement, Matty. Will you do that?"

Without a hesitation Mateo agreed. "Of course. You know I will. Soon, too, I think."

"Yes," and Pedro smiled weakly. "I am sure you are thinking that I may be getting too old and too sick to make such a trip."

"Naw, Grand Pedro, you have lots of life and energy left in you," Mateo loyally proclaimed. "It's just that I am feeling so much better and was thinking that before too long I will head back to New York to get back to work. So we should take this trip before then.

"But Grand Pedro I am still confused how my mom came to name me Mateo if she knows nothing about your past."

"I have never discussed her choice of your name with her, as strange at that may seem to you, but I have a very strong feeling she choose Mateo because I used to make up stories to tell her about an imaginary boy whom I named Mateo in honor of my friend. I had no idea those stories had resonated so strongly with your mom that she would name her son Mateo, but whether it was serendipitous or just whimsical, or maybe she is clairvoyant, I never questioned it. It has been a real gift to me to keep such a good name alive and cherished in my life."

"And Maria? Aunt Maria, was she named after your sister, Grand Pedro?"

"Of course. Of course." Pedro's face grew somber.

"And yet you didn't discuss this with Grandma Tori?"

"No Mateo. I guess that too is unbelievable for you to understand. I can only try to justify my lack of sharing by my misguided notion of protecting what was perfect and untainted, this new life of mine and those I loved, from the horror of my experience. Don't make such a mistake, Mateo. Don't."

"I hear that, Grand Pedro. I do. But, I have to wonder, didn't hearing my name daily for all these years, and saying Maria's name too, didn't that bring the pain up for you that you were trying to forget?"

"Good question, Matty, but no, it didn't work that way. It allowed my love for my sister and for my best friend to stay in my life and be transformed, be made alive again, in a safe way." Then, "And nobody else had to know. I didn't have to talk about my sadness and loss with anyone. It felt safer that way."

The wind blew up a stronger gust and Pedro came out of the trance he had been in while storytelling, and his hands shook with cold. Mateo looked around to the parking lot and was happy to see Rowan's car approaching them.

"Good, Rowan is back. We need to get you back home and warmed up. Maybe some hot coffee or cocoa?"

Pedro tried to rise, but found it difficult, so Mateo came around the table and helped him up and got his walker placed in front of him for the short walk to Rowan's car. But after a few feet, Pedro stopped and looked at Mateo. "Listen, Matty, please remember, don't share this with anyone else yet. I am learning to let things out after over fifty years of silence, but I need to do it when it feels ready to me. I'm sorry to burden you with more secrets, but this is not a secret anymore. It is just a story that needs to be held carefully right now, and I will find the right time to tell my girls and to tell Rowan and Julia, too. Do you understand?"

"It won't be easy. I can keep it to myself, but I won't consider it a secret. I can honor that, as long as Mom and the others have an opportunity to learn this soon. They deserve that, Grand Pedro. You deserve that resolution, too."

Pedro started walking again, leaning heavily on the arms of the walker. "I'll talk to everyone, Mateo. In my own time. But I can feel myself becoming more feeble. If I don't find that right time, should I die first, I will ask you, and Javier too, to tell the rest of the family. After we go to Arizona you will know me even better and understand my story more fully."

As they approached Rowan's car, he made one more comment. "You're right, Matty, let's go soon."

FIFTY-THREE

Vic left before dinner, needing to get back to rehearse for an upcoming wedding. As he kissed Cecilia goodbye at the door, he gave her an extra squeeze and murmured in her ear, "Call me later." He waved to Mateo and Rowan and left the house. He was agitated. He hoped that this would be the night Cecilia would talk to Mateo.

"So much drama," his thoughts pulsed along with his heart. As if to comfort himself, he hurried back to the sanctuary. He had several hours of vigorous organ practice ahead of him as he mastered a new piece. That would distract him and allow him to pour his emotions into the physical effort of the playing.

Vic passed Rex in the office. Rex was preoccupied with a spreadsheet, but looked up to see his organist striding towards the sanctuary looking rather wild-eyed. "Hey, Vic, you okay?"

"Eh? Oh, yes. But say, Rex, keep Ceci in your prayers tonight. She could use extra spiritual support."

"Want to talk about it?"

"Maybe tomorrow, Rex. Maybe tomorrow."

Rex nodded, trying to look nonchalant, as Vic obviously needed to be alone. Vic disappeared through the darkened pews. Soon a small light came on by the organ, followed by the surge of the pipes filling every corner of the sanctuary and going deep into Rex's bones, head to toe.

Rex figured he would find out sooner or later so he put his mind back on the spreadsheet, wishing he had more finance classes in his background, but not before giving Cecilia his most sincere prayer of strength; immediately he threw in wisdom too, figuring that would cover any situation. What now?

Back at the house, Cecilia knew it was now or never. No drop-in guests, no Catherine, no Julia. Just the three of them. She walked into the kitchen and looked at the two, innocent, relaxed, completely at ease with each other. Several empty beer bottles stood on the countertop. They had been drinking for a while already.

"Boys," she began, clearing her throat.

Just as Cecilia was about to broach the subject on her mind, Mateo spoke first, interrupting. "Hey Mom, I had a breakthrough the other night in my memory. It was kind of vague, but Rowan furnished me with the details, so now I know how I got into my coma. You don't have to avoid talking about it anymore."

Cecilia stared at him, partly because she was caught off guard, being full of her own news, and partly because Rowan had filled in Mateo on the events of his injury. She looked at him cautiously, and Mateo laughed.

"It's okay Mom, I am not going to go crazy and track down Armando to get revenge."

She still looked worried, so he continued, "I don't have it in me. Too much else to work on, and too much on my mind. As long as Grand Pedro is okay, then I'm okay. I dunno, maybe if I came face to face with Armando I would have some sort of visceral reaction, but I am realizing that some of it is my fault for letting him get to me. You don't have to worry about me doing something stupid."

Cecilia's mouth dropped open. How could things be changing so quickly? She looked at Rowan and he was grinning as well, both at Mateo's well-being and at his mother's dumbfounded expression.

Cecilia shook her head as if to clear the cobwebs and gave Mateo a huge hug. While she was at it, she gave Rowan one too. For a moment she was holding both of her sons, big tall men that they were. She tried not to cry.

"Okay guys, you got me. I'm speechless. Mateo, I've been so worried about how you would respond when you remembered or when someone told you. We kept waiting for you to ask us specifically what happened."

"Mom, I can handle just about anything these days, believe me. So let's drink to this big step." Mateo filled his mom's wine glass, and lifting his beer glass to his brother and his mother, Mateo led the toast. "Here's to Mateo Schumacher, who recovers his mind, step by step, thanks to his brother and good drink!!" Cecilia with trembling hands took a sip, wondering what was next.

Mateo continued in high spirits. "And may he, that is me, Mateo Schumacher, never lose his mind again as long as he shall live."

"Hear, hear!" cheered Rowan with feeling. "Let's call some friends and party. Are you in for some partying, Mom?"

Cecilia had no words, so she smiled with the contagious if inebriated joy of her sons. Her boys, she thought. So many years spent at a distance from each other, and now so illogically sitting across from each other at her table where she had eaten her meals alone as these young men made their way through their twenties.

Her preoccupied look and thin smile was finally noticed by Mateo, who asked her, "Hey Mom, what's up? What were you going to say when I so rudely interrupted?"

Cecilia wanted so badly to say, "Oh nothing, can't even remember. Hey, let's keep celebrating." That's what she wanted to tell her boys. Everything would be happy and nothing would ever shake their world again. She could make things work out. Sure, she could. But instead, she took a deep breath, feeling like she was about to dive off a steep cliff into nothingness. With a racing heart, she took another breath and started.

"Mateo, Rowan, sons, I have something to tell you that is long overdue."

They both put down their drinks and looked at her with curiosity. Her heart broke. She was going to shatter at least one of them, if not both. Oh, why had she waited so long to tell them? If only this moment could be in the past. Her pulse pounded in her ears, but one more breath and she really would begin.

At that moment the doorbell rang.

FIFTY-FOUR

Cecilia didn't move. She was still formulating her words. Mateo stood up and cheerfully announced, "Hold that thought, Mom. That is probably our Chinese food, my treat tonight, pork and eggplant from Very Good."

He jumped up and bounced over to the door, and Rowan grinned at Cecilia, who had no idea what there was to be happy about. "See, Mom," Rowan said quietly to her, "see how naturally Mateo is moving around now. Isn't it fantastic!" And Rowan beamed at his brother as if he was Rowan's own prodigy.

Another time Cecilia would have been thrilled beyond words, but, now, in this moment, she was just beyond words. She managed a smile.

Mateo opened the door expecting the delivery from the restaurant, but standing there was a stranger, a middle-aged man, tall as Mateo, with dark hair streaked with gray in an attractive longish style. He probably had been slender, but now his shirt buttons were snug over his belly. He wore black jeans and a white button-down shirt with a casual and somewhat ancient sports jacket. His face was worn, but he looked ruggedly handsome. His eyes were what one noticed, and Mateo found himself looking at those eyes with some vague sense of recognition, yet his mind was blank. One of his mom's friends? He racked his brain, but found nothing. Perhaps it was a remaining memory problem, he thought. So he just stood there and said nothing, waiting to see what the stranger might say.

Dane Faber did the same, not having expected Mateo to answer the door. As they stood there in mutual appraisal, Cecilia took a step towards the entry way and when she saw the man standing there under the porch light, moths fluttering around his head like a halo, she felt she had been punched in the stomach. "You waited too long, Ceci," she said to herself. "It's too late. Now it's all out of your control. You stupid woman. Why did you wait so long to speak?"

At the doorway, Dane reached out his hand to Mateo.

"Hi Mateo. I'm Dane Faber."

Mateo took the offered hand and shook it. Still puzzled, he repeated, "Dane Faber." The name still meant nothing to him, and yet he remembered with frustration that it was part of the puzzle that originally drove him out to Pine Junction.

While Rowan was innocently fetching plates and forks from the kitchen, and Dane and Mateo were shaking hands, something clicked inside Cecilia, and, as she described it to Vic later, *I knew I had to take charge of the situation.* It was now or never. Better a crisis than to feel humiliation the rest of her life.

"Dane, won't you come in?" She elegantly swept both her puzzled son and a bemused Dane Faber into the house, and on into the living room, where she sat Mateo on the couch and Dane in an easy chair without them realizing what was happening. Rowan walked in with glasses in his hand, asking for drink preferences, and Cecilia had him sitting on the couch next to Mateo before he had a chance to ask a question.

"Rowan, this is Dane Faber. Dane, this is Rowan Schumacher."

Cecilia perched herself on the arm of the sofa, next to Mateo, and it all started pouring out in a rush.

"Mateo, I have something to tell you, and you, too, Rowan, but before I do, I want to ask your forgiveness for my cowardice all these years. And at the same time I accept that you may not be able to forgive me, but I want you to hear that I love you and always have with all my heart and soul."

She went on without giving them a moment to respond, if indeed they could have in their surprise. Dane sat in his chair across the room quietly watching and wondering what might happen.

"Mateo. Warren Schumacher raised you and parented you well for many years. But he is not your birth father. Dane Faber is your birth father. I never could tell you that, because somehow I thought it would destroy you. And then I learned that the longer I didn't tell you or anyone else, the harder it was to speak of it, and as more time passed, I knew that if I told you, it would make you confused and unhappy and that made it more impossible to bring up the subject. I was frozen. I couldn't tell you, and things just compounded as time went on. And here we are. You're twenty-eight years old, and you have lived your whole life thinking you knew who your dad was, and yet, Warren isn't your birth father. It's my responsibility that you didn't learn about Dane earlier. All my fault. And now, well, I am sure this is not a good time to give you this news, right as you are rehabilitating, but now is when it must be told, right now."

There was a dead silence in the room.

"All I can do is to ask you to forgive me for withholding this information. All I can do is ask. I have done you a deep wrong to keep such a secret from you. I know that. I have known for years how wrong it was, and that is, of course, why I am so crazy."

FIFTY-FIVE

She sat motionless on the arm of the old sofa. She was only inches from Mateo yet she dared not touch him. She wouldn't have blamed him if he had raged against her, and all sorts of horrible scenes flitted through her mind. But she sat there trying to cherish what might be her last moments so close to her son, or for that matter both her sons, because it was Rowan who spoke first.

"Holy shit, Mom!" He stared at her in disbelief.

From where she was sitting, next to him but looking over his head, Cecilia could not see Mateo's face, but his body was taut. He did not move, though. From across the room, Dane watched his son carefully, not sure what he should say or do.

Finally Mateo spoke with a voice strained and wiped clean of its normal cadence. "You're my father?" He addressed the man sitting across from him in the big chair.

"Yes."

"And where have you been?"

Before Dane could reply Cecilia broke in. "In for an ounce, in for a pound" is what her mom would have said. "Mateo, I didn't tell Dane I was pregnant. I went ahead and married Warren because we were on the verge of getting engaged anyway, and we moved back to Pine Junction. No one knew but Warren, and if anyone actually counted weeks and months from the wedding to your birth . . . well, no one did."

"People need to know who their parents are, I mean their real parents." Every word Rowan spoke was angry.

Mateo looked at Dane again. "So you're telling me that until tonight you never heard of me, or knew I existed, or that I was your son?" His voice was incredulous. "Did you think I would just answer the door and you could say, 'Hi son,' and I would laugh and suggest that we go out and have a beer?"

Dane finally spoke. "That I never expected. Of course not. We have made mistakes, both your mother and I, but we are not stupid. We are also not cold and uncaring. We have been rather unwise - let me rephrase that - we have clearly been very, very unwise but it was not because we didn't care. I have known that I had a son since January. Life is really complicated but that is no excuse, and I make no excuse, Mateo. I can understand if you're not at all interested in hearing anything more from either me or your mother right now, but, if you are, we can each explain our stories and how that led us to this day and this moment right here."

Mateo stared at Dane but would not look at his mother. It was too much for him to look at her. It hurt too much. "Mom! Mom!" he wanted to wail. But he kept it all inside. Dane's voice was not challenging. But the message was screaming. And this man's existence, his very presence in the old familiar living room, was too confusing for Mateo to handle.

He stood up. From his full height Mateo seemed tall and strong, yet as vulnerable as a new-born. In a sense he was recently born, both from the coma and now from this upending of his whole identity. He walked to the doorway and Rowan immediately went to join him. As they left the room together, Rowan turned his head and looked at both his mother and Dane, his eyes more stunned than enraged. Cecilia dared not even call out, "Take care of each other and drive carefully." She had forfeited her right to behave as their mother.

When the front door had closed and the car drove off down the road, Cecilia found herself listening to judge whether it was driving too fast. There was no squeal of tires, and that relatively soft murmur of car wheels and engine was the only bit of comfort she found.

What had she thought? She had expected it to be horrible, this long overdue truth-telling. And it was. But in the midst of the heartache and fear and self-hatred, she had one small bit of relief; the telling of it was over. Whether the worst was over or the worst had yet to come, she had no way of knowing. It was out of her control. And there was a measure of relief in that fact.

FIFTY-SIX

She looked at Dane, who was watching her without a word. He always had been a quiet man. He tended to talk with his music. However, this time it was Dane who spoke first.

"Thanks for speaking up for me."

"Well, I have done enough deceiving. It's over. Unfortunately, it may all be over, my whole relationship with my son . . . my sons."

Dane replied thoughtfully. "I should no doubt apologize for showing up, unannounced, and it looks like my presence forced your disclosure. But I haven't been able to think of anything else these last months, and I just reached the end of my rope in waiting for you to invite me to come or call. Put yourself into my shoes, Cecilia."

Before Cecilia could respond, he added, "Before we get into it all, I want you to know he is a beautiful young man. Did you know I was with him in the hospital one night? Rowan, although I didn't know it was Rowan at the time, was sleeping so soundly that he didn't wake up while I was there. I came over to the hospital as soon as I got back from my tour and got your message. I know that must've been hard for you to let me know about the assault. You were very upset that I showed up in January."

Cecilia nodded her head. "I found your card in the morning, on the floor. Rowan had not seen it, as far as I know. I didn't know whether to be more overjoyed that Mateo had begun to respond, or terrified that you had been there, or relieved that no one saw you, or what." Her voice trailed off. "All these years went by and I just sank deeper into denial, and, of course, then fear. Not a good place to be. This is beyond a nightmare right now, and I am worried that they will go out and do something rash, and get hurt or hurt someone else. And then, of course, my sons might never speak to me again, and I can blame no one else but myself."

"You know, you could save some of that blame for me, Cecilia." He was finding pleasure in saying her name again. He had not allowed himself to speak it often through the years. And he was, despite the tenuous situation and the inappropriateness of his thoughts, thinking how attractive she still looked even with the suffering in her face, and the decades that had passed since he had been in love with her.

She looked at him with disbelief. "Oh sure. And what part of this mess should I blame on you?"

He shook his head at her naiveté. "For starters, I had something to do with that young man's conception. And as I recall, and it pains me a bit that you may not remember it this way, it was a glorious night that brought it all about. And I would like to blame you for being so damn gorgeous, or for substances I indulged in, or the musical high I was on after our band's performance that night at the old Franklin, you remember? I had been watching you for months serving cocktails and then running off to your library classes. Boy, you were a fantasy. I wrote many songs about you."

Cecilia's cheeks flushed. She was having a hard time balancing her despair for her sons, with her memories of being so young.

"But, Cecilia, I can't blame anyone but myself for that night. At least let me take the blame if you want to call it that . . . more like responsibility for my part. I hope I didn't completely trick you. I have always liked to hope that you came with me of your own desire. And I have always wanted to believe that you enjoyed yourself as much as I did. When you told me that you had not been able to pick up your birth control pill prescription that month, I told you I had a condom and not to worry, but, in fact, I knew I only had some that were really old. But I never told you that because I was so much in love with you."

At Cecilia's look, he clarified. "Okay, maybe it was just pure lust, but it was powerful, and I was young and under the influence of my fantasies. After our night together, you quit the club and wouldn't return my calls, and you graduated and got engaged to that schmuck attorney guy while I was out on a tour, my first successful tour, and I came back to town and found you were gone. Not just gone, but married and moved back to your home town. You used to laugh about Pine Junction, remember? And then you moved back here! I could have tracked you down, but why? You had clearly made a choice that didn't include me, and I didn't know about your pregnancy. So I let you go and washed you out of my life all these years. Or thought I had. Until I realized that we made a son that night."

Cecilia moved from the arm of the sofa and plunked herself onto its welcoming cushions. "When did you get so talkative? You sure have a lot to say tonight." Cecilia wanted to get rid of him right then, but it came back to her with a huge sense of guilt, that when she left the club to go home with Dane that night, she had not told him that she was engaged to, or even involved with Warren. She had kept that under wraps.

Dane looked at her, as if reading her mind. "I guess I have been saving my thoughts up for a long time, Cecilia, and they're all tumbling out. And hey, I didn't mean to insult Warren Schumacher. See, I do know his name. I am grateful he took my son on and raised him. For a while anyway. What happened? What does he know?"

Softly, Cecilia explained. "He knew from the beginning that I was pregnant and that it was not his child. He was angry - hurt I'm sure - but he pushed hard to get married anyway, said it wouldn't matter. I knew it wasn't the right thing to do, but I guess it was the easy way out, and it sure took care of making explanations to everyone about Mateo's father. I was wrong to marry Warren and I hold myself accountable for that, although I can never regret Rowan's birth. Warren and I reinforced each other in not talking about our secret to each other or to anyone else. Things were smooth for awhile. Then one day, when Mateo was about fourteen, it just all blew up. It was the worst fight we ever had. Truthfully, it was the only fight we ever had and it was horrific. We had no experience fighting. We didn't share much affection and had lots of experience stuffing our thoughts. Warren was a good father to the boys in his own way, but he never connected with Mateo, and Mateo was always closer to my father than to Warren. And that day we fought, it was about everything, the whole secret, his resentments, my feelings, and the sheer ugliness of that blow-up destroyed something inside of me. Probably in Warren, too. We split up after that, but the secret never came out. I think if Warren had made it public then, as bad as it would have been, it couldn't have been as bad timing as it is now."

"Say, Cecilia, do you have a drink of something, beer, coffee, water, anything? We may be here awhile and I'm thirsty."

Cecilia stared at him, uncomprehending.

"Well, I am not going to leave and have you wait this one out by yourself. It could be hours or days before those boys come home, or else you could find out they won't come home. I know you have friends, family, a boyfriend maybe, but I think this one is a shared responsibility. This could be the only co-parenting we ever do, and I will not shirk this one. Besides, I don't have to be back in New York for a couple of days."

Cecilia silently went to get a brandy bottle. "This is the only thing I have. I know you were a whiskey drinker at one time."

"Ah, this will do. Thanks. And, Cecilia, I'm sorry if I said too much before about how attracted I was to you. It's the truth, but it was a long time ago and I don't want to make you uncomfortable. I'm not here trying to get anything going now. I'm not here to scream at you or make you feel guilty. I just want to be here for Mateo, and for Mateo's mother."

He held up his glass to her. "Truce? Forgiveness, at least between you and me? We can go back to being angry at each other later if we get the urge. Or ignoring each other." He looked at her, questioning, and she found herself agreeing.

And so, not knowing what other course of action to take, they continued to sit without talking much when the doorbell rang and this time it was the Chinese food, accompanied by profuse apologies from James Chiu who was delivering the food himself, the regular delivery girl being hung up by a traffic jam on the freeway. There had been an accident so severe that it was causing a traffic back-up the likes of which had not been seen in years.

Cecilia's purse dropped to the floor at the word accident and James looked at her with concern. "Mrs. Schumacher, are you okay?"

Cecilia picked up her bag and pulled out the money, but unable to think straight enough to count it, she just handed James a wad of bills.

"Hey, we saw Mateo yesterday and he looked great. Had a great conversation and, like my mom said, 'Mateo is back to normal!' Isn't that great? You must be so happy!"

Cecilia gritted her teeth at the thought of Mateo being "back to normal" but managed a weak and civil response. And then she inquired, trying to act casual, about the traffic accident. Had James heard any details?

"Oh yeah, really, really bad. A semi-truck carrying toxic chemicals clipped a mini-van with a whole family inside. They aren't releasing all the information, but it is pretty sure there were fatalities and, even though there was only that one car and one truck involved, the freeway is completely backed up because the truck spilled chemicals all over the freeway in both directions! So they have to close down everything for hours and do a hazmat cleanup. Wow, glad I'm not in traffic tonight!

"Well, goodnight, Mrs. Schumacher. Sorry for the delay with the food." James cheerfully strode off down the walk and under the rose arbor that Cecilia used to care about during ordinary times in her life.

Cecilia put the food on the table and, walking back into the living room, invited Dane to have some food if he wanted. "It's pork and eggplant, Mateo's favorite." She could hardly keep her composure as this thought crossed her mind. And she thought of families who lost loved ones, of her own loss of her mother, and all the moments that come back like sneak punches in a boxing match. It was the small insignificant details like pork and eggplant that hurt the most sometimes, she thought. And, finally, she let the news James had given her enter her conscious mind and admitted her guilty relief at the news of another family's tragedy. The sorrow of this unknown family would always be coupled in her mind with her own relief that it wasn't her boys lying dead on the freeway. And she hated herself for that self-centeredness, thinking how out of line it was compared to her personalization of others' grief in Iraq. So many ways to experience guilt, she thought.

Dane and Cecilia picked at the eggplant and pork as the hours passed. Cecilia took a phone call from Vic to whom she told the bare facts of the evening's unfolding, including Dane's presence in the house, but she insisted that he should stay home and she would call him when it was the right time. He reluctantly agreed.

Olivia also called to talk about Pedro's meeting with Javier, but instead Cecilia took a deep breath and told her sister that if Rowan or Mateo came by to see Julia, they would likely be upset.

"What's wrong, Ceci? I can tell by your voice, something's wrong."

"Right, wrong? I don't know, Olivia. Let's just say that things are unfolding. I had to share some enormous news with Mateo tonight. He and Rowan both are very upset. It goes way back, Olivia. Not sure how much I have the energy or time for tonight. I don't want to tie up the phone lines, but tomorrow I'll talk to you and Maria, too. Trust me on that. I'm tired of holding this long secret. It has almost killed me."

There was a short silence from Olivia's end of the phone. "I'm going to be at your doorstep right after school tomorrow, as soon as the kids get on the bus. No more damn secrets, Ceci. I've had it with this family's secrets!"

Olivia sounded like she was going to either scream or cry, and Cecilia assured her that she would be waiting for Olivia in the afternoon and tell her sister everything. "I agree with you, Olivia. Enough of this. But, Olivia, you may not think too highly of me when I tell you everything. I have to warn you."

"I don't care what it is, Ceci. I just can't stand finding out that we, any of us in this family, have been living a lie."

"Agreed. Tomorrow."

"Sleep, okay?"

"Will try. Bye bye."

Everything felt suspended. Yet there was some comfort in Dane's presence. True to his word, he fell back into his quiet ways, but it didn't feel like detachment. It felt companionable. Cecilia didn't want to admit this but she finally accepted that it was a comfort not to have to face this huge parenting crisis alone. As odd as it sounded, even though she had never been in love with him, in some sense she had lived with Dane Faber secretly for twenty-eight years. Even though she had not seen him since Mateo's conception, he was not a stranger.

She knew that she alone bore the guilt of having withheld Mateo's birth from Dane all these years. She alone had harbored such a significant secret. But it did give her some relief to hear that Dane wanted to own his responsibility for creating the pregnancy. And, with tears in her eyes, she thought of the beauty of that creation. Her Mateo. She looked across at Dane, and revised her thought: their Mateo.

She laughed.

"What are you thinking?"

"How ironic, how bitterly ironic. Just when I get some help at parenting, I may not ever need it again."

Dane did not reply, but gave her sympathetic look. Later, he said. "I'm not familiar with parenting, but I am familiar with life and it is fairly bizarre at times. Makes no sense lots of the time. You better love the good times, 'cause bad times may be coming."

"All the stuff of your music writing, eh?"

"You sound like a Canadian, eh." he mimicked. "You been hanging around north of the border? I spent three months playing in Toronto. Great city, but cold. It was winter."

Cecilia didn't mention Vic and his heritage. Time enough for that later. She followed up on Dane's comments, though. "I am not sure I agree with you entirely. I think life has a lot to do with what you make of it, with your attitude. Of course, don't listen to me. I have screwed up my life royally and cannot imagine anyone ever seeing wisdom in my example."

Dane shrugged. "I wouldn't say that, Cecilia. Clearly you have done something right. I've seen a little of your sons and I think they turned out pretty cool. And you have had a good working career. Look at your book shelves and your home here, I think you have made a fine, stable life. Stable sounds insulting, perhaps. What I mean is a rich life. So when it comes to life, I won't pit my rolling stone musician lifestyle against your librarian mother lifestyle and expect to win many points."

Cecilia wasn't sure whether there was admiration or sarcasm, or even bitterness, in Dane's comments, but she decided to let it go for now. Another time, later, they could wrestle that out. She was surprised to even be thinking about "later" when it came to Dane Faber.

And so the night went on, a strange night fraught with anxiety, but quiet. They just sat and waited. No phone calls. No more doorbells. Neither watched television or searched email. Dane didn't own a cell phone out of personal preference, defiantly defending his individuality. Cecilia discreetly checked her cell phone several times to make sure it still had a full battery. And she turned up the ringer full volume on the house phone just in case someone needed to call her. Perhaps the hospital, perhaps the sheriff.

The old clock ticked on, keeping the beat.

FIFTY-SEVEN

An hour into the night, Dane looked at Cecilia from across the room. "So tell me, how did you come to choose the name Mateo?"

"What's wrong with it?"

Dane held his arms across his face as if to fend off a blow. "Cecilia, I wasn't criticizing. I actually like the name a lot, but it is unusual, especially with a last name of Schumacher."

Cecilia relaxed some. "Sorry, didn't mean to be defensive." She paused. "But it is not an unusual name with my last name, Sanchez."

"True. Still, I wondered how it came about. After all, while I know nothing about parenting, I always thought that one of the more exciting aspects would be to pick a name. It's an experience I never had, or was never given the opportunity to have."

Cecilia gave him a hard look, but while he looked a tad apologetic, he didn't back down and met her eyes squarely. She finally sighed and decided not to dive into that discussion. She melted further into her chair, put her head back and closed her eyes. Dane could see how tired she was.

"When I was a little girl, I had trouble sleeping. That's me. Always thinking, thinking, thinking. This circular whirling thought machine going on in my mind, all night long. Worrying sometimes, wondering sometimes, planning, questioning and musing, all night. Lots of trouble sleeping as a kid. Used to envy Maria. She was strong and full of opinions all day long, passionate about whatever her latest idea or project might be, and then she'd go to bed and be snoring before I could even get my blankets arranged. We shared a room, all three of us for a long time, until we got older. And little Livia. She could get scared of her own shadow sometimes, and she would whisper to me all her worst imaginations until she would make me start worrying, too. But when she went to bed, she would grab her stuffed animals, about ten of them each night, and go right to sleep.

"Not me. I rarely got enough sleep. So, my Papa would tell me stories. That was the one thing that would help me. He was a good story teller and my favorite was about a little boy named Mateo. Mateo had all sorts of adventures. Never too scary. Just fun kid adventures, very imaginative. Papa could paint a picture of forests and castles and enchanted lands, and Mateo was always in the middle of the scene. Mateo became a very real boy to me and I always asked for stories about Mateo. After a while, I started adding to the stories. They were a very special time for me to share with my Papa."

Cecilia's eyes remained closed.

"When I was older and felt I had outgrown bedtime stories from my Papa, I would still use Mateo to help me get to sleep. I would invent my own stories of our shared adventures. He was always creative and resourceful, and kind, too, just like he had been in Papa's stories. For those years between early childhood and when I became an adolescent my Mateo stories got me through the nights."

Cecilia stirred and opened her eyes, focusing back on Dane. "For many years I almost forgot about Mateo. I was busy with all the high school and college life activities. One time though, early on, I asked my Papa about Mateo. About how he had come up with the boy and whether his own parents had told him that story. And Papa pulled away from me, not physically, but just kind of removed himself. Papa did that sometimes. It usually didn't last long, those periods of disconnection, but when it happened he was definitely somewhere else. Finally, his only response to my questions was that Mateo was a Spanish word that meant 'Gift from God,' or something like that. That's what my father would do. Revert to some educational information, but not at all what I was looking for as a child. I couldn't see any relevance in what he said. But I knew better than to try to get more from Papa when he withdrew like that."

Cecilia laughed and shook her head. "Funny how kids figure out how to deal with their parents, what to say and not say, intuitively, and all the while they have no idea why. I still don't know what made my parents tick. But Papa's occasional detachment is something my mother wrote about in her journals, in her poems. I still don't know what that was all about."

"Is your dad still alive? Why don't you just ask him?"

Cecilia looked at him. How could someone see things so black and white, so matter-of-factly? For a moment, she hated him for his lack of understanding about what to her were the ambiguities of life. If Dane didn't understand the power of secrets and the history of topics that just never could be discussed, then she could not try to explain. She ignored the uncomfortable thought that he might be right, and picked up the original question he had asked, about Mateo's name.

"Anyway, when I was pregnant, I realized that there was really only one boy's name I could choose. My son would be Mateo. There was no second thought on that."

"And how about your husband? Didn't he have any say in this baby? Didn't he think he should be able to help name his son?"

Cecilia looked at him wearily. "Didn't I make myself clear? Warren knew Mateo was not his child. Until very recently, he's the only one besides me who knew. Warren was quite detached. So there really wasn't any discussion. I would name my baby. He named Rowan, our baby. I didn't object. It seemed fair at the time."

"So Warren didn't know I was Mateo's father?"

"No. He didn't know you. He may have seen you play at the club back then, but I doubt it. He was finishing law school and so busy studying he didn't go out much. We didn't go out much. And he never knew that I knew you."

Cecilia looked like she really didn't want to discuss it further, but, finally, she added. "He only knew that he was not Mateo's father. He thought it was going to be okay, and we never talked about it for fourteen years until the day things blew up. Then we divorced and that was that. No one in the world knew that you were Mateo's father. Sometimes I wanted to imagine that I had made it all up, but I could not deny the timing. And the musical gift was a link, too. Well, that I could always connect with my Papa, both genetically and his influence on Mateo, but I knew there was more to Mateo's love of music and his talent. And although I constantly pushed away from this truth, when I see Mateo, I can see you. Always could."

"I'm glad you didn't hold that against him." Dane didn't smile.

Cecilia shook her head slowly. "That could have been a possibility, I realize, but from the beginning Mateo was such a happy baby, so charming, so interested in everything. He talked early and became a great little conversationalist. And he also resembled my Papa. They were like two inseparable partners from the very beginning."

Dane nodded, but didn't say much. The two sat there in the quiet of the night house for a long time, both lost in their thoughts. Another hour passed, and Dane finally spoke, as if Cecilia had just finished her last sentence a minute before.

"Do you still have trouble sleeping?"

"Insomnia? Oh, yes, it is quite often my companion. Except recently." Cecilia stopped abruptly. She had no intention of sharing the sweetness of her relationship with Vic. It was all too new and precious.

She must have blushed. Dane seemed to know what was going on in her mind, but he didn't pry. It was, he realized, none of his business. His only business here was to sit vigil with Cecilia as they waited to hear what would happen with their son, Mateo, and his brother Rowan. It might be hours or days, but Dane was prepared to wait it out. Since January, everything else in his life had taken second place to his fatherhood. Everything else seemed superficial. He, who had never admitted loneliness, now recognized its deep grip on his soul, and since he had serendipitously learned that he had fathered a child, he was going to fight to know his son if Mateo would allow that to happen. He would be patient. He stretched out on the sofa.

"I sleep lightly myself, but I may drift off now. It's been a long drive from New York, following my flight home from St. Louis, but I'll be awake in a moment if something happens. I'm here, you know, until we find out something. It's the least I can do."

Cecilia nodded, not sure how she felt, but somehow going on instinct that Dane was the right company to have on this long night. She didn't want to do this night solo.

She fetched a blanket for Dane on the sofa, wrapped an afghan around herself in the chair, double checked her phone, both phones, for the umpteenth time, and closed her eyes. Tidbits of sleepiness mixed with her monkey-mind of musings. Finally she began singing Taize chants silently in her mind. She didn't sleep, but it helped her agitation.

FIFTY-EIGHT

A s if following some unseen script, Mateo and Rowan slammed straight out the door and into Rowan's car. Rowan started the engine and looked at Mateo. "Where?"

"Just drive. Anywhere."

Rowan nodded and slowly left the driveway, willing to just drive, but hoping for more explicit instructions from his older brother.

"New York. Brooklyn. I need to get away from this insanity."

"Sure, Mat, but we don't have any clothes or anything."

"Catherine will take us in. Someone else is living in my old apartment, but Catherine will take us in. Let's just get out of here."

Rowan moved into high gear and as his car was skimming along the country road, head-lights picking up trees and occasional farm houses, he reflected that he would need to get some employment eventually to keep this baby of his, this car that was his cherished possession. Perhaps he should follow Henry's advice and go into nursing school or physical therapy training. Dad would be pissed, but he would get over it. At least he, Rowan, still had the same father and mother he had taken on faith earlier this evening. Rowan's own mind was throbbing at his mother's revelations, and he could hardly imagine what was going through his brother's head right now. He glanced sideways at Mateo and saw that his brother was staring straight ahead, but he wondered if they were seeing the same road. Rowan was relieved that he was here in Pine Junction. What if Mateo had been alone?

They didn't talk as they headed to the freeway and merged onto the busy lanes of traffic. They didn't talk for the first twenty miles, just watched the lights and felt the rhythm of the car. Coming around a big curve in the four lane road, however, they saw red lights ahead. And then more red lights. A mile ahead of the red brake lights that amassed in front of them, they could see flashing lights in abundance.

"Damn. Something's happened up there." Rowan slowed to a crawl and then they stopped altogether, becoming part of the mass parking lot of strangers sitting in their own little capsules, waiting for what they didn't know. Rowan found a traffic report on the radio and it became clear that they had a long wait ahead of them.

Rowan looked at Mateo. This couldn't have happened at a worse time or a worse place on the freeway for them. There was no upcoming exit before the accident site. They had to wait along with all the other cars, uncertain what to do. Rowan turned the engine off and they sat.

Out of the blue, Mateo said, "Someone's having a worse day than I am."

Rowan could only think, "My brother's amazing."

Mateo started speaking, as much to himself as to his brother. "I'm so fucking outraged I don't know what to think. This is huge. What am I supposed to feel about this? What should I do? All of a sudden I have a different father! I am twenty-eight years old, and now my mother decides to tell me that our dad is not my dad. And this Faber guy shows up at the door and introduces himself as my father. One minute my mother is my mother, Mom, the mom we have known always, who was always there for us, and then just like that she is someone I don't know. How could Mom keep this a secret from me all these years? I feel like I lost my dad and my mom in one night. I know I am not very close to our dad, but at least I thought I had a dad. I mean I have some good memories of camping and fishing and stuff with him. But now, do I have one dad, or two dads, or no real dad? It's fucking crazy, Rowan. Crazy."

"Yeah. My head is spinning, and I can't even imagine what you are going through." Rowan smacked the dash board for emphasis. "How could Mom not tell you?"

After a moment he added, "It's just too weird to think of Mom shacking up with anyone else, even all those years ago." And he pushed that thought away with a grimace. Mateo gave him a look that said he wished Rowan had not even brought up the subject.

He quickly changed direction."So Rowan, you know what I finally figured out? Hah, talk about timing."

"What's that?"

"This whole time I have been wondering why the hell the name Dane Faber is so familiar to me. And you know what? It doesn't have anything to do with finding out he is my father. The whole shock of this brought it back to me. I heard him play at a club, my first year or so in the City. And now he walks into my life, seemingly as my father."

Rowan shook his head. "No shit! Was he any good?"

"What? Oh, as a singer? Yeah, well, I think. Nice guitar work or maybe that was his band. Long time ago."

Rowan stared ahead at the lights and Mateo beat out a rhythm on the dashboard but neither one had a handle on their emotions for a time. Eventually Rowan verbalized what had been swirling in his head.

"Mateo, it's all unbelievable, and you're getting this crap on top of your head trauma. You doing okay? I mean, you'd be justified in being out-of-your-mind. It's just so bizarre."

"Yeah, I should be going nuts, but despite it all, I'm still alive. Armando Jimenez, my cousin, for God's sake, threw my head against the pavement and somehow I survived, only to get this news. Yet I am still walking and breathing, and for all its screwed up nature, I still have a family, although it is hard to know what to think about them. How about Grand Pedro? I can't abandon him. But did he know about this? Or did they keep it a secret from him too? I don't want to think that my Grand Pedro wouldn't have told me, that he would've let me live my life without knowing who my father was. In fact, Grand Pedro wants me to take him to Arizona for a visit."

"For a vacation? All of a sudden Grandpa wants to go to Arizona? Doesn't he like the cold winters anymore?"

At that moment Mateo was sorely tempted to share with Rowan all that Pedro had confided in him, all the stories that were still rolling around in Mateo's mind like bouncing balls in a lottery bin. But he remembered his promise to his grandfather and just replied, "Yeah, maybe so. He was sure shivering the other day. And I think meeting Javier has stirred up his interest in his childhood home."

Then back to his Mom's bombshell. "I really don't think Grand Pedro knew about Dane. At least I hope not." Mateo thought about the secrets Pedro had kept all the years about his own past, but hoped that his grandfather would not have let him, Mateo, live all his life not knowing who his father really was. He hoped so. He hoped so.

Rowan's fingers traced the indentation on his steering wheel as they sat. Mateo continued to beat an absent-minded tap on his knees.

"You know, Mat, this does clear up one thing. Everyone always said I looked just like Dad. Even I could see that I resembled Dad, same hair, same eyes, same coloring, but even though you and Mom both have dark hair and eyes . . . there was always something different about you."

Mateo looked quickly at Rowan and then turned to stare out the window before speaking. "I never felt connected to Dad. Sometimes, I envied you because you and Dad could do things together so easily. Not me. But I didn't worry about it too much because I had Grand Pedro. He was my anchor." He gave a quick apprehensive look at his brother, but then went on. "I remember one day, I was just a kid, sometime just before the divorce, I was playing the new guitar Grand Pedro had bought me, when I looked up suddenly and Dad - well Warren that is - was looking at me with a strange look on his face. I was just a kid, I didn't know what it meant, but because kids see things really black and white, I remember thinking, 'Dad doesn't like me.'"

Rowan didn't let on how shocking this was to him. He didn't quite know what to think about Mateo's words. So he changed the direction of the conversation. "You and I have never once talked about the bad times, but I was so angry after the divorce, I thought I would explode. I hated everyone, but especially Mom because I was sure it was her fault for driving Dad away from us. But then I looked at you and you didn't seem changed at all. You just went on with your life. You were so smooth. I never saw you get angry at anyone." Rowans voice was husky. "I felt far away from you."

Both brothers stared out the front window at the red lights ahead. This revealing was too tender to be done face to face.

"Rowan, I was just cruising, avoiding the conflict, avoiding the emotions. I guess you could say I was really good at escapism. Mostly music, but also with heady sort of discussions, you know, philosophy, history and all. If I hadn't had my guitar I might not have been able to keep my cool. I just waited until I could get away. Remember, I graduated from high school early, and headed to New York. I spent four years dreaming of that escape."

He continued."I didn't think of you much. I'm sorry. I was in self-survival mode and left you out of my life. I never realized until this minute what it was like for you. I was only thinking of myself, and I wanted to separate myself from that taint of unhappiness that hung over our house and our mom. That's all I thought in those days."

"But you acted like you got along so well with Mom!"

"Oh, actually I did, and I do. I remember all the good times when we were little kids, hanging out with her at the library, reading stories with her, and playing games. But when things got so sad, I was starting high school and all I could think about was getting away, leaving all that family shit behind. I treaded water until I could leave. Yeah, Rowan, I have been good at escaping. Sounds like you had a good clean hate! Not me, I just ran away."

"Matty, do you have any good memories of Dad?"

There was a pause. "Yeah, fishing trips. I think we all enjoyed those trips to the lake. You know, it seems like we all four were happy on those trips. Even Mom. Even Dad. I remember one time seeing Mom put her arm around Dad when we were walking back to the cabin one night. That was one of my happiest childhood memories, as a matter of fact. Seeing them happy, even for just one moment."

Rowan nodded. "Dad loves fishing," he said, as if that explained anything.

Then he added a question, "You're happy in New York?"

"Yes."

"Why did you come back?"

Mateo laughed, "I was summoned. Summoned by Rex Randall."

"There's something about Rex that's very compelling."

"True, but he roused my curiosity, and then first thing you know, I started to feel guilty about deserting Mom, and especially Grand Pedro. I came back feeling obligation but then it began to feel like the right thing to do. To be here, now. And heck, look what happened!"

"Yeah, you got your very own coma and all sorts of weird news!"

"Well, yes, that's true, but, what I was thinking is that I got a brother, along with all the other shit."

Without sentimentality, Rowan accepted this tribute as a given.

Rowan suddenly realized. "Hey, Matty. Have you thought about this? This's kind of funny. Sick humor, true. But there is a sort of twisted connection here with Grandpa's situation. Let's see. Grandpa had a son he didn't know about. And Javier Jimenez had a father he didn't know was alive or, for most of his life, even who he was. Then when he did find out who his father was and tracked him down, before he can stop him, his own crazy son takes out his father's grandson, his crazy son's very own cousin." Rowan began laughing . "And our mom and our aunts suddenly have a half-brother, they never knew about. And you . . . " Rowan was laughing so hard he could hardly talk, " . . . and you find out you have a real dad you never met, and the dad you thought was your dad isn't really your dad, but still is my dad, so now you and I have a half-brother we didn't know we had before. And it's really so crazy. You can't make this stuff up!! What an insane family we have, my brother!"

Mateo turned his eyes on his brother, his face at first harsh, but then he too began to smile until he found himself laughing hard, hysterically, comically, he didn't know. For a good many minutes the two brothers sat laughing uncontrollably in the middle of the massive, impersonal highway, surrounded by hundreds of idling and stilled cars. In the darkness no one noticed the crazed occupants of the silver and black BMW. They were completely anonymous. Mateo gasped and tried to stop laughing. "Hell, Rowan, I am going to piss my pants. I need to walk over to the woods and take a leak. Don't leave without me!"

Rowan wiped his eyes and nodded. "Hurry back, I'm in the same situation. Don't want to leave the car."

Mateo opened the car door and carefully wound his way in between the other lanes of stopped cars, across the grassy shoulder of the road and into the pine trees beyond, relieving himself with a satisfaction that made him think this was the best piss of his life, next to the first good one he had after getting the catheter out in the hospital. He stared up at the stars sparkling between the branches of the pine trees and breathed in the night air. The country boy in him sensed that the seasons were changing and autumn soon would make way for winter. He wondered how in the world he could feel so content given the life-tumbling news of the day, on top of the circumstances of the summer that had just passed.

"My family seemed so normal," he whispered to himself. He contemplated this a moment and then realized that it was his family's very normalcy that made the unveiling of secrets so distressful, secrets that never needed to be secrets. As he stood there in the roadside trees, Mateo considered an idea he had not shared with anyone. Maybe he could forgive Armando. It was a niggling thought that kept passing through his mind. He was not quite ready to pursue it tonight. Still, for his Grand Pedro's sake, if not for his own sake, he was open to the idea.

Remembering his brother waiting with full bladder in the car, Mateo jogged back to Rowan. He was happy that he had found his brother after losing him for so many years: his former full brother who turned out to be his half-brother but was now truly his real brother. And as he ran he laughed with the thrill of being able to run again. He was grateful to think and to feel. Life and health were a gift. In true Mateo fashion, he decided that he would take his life in whatever form it came to him, with whatever wrapping adorned it. It was his.

FIFTY-NINE

Cecilia picked up the phone so quickly when it rang that it soothed Julia's fear that she was awakening her aunt.

"Hello?" Cecilia's voice was louder than usual.

"Hi, Aunt Ceci? This is Julia. I hope I didn't wake you up. I know it's pretty late." Pretty late for a middle-aged woman, is what Julia didn't say.

"No, No, No. I'm awake. You know me, I never sleep." Cecilia tried to make a joke, disappointed that it was Julia and not her sons. "What's up, Julia?"

Across the room, Dane's eyes opened, his ears listening, but he did not sit up.

"Well Ceci, I told Mateo it was too late to call you, that I could wait until tomorrow, but he absolutely insisted that I call you tonight. I don't get why he called me and didn't call you, but he said he would explain sometime, so anyway, he sent you a message."

"What? What is it, Julia? Is he okay?" Despite her best intentions, Cecilia's voice bordered on frantic.

"Yeah, he's fine, or I think so anyway. He sounded okay. Is something wrong?"

"What was his message, Jul?" Cecilia tried to tone down.

"It was kind of long and didn't make total sense to me - I finally had him tell me again so I could write it down. He was very insistent that I get it right."

"Yes, go on . . . please go on."

"He said, 'Tell Mom that Rowan and I are going to go hang out along the river for a few days. Rowan has a friend with a cabin. And we might go to New York and hang out. We'll be gone a few days. I need a break.' "

Cecilia breathed a little bit. "So which river, Julia, did he say?"

"I dunno. Maybe our river. Maybe the Connecticut. He didn't really say any details like that, Ceci. Maybe the Hudson if they are going down to New York. Is it important?"

"No, no not really. Anything else?"

"Yes. He said, tell Grand Pedro that I am good for my promise."

Both Julia and Cecilia stopped for a moment to wonder what that meant.

But Cecilia finally said, "Thanks so much for calling and giving me the message, Julia. Be sure to call me if you hear more. Goodnight, dear."

"Oh, there's more. And this part I didn't get at all, so I had to write it down carefully. He said I should trust him because he would talk to me soon, and that I shouldn't share this message with anyone but you. He said, 'Tell Mom not to worry. I'm not angry. I just need time.' "

"And then there was one more thing. Aunt Ceci, who's Dane?"

Cecilia paused a moment and then replied, "Dane is someone Mateo is just getting to know, Julia. Did he mention something about Dane?"

Dane sat up on the sofa, and he looked aged and youthful at the same time. Cecilia put the phone on speaker mode and set it on the coffee table between them. "What else, Jul?"

"He said, 'Tell Mom that if Dane is still around to let him know that when I'm back in the City, I might drop around to the Franklin Club so he can buy me a beer.'

"That's it, Aunt Ceci. This doesn't make any sense to me but I guess he'll explain it all to me someday."

"I know he will. Good night Julia, and again, thank you so much for calling."

Cecilia picked up the phone, clicked it off, and then held it like that little cell phone contained the key to all the future. Her eyes met Dane's across the room. He stood, stretched, rubbed his eyes, and grabbed his jacket as he walked to the door. In the doorway, he turned and smiled at Cecilia, and Cecilia could see that it was a relieved smile.

"There's hope, Cecilia. There remains hope for all of us. Let's carry on."

The End

ACKNOWLEDGMENTS

"Let's pretend. Let's pretend there was a fine family who refused to talk about the past, holding secrets that came back to haunt them and kept them from connecting fully with those they loved."

When I was young and sprawled half-way up our big mulberry tree with my book, or reading under the covers after lights out, or when our family headed off to our yearly vacation with Dad's World War II duffle bag stuffed with library books, I was simply living out the family legacy and love affair with reading. My particular passion has always been stories, real and imaginary, and the blurry space in-between. Finally, when I was sixty-one years old, I decided to try my hand at writing stories, not just reading them.

Junctions was birthed in February 2013 from a prompt in Cynthia Leslie-Bole's "Hummingwords" Writing Group, an Amherst Writers & Artists group. It became a story that wouldn't let go of me and now, three years later, the characters in *Junctions* have became my friends.

Many people walked the path with me for the writing of this, my first novel. Cousins Jinx McCombs and Paul Nordstrand, thank you for being my earliest of readers; your enthusiastic feedback made me believe in myself. It was while staying at your beloved Edgewood that I finished the first draft of *Junctions*. I will never forget where I was sitting and how I felt at that moment. Little did I know how many more drafts were to come, and how important Cynthia Leslie-Bole would be in her gifted editing work, as a writing coach, and in allowing me to use her eloquent poem. The writer friends I met through Cynthia's group continue to enrich my life. Karen Mireau, initially I was reluctant to take your clear but gentle suggestions, but, when I did, I took a step forward in my own revision skills. I also want to thank a wonderful writer friend Shari Nagi for further editing. And the painstaking task of doing the final proof copy-editing fell to our friend III, who has a talent I don't possess. Any remaining errors, are mine alone.

Over the last three years, friends and relatives encouraged me, helped me with fact checking, and listened to my updates on the process. For those who patiently helped me to word-smith, thank you. Dinah Sanders, you lent your invaluable expert advice and enthusiasm for the publishing process. Dario Sanchez-Kennedy, I love your wonderful cover design. My dear friend Judy Vargas, how attentively and intentionally you checked in with me on *Junctions*. Your interest and friendship sustain me every day. And no acknowledgement is complete without thanks to Alex and Jackson for an abundance of loving support for their Mum.

I owe the sweet flow of my writing days to my husband, David, my first beta reader, my partner, my constant cheerleader. We share this writing dream and reality. In the summer of 2013 as we lay in our tent on the bluff at Montana de Oro, with the mountains behind us and the ocean all around in front, we brainstormed titles for my story. *Junctions* emerged from the tent that day and is with us forevermore.

FURTHERMORE

All of the characters in *Junctions* have pasts, journeys that proceed their presence within the 2005 setting of *Junctions*. Thirteen of their stories are unveiled in my next book, *Journeys*, an anthology of short stories slated for publication in 2017.

Even as the author, it was only after the tale of *Junctions* was completed that my characters revealed these past and future stories to me. These details help to explain what made them behave as they did throughout the story of *Junctions*. I hope you'll find that *Journeys* will answer some questions that crossed your mind while reading *Junctions*; these are questions I also had, such as:

What happened to Warren in his childhood that brought about his painfully stoic personality?

What were the circumstances when the young Dane and Cecilia met and why didn't she tell him that they had a son?

Did Pedro's harsh experiences as a boy and young man justify or explain the secrets he held so tightly for fifty years? And what price did he pay for leaving his Southwestern roots and culture behind while trying to forget his pain in New England?

Did anyone try to keep Mateo from leaving home at age eighteen?

Rex was a settled middle-aged man when he came to Pine Junction, but what was he like as a young minister? Where did he come from and how did he end up in Western Massachusetts?

What was happening in Catherine's life during those horrifying weeks when Mateo was in a coma?

"There is hope for all of us," Dane proclaimed. Did the family drift back into their same old patterns after the dust settled, or did they become more open and connected? Did Javier become part of Pedro's life? And what did Rowan and Mateo and Julia do in the next few years?